NO WAY OUT

"There's got to be another way," Heron said to the news vendor, an obese woman with bleached-out hair. "I don't want to go through with this."

She glanced up from her TV screen. "Too late now, son. You're in it too deep."

"I could just walk away right now, take a bus back to Chicago, get work as a supervisor in my uncle's plant."

"Don't think so, son," she said, handing him another magazine and turning back to her story.

The holo showed a bloodstained easy chair; the headline said, "MURDER IN MIAMI AGGRAVATES INTERNATIONAL SITUATION." He tossed it back at her and shouted, "This hasn't even happened yet!"

❄

Praise for *Shadows of the White Sun:*

"Reminiscent in ways of a space-going Gormenghast, or perhaps of Gene Wolfe."

—*Analog*

Ace Books by Raymond Harris

THE BROKEN WORLDS
SHADOWS OF THE WHITE SUN
THE SCHIZOGENIC MAN

THE SCHIZOGENIC MAN

RAYMOND HARRIS

ACE BOOKS, NEW YORK

The author gratefully acknowledges permission from The University of Chicago Press to quote from *The Iliad of Homer*, translated with an introduction by Richmond Lattimore, copyright 1951 by The University of Chicago Press.

This book is an Ace original edition,
and has never been previously published.

THE SCHIZOGENIC MAN

An Ace Book / published by arrangement with
the author

PRINTING HISTORY
Ace edition / November 1990

ISBN: 0-441-75398-1

Ace Books are published by The Berkley Publishing Group,
200 Madison Avenue, New York, New York 10016.
The name "ACE" and the "A" logo
are trademarks belonging to Charter Communications, Inc.

PRINTED IN THE UNITED STATES OF AMERICA

10 9 8 7 6 5 4 3 2 1

AUTHOR'S NOTE

Except for such household words as Cleopatra, Mark Antony, the *Odyssey*, etc., all common and proper nouns from the classical languages have been written with their original spellings. Ordinary usage first Latinizes and then Anglicizes words from ancient Greek, but since this does violence to the phonetics involved, it has been avoided. Thus Epikouros, Herakles, Nikias, and Rhodos, rather than Epicurus, Hercules, Nicias, and Rhodes.

The verses from the *Iliad* in Chapter 7 were translated by Richmond Lattimore. The verses of Sappho in Chapter 9 and the aphorisms of Herakleitos in Chapters 13, 14, and 16 were translated by the author. The first narrative extract in Chapter 9 is from Plutarch's *Life of Antony*, translated by John Dryden. The narrative extract at the close of Chapter 18 is from *Dio's Roman History*, Book LI, translated by Earnest Cary.

THE
SCHIZOGENIC
MAN

PART ONE

CITY WINTER

1

Another Wasted Day

Five minutes before lunchtime the winch broke on loading dock Number Six. The forklift operator didn't even have time to scream before a two-ton stack of ceramic pipe, fresh out of Tropicana's righteous kilns, came crashing down around her ears like Judgment Day. Both truckers swore and one of them grabbed his luck so hard it broke off.

John Heron was on his way into the shift manager's cage, oblivious to the whole mess, when a stray pipe skipped over a bale of copper wire and glanced off his foot. It was his right foot, the one he'd broken two decades earlier on the *Kosmograd*. He swore a little louder than the second trucker had and flopped down on a wad of bubble wrap, holding his foot and scrunching up his face like the gargoyles in Fabio Pacheco's latest mural.

The pain was so fierce it gave him chills. It made him sick to his stomach, and weak and trembling everywhere else. His foot exploded to five times its normal size—at least in his imagination—and that was some pretty serious discomfort.

"Is it broken?" George Early leaned down and stared him in the face; his skin looked gray in the fluorescent light.

"I sure as hell hope so." Heron grimaced. "Is Cymbal dead?"

"Won't know till we dig her out."

Disgust vied with pain. "Should have fixed that thing long ago."

The shift manager was running around making a lot of noise; so

3

was half the shift. Echoes rebounded off damp concrete and made everything seem crazier than it was. Early kept cool, digging an ice pack out of the nearest first-aid station and strapping it around Heron's throbbing metatarsals.

"That better?"

Heron gave half a nod. "A little better, but listen, I've got to get out of here." Early winked, stuck out his arm, and helped him hop over to the rear exit.

"Looks like I've got the rest of the week off," Heron said, between gasps. "Not the worst deal in the world. Might even get a change in status."

"That depends on how bad you're hurt." Early stopped suddenly and Heron yelped. "I forgot our coats."

Heron leaned against a wall while Early ran back to the locker room. Somebody was shouting, "Don't move her! Don't move her!" The excavators had uncovered Cymbal; she looked like a deflated balloon. Her face was red and purple and a few other unaccustomed colors. Heron realized they'd never said more than hello.

Then Early was back, wearing his own quilted jacket and carrying Heron's black wool coat. They went through to the street.

As the December breeze hit Heron's face he gagged a couple times and heaved up breakfast in a neat pool next to the steam vent. Early came around with his bike, nodded respectfully, and said, "Hop on."

Heron eased himself onto the handlebars, holding his foot at a reasonably inconvenient angle, and Early started pedaling. The warehouse was on 15 de Julio, five blocks below Panamericana; the nearest polyclinic was on Seventh and Libertad. In between was a footsore army of cyclists, pedicabs, skateboarders, omnibuses, pedestrians, and trucks. "We'll be there in five minutes," Early said.

Heron didn't care. The pain was still with him, but it hadn't gotten any worse; in fact it had already begun to show him new horizons. He rubbed his luck and prayed that the injury was serious. He needed a break from the warehouse, and the next drawings were too far away. A midwinter vacation would do him fine.

Over Early's shoulder the city wobbled by in reverse, rising into the midday gloom. The sky was gray, but not dingy; it was a luminous kind of gray, full of shades and subtleties: a little silver, a little iron, some ivory and lots of slate. High overcast suited the colors of the new blocks on 15 de Julio, softening the hot reds, blending the blues and oranges into a muted rainbow. At Fuente the scrolled towers and balconies of Residencia Omega hovered against a backdrop of dissolving clouds; the Ciencia complex on Nineteenth Street, half hidden by scaffolds on Eleventh, looked like a castle guarding a hoard of gold. The more distant things were, the more dreamy they became. It was only close up that the world kept its edge.

Beyond Panamericana the traffic was absurd. Bikes, trucks, and gaping excavations were one thing; add to all that a gibbering horde of street vendors, numbers hustlers, queue keepers, and change girls, touting their wares in every language known to man, and you approach primordial chaos. Pushcarts manned by insomniac Chinese, newly transplanted from the grime of Shanghai and Xiang Gang, emitted clouds of steam and greasy odors of *dim sum*. Hoarse-throated Peruvians and Mexicans hawked cheap gloves, hand-knit scarves, and embroidered blouses. Fat tourists from Dallas and São Paulo sampled the bargains and curios, chins dripping with soy sauce, hands grubby with hard cash.

Limited capitalism had been reinstated just five years earlier, by special decree of the Junta, and in spite of restrictions it flourished as never before. All of these eager peddlers were undoubtedly fugitives from the graveyard shift; only during off hours was anyone allowed to indulge in the *economía gris*.

Round the clock servitude, thought Heron. Not my idea of how the game should be played.

After fifteen minutes of lurching and dodging and detouring they came in sight of the Xin-Xi Polyclinic at 200 Libertad. This was a handsome eight-story building with a wide arcade at ground level—fifty meters of tapering pillars and pointed arches. The pillars recalled stalactites, molded on-site from textured ceramic and finished with a honey-colored crackle glaze, very much in the manner of old Chin Leung. At least thirty bicycles jammed the racks out front.

Leaning on Early's shoulder Heron hopped into the lobby, where twice that number of people stood or squatted. Their faces had the expression—submissive, empty, all but oblivious—of those who have waited long and are prepared to wait longer. No one exhibited any injuries or seemed to be in actual pain, which was encouraging; he hoped some sort of triage was in effect.

Early tried shouting for attention. "This man needs a wheelchair! Over here! This guy's hurt! He needs painkillers!"

No one reacted.

He tried again, a little louder, with the same result.

Then a dark girl of about sixteen smiled up at them and said, "It's lunchtime. You'll have to wait till the intake staff gets back." She waved a slip of green paper. "They'll give you one of these vouchers."

Heron shook his head. "I guess it beats hanging around the warehouse."

The girl fumbled through the lumpy sack beside her and pulled out a strip of skinnies. "Take one or two of these in the meantime."

He winked solemnly. *"Mil gracias, ciudadana."* He applied a tiny blue square to his throat and caught his breath in shocked relief. "That's quite a prescription you've got there."

"Those pros know how to take care of me."

Early helped him sit down beside her and said, "They'll be missing me back at the job. See you later." The two men shook hands and he walked out.

Heron settled back on his elbows and looked up at the ceiling. The fresco depicted a series of wheels within wheels, all toothed and interlocking, all painted gold and dusted with metallic powder. Slogans ran around the edges—mostly the phrase, "Your life rests in the hands of fortune," translated into five or six different languages, with an occasional "The wheel never stops turning" thrown in.

"Not a bad place to wait," he said. "Though a few chairs would be nice."

The dark girl smiled again and started talking, telling him about the clinic she usually went to on Forty-ninth Street. That one had long benches of polished wood, initialed with two or three generations of the sick and disabled. She thought it was the nicest place in town.

"I have a blood disease," she said. "It's very unusual. They only sent me down to Xin-Xi because there's a specialist here today that they want me to see." She pointed to the name written on her voucher, showing it off like a photograph of a lover or a favorite child. "I might not live long."

Heron nodded and mumbled a few stock monosyllables. His foot throbbed profoundly, a whole separate organism that focused as much sensation as the rest of his body put together. It left him very little room for small talk.

The girl's voice—her name was Julia—droned on. Most of the

other patients were doing the same: reciting long case histories, abundant pharmacopeia, tragic prognoses. The acoustics of the lobby blended their words into a buzzing chant, a one-note hymn that rose up to the fresco of wheels and traveled beyond it, to that lower tier of heaven where luck orbits in tandem with the Lottery program. Heron felt soothed and comforted. Only a few minutes ago he'd thought he was the worst case there; now he knew he was the most fortunate.

He tuned out Julia's recitative and remembered a thousand other lobbies where he'd kept company with a thousand other lost souls. The New City had to be the world capital of lobbies and waiting. They'd been his introduction to citizenship, and they'd undoubtedly be his sendoff. He could imagine a distant day when his corpse would sit in a long queue at the crematorium, waiting for its turn in the oven, waiting to fly up in smoke to the ragged ozone.

Before he knew it a ten-year-old boy in a buff gown was circulating with a new sheaf of vouchers. "I need a wheelchair," he told him. "I can't walk."

The boy shrugged. "We don't have any more wheelchairs. Try crawling." He handed Heron a yellow slip and strolled away.

"It won't be long now," said Julia, her eyes soft and shiny with the drug. "Just relax."

In the end Heron waited seven hours. After two he thought he'd die of hunger, but then an old man next to Julia gave him a potato knish, and a couple of kids shared sips of their apple juice. That saved his life, that and the blue skinnies Julia kept offering. When her turn came, around four, she made sure he had enough to last out the evening. "The dispensary gives me as many as I want," she said. "It's in my code."

Once she was gone Heron rolled his coat into a pillow and dozed. Thoughts of Cymbal recurred from time to time; he wondered if she'd survived. He wondered which clinic they would have taken her to, and whether the staff would have recognized her as a real emergency, or whether she too would have had to wait and wait, and eventually die. That is, if she hadn't already, back there in the warehouse.

Remembering the color of her face he figured she probably had, one way or the other.

They called out his hex code three times before he realized who they wanted. Shouting, waving his arms, he started crawling toward the white screen that hid the cubicles marked EXAMINA-

TION II; halfway there a wiry Asian teenager took pity on him and helped him to his feet, supporting him all the way into CUBE A/87/KM.

Heron thanked him. The kid nodded back and said, "No problem, grandpa." It was grounds for another grimace.

Inside the cube Heron saw the same ten-year-old who'd given him the voucher, hours earlier, perched on a three-legged stool. An untidy old woman sat next to him, staring into a cathode-ray tube.

"Code?" she said, more to herself than to him. Her voice was somewhere between hoarse and inaudible.

Heron started to answer, but the boy in the buff gown nodded a curt negative and mimed rolling up his sleeve. Heron obliged, and the boy read off the ten-digit number tattooed on his left wrist. The old woman tapped it in.

"Symptoms?"

Heron explained. After two sentences the boy silenced him and said, "F seventeen, Kappa forty-four, P three." It was obvious who was pro and who was player in *this* cube. The old lady nodded and coughed, never taking her eyes from the screen. She tapped in the new code and examined whatever it was the program showed her.

"Inspection?"

The boy unwrapped Heron's foot, tossing aside the cold pack and assaying a few cursory squeezes. He recited three more sequences, waited for the woman to tap them in, and said softly, "We gotta X-ray, pal."

That took no more than five minutes. There was a camera in a closet adjacent to the cube; Heron went in and put on the lead apron, holding his breath when the boy told him to. The radiograph appeared automatically on the old woman's screen. She mumbled something about being late for supper, and called for a diagnosis.

The program had it before she could finish tapping. "Two small fractures," she said, putting on her coat. "Stay lucky." Coughing into a little pink handkerchief, nodding to the impassive pro, she walked out the door.

The boy followed her. When Heron would have hopped after him he just said, "Wait." He was back in thirty seconds with a fluttering printout.

"You gotta go down the hall for your dressing. I'll help."

"How bad is it?"

"Not bad. Just stay off it for two weeks."

Two weeks. Shorter than he'd hoped, longer than he'd feared. Heron put a hand on the offered shoulder and hopped down to TREATMENT III, a second series of cubes grouped around a big old-fashioned terminal. The boy left him there without a word.

Another hour went by before any of the technicians noticed him. Finally a pudgy guy with short crisp curls came to his rescue. He took him into a cubicle, pulled out a spray gun, and applied a partial cast; it hardened as he sprayed.

"Want me to sign it?" he asked. "It's a nice one."

Heron declined.

The technician shrugged and unfolded a wheelchair, which would take him to the Dispensary in the north wing. "They'll give you a cane there too," he promised, and Heron felt like he was in business.

By now it was close to 2100; the lines were short. Before 2130 Heron had a cane, a week's supply of blues, and the incredible luxury of a cab voucher. The cab was waiting for him when he reemerged from the long, honey-glazed loggia. He hopped from the wheelchair to the back seat and said, "Corner of Thirteenth and Segunda. And step on it. I don't want to miss dinner." The cabbie let out a long frosty grunt and started pedaling.

Downstairs the refectory was almost empty. Heron dined on soggy noodles and cold *tempeh* in soy broth, with a side of slightly oily cabbage. He was so hungry it tasted like apple pie. Thanks to the blues, the pain in his foot had diminished. Life was starting to look rosy.

As he was slurping up the end of the broth Alberto Favaloro stopped by his table in a dirty white apron. "You're here late, pal," he said, slapping his shoulder. "How was dinner?"

"Not bad. The cabbage was a little oily, though."

"But wasn't it great oil? Fresh in from Pacifica—the best I've seen since August."

Heron gave a skullhead grin. "My mistake, Alberto."

"No problem. You want to go out for a drink after I finish cleanup?"

Heron shook his head. His eyes were sinking in dark pools; his wrinkles were out in force. "Thanks, but I'm beat. Semiconscious. Try me tomorrow night."

"Stay lucky, then," Alberto said. "I'll drink one for you."

Heron saluted his back. A minute later he was levering himself up and heading home. Just past the exit he bumped into Qian the porter, who helped him into the elevator and saw him all the way to his door.

"Need help undressing?" she asked.

"I'll take a raincheck, love," Heron said. It was a longstanding joke between them. Qian was a handsome woman but she was also pushing seventy.

Inside, his screen blinked about twenty message notices. He ignored them. George Early and his current girlfriend were asleep in a tangle on the floor. He ignored them too and made a beeline for the padded alcove where he slept. Though the foot made him clumsy, he had his clothes off within two minutes. He didn't bother with a shower; semiconscious is semiconscious. Out of habit he flicked a switch by his pillow, and his ears vibrated with the strains of Shivananda's "Six Ways Out." Six bars in he *was* out. And dreaming. And sweating.

He was walking down some kind of beige-papered, taupe-carpeted hallway, his eyes fixed on the bony shoulders of the kid in front of him. Jemmy. It was Jemmy. He felt another rivulet of sweat trace a channel down his arm. This was the Hotel Drummond, and he was back again.

Jemmy stopped just short of Room 316. "Wait here," he whispered. "Don't come in unless I yell." He handed him the gun. "Put it in your pants."

Then he was knocking, with that scarred sixteen-year-old fist, and a deep male voice was saying, "Jemmy? John? Come on in."

Jemmy did. John didn't.

"But where's your friend?" The words came through the door, muffled and indistinct. Heron stopped listening.

I'm dreaming this again, he thought, staring at the pallid still life on the wall opposite. *I don't want to.* He looked at his hands, something he'd once heard you couldn't do in a dream. And they looked so real, so young and hard and efficient. *Why this again?*

The gurgling started before he was ready for it. His stubborn dream-hand tightened on the gun; his belly knotted in revulsion. And the sound kept coming, muddled and muddied by the intervening door, teasing the edge of his hearing. Its distortion made it even more horrible, because his imagination had to fill in the rest. "Just kill the fucker," he breathed. "Just kill him, you sick bastard."

Several seconds later the door cracked and Jemmy said, "Get in here."

There was a lot of blood. Jemmy looked proud. Heron kept his eyes down and said, "Jemmy, we got to move our butts." He reached back for the doorknob.

As his fingers brushed the brass it started turning. He heard keys rattling; the door swung open. He had the gun up in plenty of time.

He squeezed once. There was a popping sound and the Texan jerked back, slamming the door shut with his shoulder. A little hole appeared over his left eye and a red blotch spread across his face. He slid to the floor without a sound.

"Bonus pay." Jemmy slapped Heron's trapezius. "Both of them! They're gonna love this in Portland."

Heron took a breath and let his eyes do an inventory of the room. Both beds had that pristine, unslept-in look, unique to the better class of hotel. A large print of a prewar building hung between them. Forbus and Mitchell lay at the foot of the left-hand bed, almost head to head; neither face was recognizable.

"Nice job, huh?" Jemmy smiled. "You fired that slug like a real killer, John." Then they were walking calmly out the door, down the back stairs, and into the waiting car.

Daylight seeped in, softly, surreptitiously, sneaking under white shades and glowing off white walls. Shivananda's adagio buzzed and whispered. Heron opened his eyes, flinched away from the light, and swore. His foot throbbed and his back stuck to the sheet. *Why that dream again?*

He fumbled for the strip of skinnies and applied two at once. Two weeks vacation, he thought. Two very drugged weeks with nothing to do.

He glanced at the floor. Early and whatsername were already gone. Good. With the help of the cane he managed to stand, careful not to put any weight on the foot. He hobbled over to the window and let the shade fly up, staring down at the courtyard. It glared back at him in December sun.

Two weeks isn't long enough, he thought. I have too much resting up to do.

He took a breath and kicked the wall, very hard. A cry twisted out of his lips; tears overflowed his lashes. He took another breath and kicked again. This time he heard a substantial crack. Abruptly he was so nauseated he couldn't keep standing, so traumatized he wanted to sit and cry. But no, that's not how John Heron bought player status; that's not how John Heron played city games. He crawled to the door, made sure no one was in the corridor, and dragged himself down to the stairwell. It would be nice to stop right there but it was just too unlikely. So he sat on the top step and bumped his way down, one by one, till he made the first landing. Then, *then* he started shouting.

Another day wasted in the Xin-Xi Polyclinic. He figured it was worth it.

2

The Christmas Club

Cymbal died, of course. Afterwards the Bureau of Safety questioned everyone who had witnessed the accident. Heron's appointment lasted about ten minutes. Since he'd had his back turned at the crucial moment, he had nothing concrete to say, beyond a few sarcastic observations on shift management. The bureaucrats accepted his testimony and released him without comment.

It was the same thing at the Bureau of Disabilities: ten minutes and he was out again with a month-long deferral from the work pool, and a year-long reclassification to Strictly Non-strenuous.

"Given your age, Citizen Heron," said the owl-eyed young lady in the sea-green cubicle, "it's doubtful you will ever be called for manual labor again."

Heron smiled. "No more dirty hands. No more aching muscles."

The young lady sniffed. "All labor performed for the common good partakes of the same dignity, Citizen."

"Though some assignments are more conducive to backache than others." Heron rose and leaned on his cane, looking very dashing in his black one-piece and wild silver-gray hair. "Stay lucky, Citizen."

He limped out, waving his hand and grinning wickedly. Some people took their jobs too seriously.

Christmas came two days later. Though the Junta did permit its

13

religious observance, behind the closed doors of specified houses of worship, any public demonstrations were taboo.

But Heron had been raised in Middle, and there are some habits you can never shake off. As a child he had anticipated the winter solstice with impatience and awe; the magic day was a dream of candles and presents and evergreen boughs, of hymns and prayers and big crowds gathered around a big table holding more food than anyone could possibly eat. As a newly landed immigrant in the Oz of the East, he had missed all that (and only that) and taken steps toward forming a Christmas Club of like-minded individuals. Two decades later the Club still existed, much altered in membership but little changed in spirit.

The basic idea was to get a bunch of people together, put up a tree, eat a great deal, and drink slightly less. Sometimes the priorities of eating and drinking got mixed up, but as long as people's hearts were in the right place, it caused no problems.

By unspoken agreement the venue was always the biggest apartment available to the collective run of luck. Five years in a row Heron had been the tenant of an upper-floor suite in Residencia Omega, next-door neighbor to some of the top pros in town; that was back when he and Sally had still been married and they had the extra housing credits. With such a palace at his disposal it was inevitable that he would take the role of Father Christmas. And what days of decadence those had been! Bottles of vodka and whiskey vied for space on his kitchen counter; ice cascaded from his Green-manufactured refrigerator; an actual antique plastic Douglas pine, with a skirt of Chinese silk, stood magisterially athwart his entrance hall, casting fairy-light in six colors over the gaping face of each new arrival. In the dining room casseroles of soy and lentils emitted clouds of savory steam, swimming in sauces of *kuzu* and garlic; cranberry puddings gleamed like blood, and yams shone yellow as candles. Those parties had carried on till the neighbors complained, and then some; Texan vodka will bribe even the most jaded pro.

But the days of John Heron's good fortune had dwindled into memories. His studio on Thirteenth was adequate for himself, and for occasional overnight guests, but not for the twentieth annual gathering of the Christmas Club. This year the honor fell to Minoru Fukunaga, whose luck had brought him three large rooms halfway up Libertad.

A smile of paternal delight lit Heron's face as he shuffled through the flat. Fukunaga might be a newcomer to the idea of

Christmas, but he already grasped its essentials. Every wall was covered with murals of boreal forest, every room was ankle-deep in styrofoam peanuts, which furnished an exquisite facsimile of snow—especially for people who had only seen it melting, on rare occasions, in heavily trodden parks.

"Minoru, this is amazing." He bowed very low; Fukunaga replied in kind.

"Amazing! It's a lot more than amazing. It's a masterpiece!" Pacifico Ortiz clumped in, still swathed in an ankle-length cloak. He pumped Fukunaga's hand while Heron stood by to take his wrap. "If the Aesthetic Council got a look at this they'd set you up as a five-year Art Pro. I'm not exaggerating."

Fukunaga's eyes disappeared in a grin. "I photographed everything in its pristine state just for that purpose; I've already applied for a presentation. The prints are on display in the bathroom."

"Oh, but nothing can compare with the actual experience. This is a living environment. Let's see, who do I know on the current Council? Maybe I could make a quick call and turn this party into a *real* celebration. . . ."

Pacifico liked to boast of his connections, a common failing among players. He rarely came through.

"Not necessary, Pacifico." Fukunaga radiated patience. "Just relax and enjoy yourself. This is supposed to be a day of rest, isn't it, John?"

"Rest for the bones, pleasure for the flesh, solace for the spirit." Heron draped Pacifico's cloak over his arm and headed for the growing mountain of winter fashion in the far room. "Drinks are over there, Pacifico."

At least fifty people drifted through a haze of tobacco and cannabis smoke. Fresh leaf costing what it did—in counters as well as connections—it was evident how highly they valued their fun. Most were in their first decade of player status, the years of the roughest and least desirable assignments, so they had a lot to escape from. Conversation ebbed and flowed from such shores as Pacheco's new show, the current offering at the Cine Popular, roommate aggravations, the Texas-Tropicana crisis, romantic entanglements, job hassles, and inevitably, the prospects of the New Year's Lottery.

"I'm bound to get a residential reassessment," Pacifico said. "I've been living in one room with seven roommates for eighteen consecutive drawings. I graduated to the upper bunk last spring but it's still substandard housing."

George Early shook his head. "I heard a rumor they were going to amend the Code to include situations like that. As long as you have a roof over your head and a bed to sleep on—"

"But what about that new block that's going up on Fifty-second Street?" Ursula Schell's voice already had a giddy edge; she obviously wasn't limiting herself to smoke and alcohol. "There must be a hundred and fifty units opening up."

"Ah, but what about the new immigration quota?" Alberto Favaloro loved to bear bad tidings. "It was on page ten or twelve of *Luz y Verdad* last week, a five-line piece near the bottom that you were supposed to overlook. The Junta is increasing the landing fee to ten thousand Middlebucks and creating space for five hundred new players in the game."

"More Chinese," said Ursula. "I can just see it. Pretty soon Spanish will be a minority language, and English will disappear. I'm too old to start memorizing six million characters. I'll die illiterate."

"They have drugs." Early was solemn. "Teach you overnight. Wake up using chopsticks and quoting from *The Little Red Book*."

Ursula made a disgusted sound, but Alberto seconded Early's statement. "It's true. They can put you through a crash program. My friend Rita once drew a spot as a translator—don't ask me how, even MEQMAT makes mistakes—so instead of canceling the assignment and redrawing, the Adjustment Council had her take this week-long course in Basic Mandarin. She started seeing characters in her soup, in people's eyebrows, under her bed. Took her a year to calm down."

"The Junta is always trying to scare up foreign exchange, any way it can." Heron joined the circle, offering a tray of cookies in the shapes of stars, snowmen, and Christmas trees. "Five million Middlebucks could buy a security contract with one of those cut-rate Mexican outfits."

"You're an immigrant yourself, aren't you, John?" Pacifico's eyebrows moved a little closer. "How much did landing cost when you came over?"

Heron grinned like a kid. "A lot less than it does now."

"Five thousand?"

"About that." The grin didn't waver. "But back then it might as well've been fifteen."

Ursula copied Pacifico's frown, but neither one pursued the subject.

Fukunaga's front door picked that moment to chime. Heron winked at Ursula and limped over to do the honors.

It was none other than Fabio Pacheco, with two stylish women in tow. Fabio became the immediate center of attention and the party moved into higher gear. Here was living evidence that you too could see your dreams come true. Fabio Pacheco was an old-time habitué of the Segunda bars, a founding member of the Christmas Club, a long-suffering player who'd had his share of shit along with the gravy. He was now in his second term as Art Pro, selling sculptures and canvases everywhere from Beijing to Buenos Aires and earning the Junta a nice fat wad of foreign exchange. He had a studio on Panamericana, a flat well up Libertad, vacations every February in Puerto Rico, and a private account in the Banco del Hemisferio. This last distinction put him a few rungs below current and former members of the Junta.

Fabio brought a kiss for every woman in the room and three bottles of Argentine champagne. He embraced Heron—"You're looking great, man!"—and complimented Fukunaga on his installation. Pacifico Ortiz gaped ("*We* know *him*?") but Ursula just smiled appetizingly.

Fabio's companions were Stella Cranach and Galina Fyodorovna, both raven-haired and svelte. "I just picked them up in the corner bar," he said. "I figured this party could use some new blood."

Heron offered a facetious bow and shook each woman's hand. Galina nodded back and started talking to Fukunaga; but Stella's handshake lingered, and she said, "What a pleasure to meet you, John." Five minutes later they were head to head in the smokiest corner of the room.

Citizen Cranach was tall and self-composed. Her smallest gesture betrayed how well she knew her best angles. She moved like an actress or a dancer and dressed like the Queen of the Night—that stark monochromatic mode favored by city women of a certain disposition, always stylish and never in vogue. Her hair was jet-black, her face corpse-white, and her eyes (anomalously blue) sparkled with Mexican kohl. Her lip rouge was such a deep magenta it approached ebony. She wore a simple dress of crisp black Shantung, whose cut revealed an expanse of smooth white back and a pair of shapely calves. Whether she stood or sat, it always hung in perfect folds; no flashcube could ever catch her by surprise.

"Fabio is such a liar," she said, sipping her vodka. "We've

actually known each other for years. I've been hearing about these Christmas bashes ever since I met him, so it's a treat to be here at last. And it's every bit as good as I expected. Where did you get the idea? Are you a student of historical ethnology, or just an old-fashioned boy?"

Heron's eyebrows lifted. "Exposed so soon! In fact I'm a very old-fashioned boy. Born and raised in the prairie—a real Middle-man. When I was a kid, folks still imported trees from Canada and even ate turkey once or twice a year."

"Good God! You can't be that old."

"Forty-three last month."

She smiled. "And here I thought you were a fine young trendy, with all that silver hair. I never guessed it was real." Her eyes wandered up to the ceiling. "Though forty-three is hardly moribund. Fabio's pushing fifty."

"While you must be a mere babe of twenty-six."

"Keep talking. I'll be thirty-one in April."

"And I've been this gray since twenty-two, so none of it means a thing. Now that *that* sensitive subject is disposed of . . . ummm . . . what do you do when you're not playing the game?"

She smiled wider. "I see I'm in for another round of Twenty Questions a la Nueva Ciudad." She settled back on the couch and straightened her dress. "I guess you could call me a compulsive spectator. Film, theater, gallery openings—you name it, I'm there. I figure, here I am living in the new Athens—"

"The new Florence—"

"—the new New York, so why not plunge into its pulsating heart? It keeps me from feeling bored." She spread well-manicured hands (no forklift duty for *this* girl). "I also read a lot."

"Poetry? Novels?"

"Mostly history. I have a passion for knowing how things got to be the way they are, and how irrevocably they've changed from the way they were."

Heron pushed out his lower lip. "I wouldn't have expected so much cogitation from a lady with vampire eyes."

"Isn't it fun being other than you seem?"

"I'm not so sure I am."

"You mean you're neither an iconoclastic poet nor an experimental novelist?"

"I'm not an artist of any description whatsoever. I just play the Lottery and get drunk in my spare time."

"Not the worst life in the world."

He suddenly felt a little silly, which wasn't a good way to be around an attractive woman he'd just met. He also felt his defenses going up, and he knew from long experience how poorly that state mixed with vodka.

But she read him chapter and verse. "Relax, John. I'll back off." She put her hand on his arm, an insect touch. "All my teeth are in my mouth, believe me."

He laughed. "You're full of surprises."

"I do my best."

A few sentences later, without wanting to, but completely unable to resist, he started telling her the story of his life as a player. How he came into town with stars in his eyes, hoping to win a spot in the new orbital colonies: one of the Lottery's original grand prizes. How he married a young pro and qualified for the fifth go-round. How he and his wife passed the first cut, the second funneling, and the final squeeze, and one bright morning found themselves lifting off from the Tropicana Space Center on a joint Pacifica/New City mission.

"Teofila and I spend six months crewing the *Kosmograd*," he said. "Teofila was the one with the skills; I tagged along because they only accepted married couples. But I pulled my weight. I learned as much as I could about the day-to-day realities of L-5 habitat maintenance, and my weekly assessments were never less than excellent. That tour of duty was the peak experience of my whole goddamn life."

"You only got one assignment?"

He nodded. "Sad but true. Right at the end of our tour I had a freak accident in free fall. Broke my foot. This one—see? It still gives me trouble. That hurt my ratings and kept me out of the pool for five years. By then the New City had phased out most of its L-5 investments and wasn't supplying any more non-technical staff. The program didn't heat up again till six or seven years ago, and by then I was over the hill."

"Pretty rough."

"Yeah. At twenty-five I had achieved my wildest fantasy. At twenty-six I was history. It's taken me all the years since then to get over it."

"One of heaven's exiles," she said. "A fallen angel."

Heron winked. "That's the spirit. My wife divorced me, of course, and I went back to playing the game. In the last seventeen years I've been everything from a futures analyst to a gourmet chef to a garbageman. I've been a husband twice, a father once, and a free man more times than I can count. I've been kind of a compulsive spectator, too, especially from the wings. When I'm not working I usually trade sarcasm with the local roundup of dissolute painters and death-bent musicians. Funny how no talent ever rubs off."

"I'm not so sure," she said. "You seem to have a flair for the art of living."

He met her eyes and smiled. "You're a kind woman."

"Oh, no. I'm frank, not kind. You'll see that when we know each other better."

"Sounds like a threat."

"It is!"

Heron chuckled into his drink. This was definitely what you'd call a disarming woman. It was almost scary the way she could draw him out.

But Stella's turn came next. She spoke, a little more guardedly than he had, of her own dreams and disappointments, describing her four attempts, and four failures, at attaining Art Pro status.

"I tried assemblage, I tried video, I tried confession, I even tried comic books. The Chinese love Hemispheric comics, you know. None of it was quite what the bureaucrats were looking for. But the Council is endlessly patient." Her lips twitched. "I could ask for another review tomorrow and they'd give it to me. Trouble is, I've run out of ideas."

"Maybe you're better off in the audience. There's no rule that says artists are better people than anyone else."

"In fact sometimes they're much worse. You're right. I've got to accept myself as a moderately talented dilettante with an overdeveloped aesthetic faculty. Not the most comfortable neurosis to live with, but it can be done."

Heron gave his head a quick shake. "How did we ever get so serious? This is supposed to be a night of frivolity." He examined Stella's empty glass. "Let me refill that and see when the food's coming out."

He was halfway to the kitchen when the front door resounded as if struck by a miniature battering ram. He exchanged glances with Fukunaga and started fiddling with the bolt.

The pounding continued as he drew it back. "Hey, didn't you ever hear of doorbells?" he shouted.

Three figures stood framed in the doorway. All wore elaborate headgear, short capes, and high boots. The only things missing were the myrrh and the frankincense.

Someone stage-whispered "*Los Reyes Magos*!" and the general company stifled laughter. Actually it was the police.

"Guardia Civil, Officer Vigneault here." The flat-voiced woman waved her badge under Heron's nose.

"Not the Celeste Vigneault who used to live at Panamericana and Libertad?" Heron made a palsy face and would have offered her a drink, but she didn't give a centimeter.

"Where I used to live or who I used to know has no bearing on this assignment," she said in that same flat, patient voice. "We're here to investigate a complaint that you people are holding some kind of religious ceremony."

Fukunaga came forward with a sour look. "My neighbors love to cause trouble," he told Heron out of the side of his mouth. To Officer Vigneault he said, "Take a look around, then. We're just having a party."

The three cops eased in; the party crowd fell silent. Quickly, quietly, with practiced efficiency, they gave the flat a thorough once-over. They ignored the drugs and alcohol—legal-enough substances, though often obtained by illegal means—passed the exotically decorated tree without a glance, and stopped dead beneath the *piñata* hanging in the center of the main room.

"This looks like an icon or a cult object," said Vigneault.

"It's not," Heron said. "It's just a *piñata*. Section 489 says nothing about party favors."

"How did a civilian get so familiar with the Code?" Vigneault's hostility rose a few notches.

"Celeste! I used to be a cop too, back when you were in the Network. Don't tell me you forgot."

Vigneault studied him. "Okay, Citizen, you begin to look familiar, and I could probably even summon up your name, and the names of both your wives, too. But if you were ever a cop you must remember what it's like to go out on duty. We function as peace officers, period. Our private lives don't enter into it."

He nodded. "Yeah, I remember the drugs. I avoided taking them."

She shot him a look and spoke into her headset, too softly for anyone in the room to overhear. Her companions idly fingered their truncheons. When her answer came it closed the case.

"Headquarters has decided you're clean," she said. "Sorry to disturb your fun." All three turned and walked out.

Fukunaga listened at the door for a second to make sure they were gone; then the party at large erupted into loud talking and louder laughs. "You guys planned this, didn't you!" Pacifico said.

"No chance." Heron fingered one of the long streamers hanging from the *piñata*. "But it *is* an interesting comment on city life."

Stella was at his side. "More sociology from the Middleman?"

He glared at her until he had to smile. "That's right, you painted Jezebel of the streets. In this town pretty much everything is allowed except murder and religion. Anywhere else on the continent it's the other way around."

"Come now."

"Well, almost. They sure don't stand for any drinkin', smokin', or dancin' out in those God-fearing realms to the west. Just tune in to Reverend Joe Bob Lewis's show someday if you don't believe me. And as for fornication——"

"But there's none of *that* going on," Pacifico said.

"Not yet," Heron conceded. "But just wait a while."

Stella laughed. "Fabio warned me that these parties can get pretty wild. I can't decide whether I want to see if he was telling the truth or just head home with my illusions intact."

"Suit yourself," said Heron. "I've gotten too old for that kind of nonsense anyway."

The food appeared shortly afterwards, an ersatz Mexican fantasy of burritos and tostadas and *frijoles resfriados*, served up with a choice of red or green *salsa picante* "to add that special Christmas touch," as Fukunaga put it. Alberto cried out for *aguardiente* as well, but even connections have their limits. At least there was plenty of *cerveza fría* to wash it all down, and there were no leftovers.

When the dance music came on Stella and Galina made their apologies, pleading early appointments the next day, and said good night. Stella gave Heron a firm handshake. "It's been a pleasure," she said.

"It certainly has. And since it's Christmas I'd like to make you a present." He produced a card. "Here's my call code. Use it. Maybe we can get together later on in the week."

"I'd like that. You'll hear from me tomorrow."

"It's a deal!"

Then she was gone in a swirl of teased hair and black gabardine. As far as Heron was concerned the rest of the party was another waste of time.

3

Imperfect Evidence

He got up early the next afternoon with a mild hangover. Breakfast cured that; but when he returned to his room around 1500, a flashing green light told him he'd missed Stella's call.

The recording showed her in a shapeless steel-gray tunic, eyes minus the kohl and hair pulled into a messy bun. "Hi John," the image said. "If you're free, and if you feel like it, how about meeting me this afternoon at the Museo on Quinta? Let's say 1800, at the entrance to the Egyptian collection. Unfortunately I'll be out all afternoon so we won't be able to confirm. Just show up, if you can, and we'll have dinner afterwards. For future reference here's my call code." She recited a string of digits and signed off.

"Strange woman," Heron murmured. He replayed the message a few more times. The background was fuzzy, as usual, but the smears of light and color hinted at a well-appointed office. He realized she'd never mentioned her current assignment; it was probably one of those stuffy institutional jobs, all appearance and manners. He shrugged. "I'll be there, Stella."

He left the residence at 1725 and limped out into a damp, inhospitable night. The wind whipping up Segunda promised snow. He caught the metro at Fourteenth Street and squeezed into an overheated car. No one took pity on his gray hair or cane; he stood the whole way.

The Museo de la Ciudad housed the leftovers of five earlier museums, covering everything from Cro-Magnon *art mobilier*

23

through medieval choir-screens to Rauschenberg flags. It incorporated a crumbling prewar building, vaguely snail-shaped, within its eclectic sprawl of domes, pyramids, and reinterpreted Mozarab colonnades. Climbing up the entrance ramp he realized he hadn't been there in years. A huge banner proclaimed the current special exhibition: Greek and Roman sculpture recovered from the ruins of London. He didn't miss the irony.

Inside the echoing marble atrium he craned his neck for a glimpse of Stella. The crowds were thin; once he'd picked out the lotus-crowned pillars flanking the entrance to the Egyptian Wing it was obvious that she wasn't there. He checked the wall clock: 1805. He was late, as usual, but not so late that she would have given up and gone. No; he was late, she was later.

And later. And later. By 1820 he was irritated; by 1830 he was depressed. He figured the safest thing to do was call her.

There were four callboxes in the museum lobby. Three of them had *Fuera de Servicio* signs; the fourth had a queue. What the hell, he thought. Queues, waiting rooms, wasted time: that's life in the New City. He stepped to the rear and sighed.

Fifteen minutes later he was inside, tapping out her code. When the snow cleared, the screen showed him a black and white collage of the city's architectural highlights. Color seeped in and the images rotated at high speed, blurring and then resolving into words:

STELLA CRANACH
6A30BC5582
ADJUSTMENT COUNSELING

That screen faded to an image of Stella herself, teased and kohled and painted just as she had been at the party. "This is Stella Cranach," she said in round professional tones. "I have temporarily discontinued my private practice, but if you need counseling I can refer you to Claire Vanderveer at 92D4CC7219. Otherwise you may leave a message during the next screen."

A light flicked on overhead; the screen said, "Your message now."

Heron scowled and then did his best to neutralize the expression, all in the space of a split second. Unfortunately the camera always caught that stuff. "Hi Stella," he said. "I'm here; you're not. Call me." He would have clicked off, but at the last instant he decided he'd better repeat his code—just in case she'd lost it.

Though in his experience people never lost call codes they wanted to keep.

He finished; the box beeped; and Stella's image returned to say, "Thanks. I'll call you as soon as I can." He found that bit particularly annoying.

He turned away muttering a stream of four-letter words, and once more faced the Egyptian Wing. What the hell, he thought. Here I am. And he shuffled through the lotus pillars into the halls of Nilus.

Peering at the Gerzean bird-goddesses and flamingo vases he decided Stella was a manipulative bitch. What kind of ball-busting stunt had she pulled? Number one: she was obviously a pro, not a player. Her machine message made that clear. It looked like she'd been having a little trashy fun, slumming with the other half, pretending to be as folksy as he was. Of course she'd never actually *claimed* to be a player, but she'd never contradicted the attribution either. And what about that sob story of how she'd tried and failed to become an Art Pro? How could it be true? She must have invented it on the spur of the moment to conceal her status. There was a basic lack of sincerity in operation here, and he didn't like it at all.

Number two: well, number one covered most of the territory, so number two could just be an underscore. Citizen Cranach was not playing fair. She was posing. He didn't know what her motive was but it didn't seem to be charitable, especially where he was concerned. It looked like she had deliberately set him up for a stiff—and there was nothing he hated more than being stood up. Pretty childish behavior for an Adjustment Counselor, wouldn't you say?

Indeed he would. He drifted over to a glass case filled with rank upon rank of mummy-cases, fuming internally but doing his best to distract himself. How grotesque they were: massive, smiling, reconciled by death to the outrages of life. Well-adjusted corpses. Well, the twenty-first century could teach those ancient Egyptians a few things about fake smiles.

He remembered his own brush with the Bureau of Adjustment right after his unhappy return to Earth. Three of the four shrinks he'd seen had been mindfuckers. Their basic message was, "Do as you're told and don't question the system." At least on his fourth try he'd found a decent human being.

Other players he'd known hadn't been so lucky. A lot of

would-be artists had ended up as drugged-out vegetables, slogging away at big collective farms on the Island.

He left the mummies and turned to a long papyrus scroll: a Ptolemaic edition of the Book of the Dead, prized possession of Imhotep, son of Pshentehe. The fluid hieratic script recalled Arabic. Interesting long-term continuity. The more things change, etc. The more things don't change, etc. Hmm.

Maybe there was more to Stella's story than he understood. Maybe he should trust his initial perception. She hadn't *seemed* like a ball-buster or a mindfucker. She'd seemed like a mature and intelligent woman. And such a good listener: so much empathy, such a healthy sense of humor . . .

By the time he reached the Hall of Sphinxes—images of the androgynous Hatshepsut, master-mistress of all the known world—his judgment was in a state of suspension. It was foolish to jump to conclusions. A man his age, someone who'd seen and done as much as he had, should realize how uncertain appearances are, how unwise it is to make assumptions before all the facts are in. Being an Adjustment Counselor wasn't automatic proof of dishonesty. A mystery was a mystery and time would tell.

He made the circuit of a room full of fragments, bits of sculpture recovered from prewar excavations, tantalizing in their incompleteness, teasingly suggestive of lost power and beauty. One piece was simply a pair of lips on top of a chin, chiseled out of yellow jasper and polished to a silken finish. Its sensuality amazed him. "Fragment of a life-sized bust," the card said, "possibly of Queen Tiye." Or possibly not, Heron thought. Who could claim to recognize the lips of a woman dead thirty-five hundred years? They can still give us a carnal quiver but they can't tell us her name.

The final galleries were just window dressing for his reflections. Artifacts of the Roman occupation: tawdry coffins of plaster and gilt, funereal portraits in cracked tempera, imperfect evidence of past lives and deaths. History was a big puzzle with half the pieces missing. Each of us must reconstruct the picture according to our own expectations and eccentricities.

So much for yesterday. Today offered a little more to work with, but it was still a matter of intuition and fantasy.

He left through a side door and crunched over frosty grass to the metro stop. Sally Kuo, his second wife, had shared her days and nights with him for nine years, and even now he wasn't sure how they'd fallen apart. And if Sally was a question mark, Stella

Cranach was no more than a blank space on the page, *to be filled in by the student* out of the depths of his imagination.

The downtown train was pretty empty. He sat in comfort all the way. At Fourteenth Street he debated calling Stella and decided against it. Then he thought of calling Ursula to join him for a restaurant dinner and decided he didn't want to use up his stash of Middlebucks just yet. So he ambled home, greeted Qian on his way to the elevator, and rode up to his room.

Where, naturally, a message from Stella awaited. It had come in at 1730, five minutes after he'd left.

The image was the fuzzy product of some public booth badly in need of repairs. "So I missed you," she said. "I'm sorry, John. My meeting lasted longer than I expected and now I'm on my way out of town. Life in the fast lane, I'm afraid. That's what it means being an organization pro during the last week of the year. They're sending me on a quick trip to Miami—but don't envy me, I won't have time for the beaches. I'm really sorry. I thought this might happen but I hoped I'd be able to squeeze in a date with you. Anyhow. I'll call you when I get back, probably the beginning of next week. Happy New Year."

Her hair was messier than it had been that afternoon, and even through all the static she looked tired. "Well, Stella," he said, "I guess I'm gonna have to forgive you. But I'll know better than to count on you in the future."

He pulled off his coat, sat down in his favorite chair, and propped up his foot. A minute later the screen beeped. For an instant he hoped it would be Stella, but when the colors cleared it was just Alberto. "Hey John," he said, "you wanna go out for a drink?"

He went to bed late and tight. Halfway through the night he roused to make a quick trip to the bathroom; en route the floor chilled his bare feet to a temperature not far above absolute zero, and there he was, wide awake and shivering.

Blinking blue digits said 0505: the butt end of time. He turned on a light and examined himself in the mirror. The clarity of his eyes astounded him. Even at forty-three, dissipation had yet to take its toll. Must be those solid midcontinental genes. He thought of going out—La Puerta Negra was still serving, and he could sleep all day if he wanted to—but a glance out the window showed a heavy snowstorm in progress. He turned off the light again and sat by the glass, watching icy white specks swirl through the streetlamps' glow like a rain of ashes. It soothed him, recalling, as snow always did, his childhood in the prairie, his idealized memories of a time that existed in the great dim vastness between always and never.

He felt deliciously isolated from everything real. The falling snow was a curtain between him and the city, between him and the Lottery, between him and three million other victims of fate. Whiteness in constant motion, never changing, hinting at pattern but ultimately formless and unresolved: it seemed to whisper as it fell, lulling him, soothing him, dulling his senses, filling his body with a voluptuous weight, wrapping him in a heavy blanket of flesh.

His head drooped against the pane, and the cold shock made him realize he wasn't wide awake anymore. He crawled back under the covers and lost consciousness.

In the dream he was with Jemmy again, a slightly older Jemmy, a much better groomed Jemmy. They were on an airplane, stiff and uncomfortable in new gray business suits, knees drawn up almost to their chins. A saccharine female voice with an *r*-dropping drawl addressed them over the loudspeaker.

"Captain Kramer is initiating our final approach to Atlanta International Airport, where the temperature is a balmy twenty-two degrees Celsius. There will be a forty-five minute layover for those of you who are continuing on to Miami. Please extinguish all smoking materials, and do remain seated until the captain turns off the seat-belt sign."

They exchanged nervous grins. "Miami's just two hours away, pal," Jemmy said.

Heron felt something blocking his throat. He said nothing. Between one thought and the next they had landed. He rose painfully and shuffled off the plane into the bright bland terminal. For some reason he wanted to buy a magazine.

But the newsstand held such an enormous selection that he didn't know which one to choose. Glossy 3-D covers showed starlets with plunging necklines, theocrats with string ties, slant-eyed children with swollen bellies and twiggy limbs. He reached into the confusion and pulled out something called *New City News,* whose cover holo pictured a late-model shuttlecraft lifting off the Kissimmee launch site in a blaze of orange and red. The headline said, "RETURN TO THE SKY!" The caption said, "Sixteen winners in the April Lottery land crew assignments in the *City of*

Light, the joint New City–People's Republic orbital habitat. Find out how YOU can join them on Page Three."

Another saccharine female voice announced the last call for Flight 009 to Miami, now boarding at Gate 16, but instead of paying the news vendor and hurrying away, Heron turned to Page Three. A box on the top right listed all the information you needed in order to apply for a share in the New City Lottery. The bottom line was 4999 Middlebucks: a year's salary at a well-paying job.

"There's got to be another way," he said to the news vendor, an obese woman with bleached-out hair. "I don't want to go through with this."

The woman glanced up from her TV screen. "Too late now, son. You're in it too deep."

"I could just walk away right now, take a bus back to Chicago, get work as a supervisor in my uncle's plant."

"Don't think so, son," she said, handing him another magazine and turning back to her story.

The holo showed a bloodstained easy chair; the headline said, "MURDER IN MIAMI AGGRAVATES INTERNATIONAL SITUATION." He tossed it back at her and shouted, "This hasn't even happened yet!" She didn't pay him any mind.

He walked away, looking right and left, up and down. "Taxi!" he yelled. "Taxi!" Overhead the big video screen flashed from 009–BOARDING to 009–DEPARTING. As he swept through the glass doors that led to the parking lot, a hack came up to him and said, "Where you going, brother?"

"Home," he said. "Home."

He woke slowly, grasping at shreds of dream. *A new one,* he thought. *Not as bad, but still pretty strange.* He sat up carefully and put his feet on the floor; the heat was on full blast, the rug was warm and welcoming. *The past reinhabited. What if I had it to do all over again . . .*

"But I don't," he said aloud, and headed for the bathroom.

After some internal debate he decided to shave. He did a careful job of it, paying for his care with a long appraisal of his face. It didn't look like the face of a murderer.

"Assassin," he said. "Killer for hire." The words fell flat, awakening no remorse.

Then why these dreams, he thought. Has some part of me decided I need to atone? It made sense. However blameless he might feel on the surface (because really, hadn't he and Jemmy done the world a favor, hadn't they rid the planet of its worst warmongers, its fiercest haters?), however justified he might feel for those twenty-year-old crimes, there must be some residue of guilt buried inside, as deep as the place where he dreamed.

He washed off the soap and ran his hand over scraped skin. Smooth enough. "Maybe I should fly down to Miami and turn myself in," he said. No. That wouldn't accomplish any more than a quick suicide would, right here in the New City.

"Maybe I should make an appointment with Stella, then." He laughed. That sounded more like it. He winked at his reflection and turned away.

By a freak of nature it snowed for the next three days. His foot bothered him, so going out in the slippery damp was not an option. And since George Early and his girlfriend had wrangled their way back into her place again, he was completely alone: a rare state of affairs for someone as gregarious as John Heron. The only person who visited him was Alberto, and he tended to leave almost as soon as he arrived.

Mostly he stayed in bed, punching up videos and drinking Irish coffee till sundown, then straight vodka till midnight. The dreams stayed away. After the first night he was surprised. After the second he was relieved, and after the third, merely oblivious.

4

Shut Up, Alberto

George Early was beating him, but that was just as well. Most players figured that bad luck on New Year's Eve meant bad luck on New Year's Day, and Heron, for once in his life, didn't give a damn. His number wasn't in the running; he was momentarily immune to fortune. So let Early feel the glow.

He laid out his hand. Two tens, period. Early had a pair of deuces and three jacks, netting him the jackpot: two bits Texan.

"John, this is no fun. Your heart's not in it."

"True, true. Find another sucker."

"Hey Ursula?"

But Ursula was deep in conversation with Pacifico Ortiz at the next table and couldn't be bothered. And Lola Achebe, Early's girlfriend, was too fidgety to sit still.

"You know I'm singing tonight, baby," she said. "I can't concentrate on that shit. This is a big gig for me."

Early shook his head. "Can't drink, can't smoke, can't play cards, can't f—"

"Now watch yourself," said Lola, but she said it sweetly.

They abandoned the game and ordered fresh drinks. That took longer than it should have; while it was only 1800, the Rincón was already packed, and service had started lagging. With second shift suspended for the holiday, there was twice the usual number of players wandering the streets and drifting from café to bar to nightclub, in serious pursuit of the good life. Tonight, at least,

they mostly found it. Even Heron, with nothing at stake, felt
intoxicated by the pervasive spirit of fun. Over the past few days
his foot had improved, restoring most of his mobility, and the
weather had mellowed to an almost springlike softness. He was
getting out and around again, rubbing shoulders with the whole
Barrio Violado, in his element once more. He had a whole string
of parties to check out before the old year passed.

"All I want this drawing," said Early, gathering up the cards,
"is an apartment as nice as John's."

"That dump? Big enough for a bed and a table, and then you
can barely get the door open."

"Listen to this fat cat!" Ursula leaned over the back of her chair.
"John, my friend, I don't think you remember what dormitory
living is like."

"Yeah," said Pacifico. "You even got your own personal
callbox. That's splendor, amigo!"

He decided not to argue. The kids were right, of course; he
tended to forget how seriously the housing situation had declined
since he immigrated. His over-thirty-five status spared him the
multibunk rooms and the ten-way toilets.

"But I'm setting my sights even higher," said Pacifico, who in
spite of the hour was fairly drunk. "I want one of those Caribbean
vacations. Palm trees, grass huts, klick after klick of shimmery
sand . . ."

"Good luck, pal." Early shuffled idly. "MEQMAT gives out
just ten of those a year, and there are three million of us drooling
at the prospect."

"So maybe I'll get lucky." Pacifico smoothed back his long
blond hair. "Maybe I'll meet somebody on the Junta at some party
tonight, um, *y después nos hacemos muy amigos*, right?"

Lola cackled. "That's the spirit, Pacifico. Whore your way into
the top slot."

He ignored her. "And then I'll get invitations to those secret
island hideaways every other week."

"And maybe I'll meet MEQMAT," said Early, "and be invited
to tea in the Black Tower."

That set off a flurry of frivolous speculations about how
MEQMAT would look and behave if MEQMAT were an animate
being (would he be male, would he be female, would he be
well-hung, would he play a vicious game of poker) until finally
Ursula confessed, "You know, I haven't the slightest idea what

MEQMAT stands for. I suppose they told me in school but I forgot."

"Multi—" said Early, and was stumped.

Pacifico raised a smug eyebrow. "Monster Extraordinaire, Quintessentially Malevolent And Tyrannical."

Ursula laughed. Early said, "Mangles Every Quality, Motivates All Tears."

"Makes Everyone Quake in Misery And Terror," said Lola.

"Very pretty, very clever," said Heron. "But obviously none of you ever had to qualify as a landed immigrant."

"Oh yeah, Mr. Smartass?"

"Yeah. I quote from the New Citizens' Orientation Manual, twenty-third edition: 'Sociometricians agree that our Lottery is what makes the New City the most desirable place on Earth to live and work. To ensure its fairness, our Lottery is conducted by an incorruptible artificial intelligence, MEQMAT: a Multi-Elemental Quasi-Macrocognitive Aleatory Transformer.' "

Lola and Early applauded.

Ursula said, "What the fuck is that supposed to mean?"

Pacifico said, "Manufactures Excrement Quietly, Masturbates Adroitly, Too."

Heron said, "Bravo, but I was right."

And they debated the nuances of "aleatory" and "macrocognitive" for at least ten minutes. Just past the point of tedium Lola begged them to stop. "Big deal—you can talk yourselves silly, but all it means is MEQMAT is one smart machine and we got to do exactly what he says." She surveyed them archly. "Unless we make Art Pro, which is *my* New Year's wish. And that's got nothing to do with luck."

"And everything to do with talent, as we're about to see live on stage at the Siete Pecados Mortales." Heron stood and surveyed them benignly. "Shall we get the hell out of here?"

Much later and drunker he shared the same corner table with Alberto Favaloro. Ursula and Pacifico had long since vanished, off to bigger and better parties in the Barrio Amarillo; Lola and Early had gone on to join the thronging queues in the Plaza de la Paz, impatient to read their new assignments in the Lottery.

"So look at you, Alberto—not even curious about the headaches MEQMAT has in store for you."

"Tomorrow is soon enough to find out. Who needs the crowds?"

Heron laughed, a dry rumbling ha-ha-ha. "What a pair of old farts we are. Grizzled veterans of the battlefields of fortune."

"It could be worse. I could be eating rats in Miami with the rest of my family. Things haven't been so bad for me here."

"I guess it takes a refugee to appreciate what the Junta has to offer. But you should have been here earlier to hear Pacifico and Ursula bitching and moaning about the system. Misery and terror, they called it. Cybernetic tyranny."

Alberto spread his hands. "Any time they want to they can leave, right?"

"Yeah." Heron slid his elbows out over the table, resting his chin on his wrists. "But I can't. And I wonder sometimes if that's a problem. I wonder if I've accepted the city's limits a little too tamely."

"Don't be silly."

"I'm not being silly. I'm just—wondering."

"Okay. What if you did live in Buenos Aires or Sacramento? Where would you be now? Working as a sales rep for some munitions concern, with ulcers and a pot belly? Sitting in a national ministry, twiddling your thumbs and taking bribes to support your teenage mistress? Or maybe you'd be on the other side of the line—sweeping floors, collecting garbage, begging in the streets. Who can say? But whatever you did, that would be *it*. You'd be locked into it forever, and you'd have no time for anything except a few minor vices on the side. All class societies are straitjackets, amigo. What could be more liberating than the rule of chance?"

"You sound like Citizen Zhang on a good day."

"Shit, I mean it. You'd prefer sucking up to an elite whose motto was 'Why tell the truth when you can lie?' and whose guiding principle was greed? Because that's what it's like out there in the wide world, from Dallas to Shanghai."

"Enough, enough, I give in. I guess I've been asking myself too many questions lately. I've been too much alone, yeah, that's it, just a little too inward."

"Oh, come on. Your problem is very simple—you just don't want to face it. You still got that woman on your mind." He looked up sharply. Alberto chuckled. "Oh, you think I haven't noticed how you've been ever since Minoru's party. But I know you, John. I've watched you operate for fifteen years. You like having a steady woman, and you haven't had one for a long time. You're ripe."

"Huh. I didn't think it was so obvious."

"Well, it is. Don't worry. She seemed like a pretty hot catch, and she also seemed to like you. So you might be in for a very pleasant New Year."

Heron blushed fiercely. "Shut up, Alberto." And they both laughed out loud.

5

The Black Tower

A squawk from the callbox wrenched him out of sound sleep the next afternoon. Consciousness had rarely been so repugnant. As his eyes shot open, searching for the source of the torment, he caught the tail end of a message fading from his screen. He was too slow and squinty-eyed to spell it out; instead he grabbed the printout and held it up to the light.

The first few lines were markers for his address in the Lottery matrix. He skipped them and went for the meat of the text. Its menace was unmistakable. "You are to report to the Torre de la Raza, Room 3624, at 1700 on January 1, for your next assignment in the Lottery of the New City."

He groaned, swore, and pounded his mattress. Seventeen-hundred was four hours from now, when according to the Bureau of Disabilities he should have another full week of rest before resuming active status in the Lottery. It wasn't fair. There had to be a glitch somewhere—of course, that was it, some codes had been transposed, some commands rerouted; this summons couldn't be intended for him at all.

Unfortunately he couldn't ignore it. If he even tried the Guardia Civil would be on his ass in minutes. Mistake or no mistake, players didn't disregard Lottery directives. That kind of cheek could result in a long-term assignment to the collective farms, in an enforced tour of duty at the waste reclamation sites, or even in exile.

No, he'd have to appear in person and clear this up himself. He had a ready-made case. With one hand on his luck he tapped out the commands accessing his Lottery status. As it flicked down the screen he pressed PRINT, and a minutely detailed history of his disability scrolled out of the box.

It looked impressively nasty. His mood picked up a little and he pulled on some clothes. The box could keep processing while he went down for breakfast.

In the refectory there was only one subject of discourse: who got what.

Alberto was in ecstasies. "John!" he called, over a plate of pancakes and scrambled tofu. "I'm out of this dump. I've been reassigned to Propaganda, with a suite in Y Block. Seventh floor!"

"Great, Alberto. And you're not even married."

"No. But something tells me I'm going to be very popular with the ladies this year."

"Sounds good. But listen to what happened to me. . . ." And he told his tale of woe.

Alberto wasn't impressed. "That's nothing," he said. "It'll all be cleared up by tomorrow. If you want to hear a *real* hard luck story, talk to Pacifico. MEQMAT's made him a hack—he'll be doing twelve-hour graveyard shifts four nights a week, from now till April. And he still hasn't been reassigned to new quarters."

"Poor sucker," said John.

"Don't mention suckers around me." Qian appeared, wearing a smile bigger than her face. "The Lottery just retired me with full benefits. I'm getting a garden apartment with a river view."

Cheers echoed from every corner of the room. "When's the party?" shouted Alberto.

"Every night from now till the new century! Stop by this evening, if you can stand to be in the same room with five of my grandchildren."

Alberto laughed. "As long as there's liquor I'll be there."

"How about you, John?" she asked.

"I don't know. I'll try."

"You better do better than try!" she said, and sailed off to the next round of congratulations.

Fortified by Alberto's optimism, Qian's relief, and four or five cups of coffee, Heron limped across Ninth Street to the Plaza de la Paz, papers clutched against his chest. Dusk was already deepening into night. Amber floodlights played across the sleek black surface of the Torre de la Raza, looming against a sky full of crisp stars and shredded clouds.

Even in a bind this dodgy, the sight of the Tower recharged him. Rising in seven tiers, crisscrossed by broad ramps and ornamental buttresses, it resembled a combination Babylonian ziggurat, Toltec sun-temple, and Bauhaus factory. Chin Leung, its architect, had been no candidate for false modesty.

The Tower was the tallest and most massive building ever constructed: four hundred meters square, five hundred twenty meters high, capable of swallowing the Great Pyramid and the Houston Astrodome in a single bite. Its basements were a labyrinthine underworld of corridors and levels and passageways, delved deep into Tertiary bedrock. Its upper stories were a three-dimensional maze, containing uncounted thousands of offices, studios, bathrooms, libraries, reception halls, lobbies, auditoria, and residential suites. Each of its terraces sported enough trees and flowers to rival Nebuchadrezzer's hanging gardens, and its fourth tier contained a zoo stocked with every surviving species of terrestrial animal.

For Heron the Black Tower embodied all the promise of the New City. Beyond that, it was a metaphor for mankind, a challenge to heaven, an expression of the nobility and daring of the human race. For in tasty irony Chin Leung had built it, not of granite or steel, but of clay, of common earth—just like Adam. Its construction had pioneered the ceramic technology that now housed most of the world.

He entered through the north gate, passing bare trees and antique statuary culled from the ruins of Europe and Asia. A team of security guards confronted him just inside. One gripped his wrist and held it under an ultraviolet scanner, frowning all the while. The scanner beeped; the guard said, "You're clear. Elevators are that way. Bank Seven."

Holiday though it was, the Tower swarmed like an anthill. Heron brushed past organization pros in sober tunics, Chinese businessmen in three-piece suits, and Texan sightseers toting gray-market video cameras. He squeezed into the first available lift and said, "Thirty, please." Hidden speakers played Marpus Lilling's "Suite for Saxophone and Silverware"; plump matrons kept time with booted toes. At his stop, another set of functionaries detained him and ran another scan of his hex code. Again he was cleared. Colored bulbs inlaid in the floor flicked on to guide him through the maze of corridors and the crush of supplicants and bureaucrats.

Room 3624 was the anteroom of an enormous suite, guarded by a security detail armed with truncheons and automatic rifles. The rifles made him nervous. Once more his tattoo was examined; once more he was passed to the next station of the labyrinth. A sober young lieutenant, face hidden by a bullet-proof mask, delivered him to a door marked ASSISTANT TO THE PROGRAM DIRECTOR.

He hesitated before knocking. The rigmarole of security had unnerved him more than he thought possible. He was no longer as confident of his case as he had been at ground level; funny what one elevator ride can do to you. What if he never saw Thirteenth Street again?

He knocked. A voice said come in. He did.

The office was as luxurious as he feared. The far wall was curtained in Chinese silk; the floor was muffled in a thick geometric rug, product no doubt of Tucson's Navaho ghetto. Behind a huge oak desk, wreathed in a blue cloud of tobacco smoke, sat Stella Cranach.

She smiled shyly. "Hi, John."

"Uh, Happy New Year, Stella."

"Sorry about our museum date."

"I had a good time without you."

"Oh." She gestured with her cigarette. "Sit. Please."

He lowered himself into a lacquered armchair, very slowly. Then their eyes met through the haze and they both started laughing.

"Jesus, Stella! I don't believe this."

"You will." She waved at the sideboard. "Coffee? Smoke?"

He accepted one of those expensive Cuban cigarettes and lit it off hers. "First indulgence of the New Year," he said, inhaling deeply. "Now tell me what's going on."

"Well, I'm about to offer you a job."

"Offer? You mean I get to say no if I don't want it?"

"That's right."

She blinked; her eyes looked tired, and there were lines in her forehead. She was wearing a loose ponytail and hardly any makeup. She didn't look like an official with an office deep in the Tower. She didn't even look like the demimondaine he'd met a week earlier. He felt off balance.

"I'm not sure my ears are working right." He waved away a

fresh cloud of smoke. "Who are you, some secret member of the Junta? Because I never heard of any private citizen who could pass out assignments. That's MEQMAT's job."

"True, but there are, shall we say, certain technicalities."

His eyes questioned. She drew a breath.

"Let me start at the beginning. Until a month ago I was just an ordinary shrink. My rating was high, but I'd never been singled out for anything special. Then it happened. A prominent official from the Bureau of Adjustment invited me to collaborate on an experiment in memory enhancement. I'd just written an article on computer models of human memory; it appeared in the *Pacific Journal of Medicine,* and this official had read and admired it. She asked me if I'd like to join her own research team. It was a big step up, lots of perks, and I was getting frustrated with my private practice. So I accepted."

"How come you never mentioned this when we met at Minoru's?"

"I didn't want to alienate you. Once we started talking I realized you didn't care much for pros, so I kept quiet about the work I was doing. It's not like I was going to hide it forever, but we had enough to talk about for the time being."

"So that story about your four tries at Art Pro status was just a fiction?"

She frowned. "Not at all. Pros can be artists, just the same as players. Do you think I'd lie to you?"

"Maybe."

They exchanged a long look. Stripped of its paint her face was solid and wholesome. In fact she had the same down-home bones as he did. He'd be willing to bet money—real money—that underneath that dye her hair was mousy brown. Whether she was a liar or not, she certainly liked to embroider the truth.

She pulled on her cigarette and gazed off to the side. "Well. Maybe we have nothing more to say to one another."

"Oh, Stella, I'm sorry. But you must realize that this is all pretty strange."

"True." She shrugged. "Okay, I'll go on. So now I've got this position on the Subcommittee for Simulation and Modification and I'm up to my ears in work. Citizen Liang's experiment is very complicated, very detailed and time-consuming. We need dozens of subjects and they all have to fall within narrow psychological parameters. Among my responsibilities is determining who fits and who doesn't. Given the random selection process necessitated by our delightful society's basic tenets, it means that I disqualify four out of every five candidates. Which translates as four lost hours for every new subject I find—and I have lots of other responsibilities, too. But that's *my* problem. The reason why you're here is—I know you'd make an ideal subject. Just talking to you I can figure out your approximate psychic indices, and they dovetail nicely with Liang's guidelines. So the job is yours if you want it."

"Wait. You still haven't told me what that means. Memory enhancement? Experimental subjects? It sounds like you want me to be a guinea pig for some mindfucker drug."

"No! There are no drugs involved. It's more like a course of study, pursued in direct neural link with the system."

"A crash course in the art of memory?"

"More or less."

He waited for her to elaborate, but she didn't.

"See, I can't tell you much about it in advance, because preconceptions will spoil your response. Believe me, it's a harmless process."

"But you just said it's still in the experimental stage. I don't know, Stella. The Bureau of Adjustment doesn't have the cleanest reputation in town. What if this experiment backfires?" He looked down at his hands. "Everybody has things they'd rather forget. What if I end up with total recall, and my unconscious keeps playing inner-eyelid movies of all the shittiest scrapes I've been through? I could go nuts."

"No, no, no. It's not like that at all. Listen, I've done three dips myself—"

"Dips?"

"SSM jargon. I've plugged in three times without any ill effects. You'd be in no danger."

"Hmm. What enticements are you offering?"

"Aha! First off, it's a six-month assignment, and in that period you'd have to do eighteen dips. With briefing and debriefing, each session takes about four hours. So that means four hours of work—if you call lying around with electrodes on your head work—every ten days. Period. Sound interesting yet?"

"Jesus. It sounds boring. What would I do with myself all that while? With this foot the way it's been, all I do now is drink and watch the box. I don't need six more months of that."

"Oh, but I haven't finished. During the course of the assignment you'd have full Remedial privileges, same as a new immigrant or a baby pro. You could study whatever you wanted with any teacher you chose, and you'd have unlimited access to the Tower fitness complex. So you could certainly sweat off all the liquor you've guzzled in the last month."

That got him. He rubbed his chin and focused on the print hanging from the left-hand wall; it was a recolored version of Breughel's "Tower of Babel." Funny how a minor painting like that had survived the wrack and ruin of the war years. He imagined himself gliding up the spiral ramp, round and around, passing through the zone of clouds into free space, floating in the vacuum, high as a kite and wise as a god. Stella's offer sounded that good.

"There's got to be a catch."

She rolled her eyes. "Maybe my estimate of your paranoia index was off. Maybe you wouldn't make a suitable subject after all."

"Come on, Stella. I've been playing the game too long to imagine that any plum could fall into my lap this easily. Your process must have side effects. Severe depression, delusions, hallucinations. Otherwise why would they give you ten days to recover between sessions?"

"There often *is* a brief period of disorientation after the dip—I'll grant you that. And it is conceivable that some people might develop psychological disorders; that's one of the things we're looking out for. So I was exaggerating. It's not one hundred percent safe. But it's shaping up very nicely so far."

"Okay. It's sounding better and better." He looked at her squarely in the face and softened his voice. "But why me?"

She smiled. "I'm trying to do you a favor, John. Is that so mysterious? You're a good man. You deserve a break."

They both sat still for a while, staring at opposite walls without talking. John felt a tingling in his ears, a prickling in the hairs on his neck. She liked him. She wanted to have him around for a while.

Finally he glanced up and said, "When do I start?"

"Right now, citizen." Suddenly she looked very businesslike. She spoke into the intercom. "Grishka. How's our status? Yes? Lots of memory? We'll be right over." She stood up briskly. "Before we can officially inscribe you we've got to take a look at your brain—"

"Wait a minute—"

"With the EEG. It's completely painless and non-intrusive.

Safer than an X-ray." She started for the door. "The lab's in Section Forty-four."

He hesitated. "Hold on, Stella. It's New Year's Day—I mean night. What's the hurry? You promised me a cushy score, and now you're asking me to work night shift on a holiday."

She looked tired again. "Listen, with this job one of the tradeoffs is odd hours. Come on, John. We'll be done by 2200. I'll take you out for dinner afterwards. Deal?"

He had to hurry to keep up. "Um—yeah. Deal."

She swept ahead of him, passing armed guards and doors marked DO NOT DISTURB. He decided the easiest thing to do was just trust her.

They took an elevator somewhere—the ride was so smooth he wasn't sure if they went up or down. After another security gauntlet they negotiated a door that said MEQMAT-IV. Inside, everything was cool, quiet, and unnerving.

The room was a sprawling cave whose nether reaches faded into shadows. Its ceiling was low and festooned with a tangle of pipes and tubing. Soft lights below eye level created an air of mystery. Scattered throughout were padded couches, potted plants, computer terminals, and several kilometers of electronic spaghetti.

Grigori Arkadyevich Likhodeyev waited for them beside a vase of lilies. He was unbelievably boyish and fresh-faced, the earnest young scientist defined.

Stella made the introductions. "Citizen Likhodeyev runs the lab. Call him Grishka. He's kind of square but he's not a bad guy."

Grishka kept smiling, hands clasped behind his back, standing there all solid and Slavic in his white lab coat and perfectly combed hair. He did look pretty square. At a nod from Stella he started—suspiciously like a still hologram brought to life—and gestured toward the nearest couch.

"If you'll make yourself comfortable here, John, we can start the EEG." His accent sounded more like Buffalo than Moscow. "You've done this before, haven't you?"

"Eighteen years ago, I think."

"Hmm. Well, things haven't changed that much. Just lie down, that's it, and turn your head. . . ."

Deftly, Grishka began attaching the electrodes, glancing back at a bank of screens to make sure he had them in the right places. Stella leaned over the main display, nodding to herself and fiddling with the controls.

"Okay, Grishka. That's it."

He joined her and they passed some jargon back and forth. Heron felt stupid—yes, and off balance. Stella certainly had a talent for keeping him that way. He closed his eyes and tried to tune them out.

After about ten minutes she came over to him and said, "You look fine so far, John—perfect induction material. Are you by any chance prone to vivid dreams?"

"Um, as a matter of fact, I am. At least lately. Why do you ask?"

"Oh, because your configuration suggests it, and because vivid dreamers make our best subjects. So that's one more plus. But we need a complete reading. We have to monitor your brain while it's actually in REM state, and we can't do that unless you fall asleep."

"I'm not tired."

"We have ways. Are you game?"

"You said no drugs."

"I meant no experimental or mind-altering drugs. I'm just talking about a simple hypnotic. Enough for a short nap."

"Well . . . I guess if it's the only way . . ."

She smiled. Grishka produced two skinnies, one pink and one green. "The pink is aphypnone," he said. "A mild soporific. The green one is peronirine, an acetylcholine analog. It makes you dream."

Heron shrugged. "Fire when ready."

Stella applied the skinnies while Grishka called up the induction program. "We've got all the core you could possibly want, Stella."

She chuckled. "You mean from here to Mars and everything in between?"

"Almost. We've got *City of Light*, *Kosmograd*, *Yama's Gate*, and *Yueh Cheng*. Not to mention Bolinas and Bakersfield."

"Sounds good."

Grishka turned back to Heron. "How are you doing?"

"Sleepy."

"Fine. Now, before you nod off, I want you to look right up at the ceiling—that's it, directly overhead—and imagine it as a screen. Now imagine your eyes as two projectors. Think of two rays emanating upward, one from each eye. . . ."

Grishka's flat tones skimmed over him, leading him through a simple visualization exercise. Though he felt duller and more sluggish with every passing second he did his best to concentrate. First he drew circles with his eyes, then figure eights; then he pictured himself tracing their course with his feet. He fought the urge to drift off, and pulled the image into tighter focus. The drugs gave his synapses seven-league boots.

He was walking on the ceiling, on the floor, out the door, through a bright new landscape. He was walking the path of infinity with lengthening strides, covering kilometers at a step, centuries in a heartbeat.

A distant voice that didn't sound at all like Grishka's was whispering in his ear. "The road into Egypt is a long and painful one; so the poet warns, so the traveler confirms."

PART TWO

ALEXANDREIA-BY-EGYPT

6

As Above, So Below

The first thing he felt was the bottom falling out of his stomach. The rest of his organs came next. Then, after several eons of visceral anguish, after an interminable nightmare of churning and wrenching and bubbling, the pain just stopped, just went away, taking his somatic awareness with it.

Time switched off for a while.

When he could notice such things again he was walking down a dusty lane in warm darkness. The dust he recognized by feel; his eyes didn't seem to be working, or at least not yet. Noise he could sense, though, floating gently down his auditory canal, growing steadily louder and harsher.

"You dirty Greek! Where's your money, you son of a bitch? You think you can take what you want for free? I bet you'd go for my ass too, you filthy shit-licker."

Light flickered up, yellow and red, casting shadows at his feet. He saw pale flaking walls in bright torchlight, with an expanse of black dirt between.

"Where's your money, you Greek bastard? Are you so drunk you forgot what you were doing?"

His nose twitched. He smelled sweat, sour wine, rotting garlic, and stale piss, all mixed together in a vivid bouquet, with the faintest, most delicate undertone of fish.

"That wineskin's spent, you clown, and so's your balls! Pay up! Pay up!"

Something tugged at him. He was wearing a loose tunic—no, *chiton* was the word—a comfortably familiar garment. Two children were pulling at his hem, screaming at him with gutter accents.

"Your coins, you buttfuck! Doricha doesn't put out for free!"

The owner of that earsplitting little voice seemed to be a boy of about ten—brown-skinned, black-haired, naked except for a rag around his hips. With him was a girl of similar age and appearance, most likely his sister. Both glared at him with undiluted malice. Then the boy reached down, scooped up some dirt, and threw it at his head.

"Can't you hear? Can't you talk? Answer me!"

John Heron figured it was time for a change of scenery. He started running.

After a dozen meters he remembered his bad foot and wondered why it wasn't complaining. He was hauling ass like a fifteen-year-old, as quick and light as he'd ever been.

But the two urchins were almost as fast, and they were throwing rocks, broken tiles, and garbage. Their screams had roused the neighborhood. Heads appeared in upper windows.

"What is this racket? Call out the watch!"

Rounding a corner, Heron almost collided with two men, dressed alike in leather cuirasses and steel helmets. One held a torch overhead; the other drew a sword.

As he recoiled Doricha and her brother came hurtling up behind him and slammed into his legs. Heron went sprawling. Only luck and an agile dodge saved him from being skewered; he was on his feet again in an instant. He turned on his tormentors, and had begun repaying them with some invective of his own, when they both looked up, took in the soldiers, and fled in the opposite direction.

A stream of laughter cascaded after them, falling in intervals like a song.

"Such a pretty picture!"

Four more individuals appeared behind the soldiers. The first was a woman with thick black hair and a face so painted she had to be a whore.

"Well, my good man," she said, "what have you got to say for yourself? Brawling with street trade? Flushed with drink? Really!

I see silver in your hair. Have you no concept of the dignity of age?"

"They jumped me," he said, shrugging. "I ran."

She nodded. She was wearing a scarlet gown whose folds barely contained the ripe pendulosities of her bosom. Her expression was at once mocking and sympathetic.

"Prudent, if not heroic."

Of her companions one was a woman, one a man, and the other something in between. The woman was about twenty-five, draped in a rose-colored chiton with a yellow peplos on top. The in-between was somewhat older, wearing a voluminous robe of midnight blue. Heron now recognized the smooth jaw and plump contours of a middle-aged eunuch.

A eunuch, he thought. Why didn't I realize that before?

The man was over fifty, a broad-shouldered, swag-bellied giant with curly hair and a big red nose. Traces of boyish charm still lingered in the ruin of his face; the remains of an Herculean physique persisted beneath the sag and bulge of his flesh. He wore a whitish tunic and a purple chlamys, clasped with a large gold brooch. He ambled forward and put his hand on the whore's shoulder, glancing at Heron with watery blue eyes.

The soldiers meanwhile stood at ease, paying him little attention. Nevertheless Heron felt edgy, confused, threatened. Something about this tableau—something about these people—

A light went on in his mind and he caught his breath. "*Kale Kleopatra!*" he said, falling on his knees in the dirt. As he spoke he knew that he was quoting from the *Iliad* (Book Nine, line 556, with a change of case from dative to vocative), that the words meant, "Cleopatra the fair," and that Cleopatra was the whore's name. Also that she wasn't a whore at all, but Queen of Egypt, scion of Alexander, daughter of Amun-Re, earthly manifestation of holy Isis.

Cleopatra laughed again. "Stand up, mate. We're on the bum tonight."

He rose stiffly and looked her over. The makeup was obviously a joke, part of her disguise. She was famous for these sprees in the rougher parts of town. Beneath layers of rouge and antimony he could make out the large brown eyes, the fierce hawklike nose, the full lips and wide forehead of the most brilliant woman alive. She was close to forty by now, and it showed; but even in sluttish rags she retained an awesome majesty.

"Like what you see?" she said, cocking an eyebrow. "You're

lucky I'm in a good mood, or I'd have my boyfriend here punch you in the nose."

"I beg your pardon, Your Majesty. I couldn't help but stare. You're a legend."

"True. And what are you?"

"My name is Nikias of Rhodos." The words came automatically. "I'm a teacher of rhetoric."

She turned to Antony. "An omen, my love!" *Nikias* came from the word *nike*: victory.

"Too bad he's not a soldier, then," said Antony, with a touch of a slur. "It's soldiers we need in Egypt, not rhetoricians."

"Well." Cleopatra played with her rings. "You're not part of the Mouseion, are you?"

"Unfortunately, no. I teach privately."

"In Rhakotis?" She cackled. "Walking home after a late lesson?"

"Uh, not exactly." What *was* he doing in the Egyptian ghetto, anyway? His mind was foggy, but his tongue knew exactly what to do. "I'm returning to Gamma from the temple," he said. "The Sarapeion." It sounded plausible. "I gave an offering at the evening service."

"Oho!" Cleopatra turned to the younger woman. "Charmion! We should take this one home with us. He makes a better fool than that Roman Plancus ever did." She glanced back at Heron. "It's close to dawn, my friend; the clepsydrae of Alexandreia keep trickling, even though your fuddled mind has stopped. If you attended the evening service, you've done several hours worth of wandering since then."

Charmion yawned ostentatiously. "Since he's such an amusing fool, madam, you should hire him as your son's tutor. At least he's honest in his foolery. Unlike those scoundrels Rhodon and Theodoros."

"Tch, tch. What an uncharitable heart! So ready to believe the worst!"

"I know what I know, madam."

"As do I." Cleopatra settled down on an overturned pithos with an unqueenly grunt. "So, good Nikias. You've been whoring and carousing with the children of the Nile. I must say, you prefer partners of unusually tender years."

"That was just the boy's slander, madam. I'm no fonder of wine and virgins than any other Hellene."

"That's still a considerable fondness—though none in this

company is immune to it." She winked at Antony. "But the night dwindles while we talk nonsense, and the morning service for holy Isis is no more than an hour away. What do you suggest, my friends?"

The eunuch spoke. "Perhaps we could send Derketaios to fetch some carrying chairs, and attend at the Iseion by the harbor."

"Too far away. We'd never make it."

Antony said something in Latin; Cleopatra laughed and replied in Greek. "Soon enough, soon enough, my love. But what's your opinion, Charmion?"

She was adjusting the folds of her himation. "As good master Nikias reminds us, the Sarapeion is close by. What better destination?"

"I won't argue with that," said Cleopatra. "Any dissenters? Good! Master Nikias! Will you lead the way?"

It occurred to Heron that he was drunk and dog-tired, that he had no idea where he was or what he was doing—but once again his tongue came to the rescue. "It will be an honor, Your Highness. We can take Philopator to Our Lady of Plenty and be there in a quarter-hour."

They set off down the street, Derketaios leading as before with the torch held high. Cleopatra walked along with Heron, thrusting her arm through his as if they were old drinking companions.

"Well, then!" she said. "I suppose you're a disciple of Zeno, like every other learned man of the age?"

"No, not I. My heart still rejoices in good fortune and suffers in adversity. I'm too frail a vessel for Stoicism."

"Then perhaps you've wandered down the flowery paths of Epikouros?"

"Some distance I've gone, but turned aside in the end. His teaching, I think, fails to reconcile its own contradictions."

"You have eccentric leanings. Do any of the philosophers satisfy you?"

Heron thought a minute. "Pyrrho, maybe."

"Hah! 'Nothing is certain, not even that.' If I felt that way I'd never get out of bed."

Heron smiled. "You wouldn't have to. You're the Queen."

Cleopatra gave him a withering look. "Only in poetry or stage plays are queens allowed to rest on their majesty. Any heir of the Lagidai must keep his head or lose it. Perhaps you know our history? I could never have kept the serpent of Egypt on my brow, these past twenty years, without a few certainties."

"I concede the point. In any case I find philosophy a hollow substitute for religion. Men may argue over causes and conundrums, but only the gods hold the final truths."

"Why, Nikias! Either you're extremely old-fashioned or extremely up-to-date."

Heron shrugged. "As above, so below."

Cleopatra's face assumed the expression of a predatory cat. She made a sign with her right hand. Heron made the proper countersign. She made another, and again he answered it. At her third challenge he faltered, saying, "Only the Maiden and the Harper have granted me their light; I've delved no deeper into the Mysteries."

"Deep enough, though, for a wandering rhetorician." She nodded to herself. "You've danced away death at Eleusis, and sung the hymns of Orpheus at Mytilene. You've done good service for your soul. Are you as well versed in literature as you are in the Mysteries?"

"Oh, I know my Homer pretty well, and a good piece of Euripides, and a few books of Archilochos, Alkaios, and Theognis. And of course the moderns, Apollonios, Kallimachos, Theokritos, and the rest. Not to mention Plato and Aristotelis. My head is full of old words."

"You're not as big a fool as I thought."

Heron showed his teeth in a wide grin. "Nor as big a fool as I used to be."

She pushed her face right up to his, so that for a moment they breathed each other's exhalations. "Then stay by me, Nikias. I need men like you around me in this miserable season." Without waiting for an answer, she disengaged her arm and strolled over to Antony, speaking softly to him in Latin.

Heron walked on alone, calm and quiet for the first time since his irruption. Some weird stuff was afoot, no doubt about it. He should probably be confused, distraught, racking his brain for reasons and explanations, but instead he was as relaxed and optimistic as he'd ever been. He was actually having fun.

The best part of it was the torrent of information flooding his brain. Fluent *koine*. Total recall of the *Iliad*, the *Odyssey*, and a few dozen lyric poets and philosophers. A complete street map of Alexandreia-by-Egypt. A host of personal memories belonging to this fellow Nikias, including details of daily life, current events, geography, and religion. It was like wandering through a museum that contained the whole world. He'd never realized how sensual, how exhilarating pure knowledge could be.

He was seeing and thinking and feeling from two separate points of view: that of John Heron and that of Nikias Rhodios. It wasn't the least bit confusing or frightening; he had no sense of being an invader in another mind. Instead it was as if two discrete entities had combined to create a new consciousness, a two-headed beast in which Heron's personality guided and dominated, without obscuring Nikias' responses.

Could this be what Stella meant by a crash course in the art of memory? With an act of will he plunged deep into the tangle of neurons beneath his skull, parting threads of tissue like vines and tendrils in an overgrown garden, blundering through the undergrowth till he came to a clearing where the sun shone brightly. Alexandreia's walls and alleys faded; Nikias receded; Heron grew and solidified. Memory: a black-haired woman in a plush office making promises and reassurances. Memory: a padded couch in a room full of screens and wires. Somehow he'd bridged the gap between this and that.

But how? Was it all just a stroll through his cortices, an electronically enhanced dream of Alexandreia, a movie projected directly into his mind? Or was it something else?

He'd heard such deceptions might be possible. Perhaps they were fact already, in the secret laboratories of Chengdu and Lubbock, behind massive doors marked MEQMAT-IV. A dream as real as life . . .

The sensation of a human hand grasping his forearm brought him back to Alexandreia-by-Egypt. Charmion had come up behind him during his reverie, and she regarded him through long sapphire eyes.

"Master Nikias?" she said. "You stumbled." The curve of her lips suggested mischief.

"I—" he said. His mouth opened and closed a few times, like a fish short of oxygen. This woman's face looked familiar, very familiar indeed. "You're Stella," he said. "You're Charmion but you're Stella too."

And she was. There was no mistaking that nose, those eyes, that smile.

"Hush," she said.

"Why? Will I break the spell?"

"In a way. You almost did just then, with all that introspection."

"I could snap myself out of this at will?"

"Not now." Her eyes were playful. "The program has learned to compensate for you." Her lips were stained with a creamy red paste. "It's very smart, you know."

"Is this some kind of interactive game?"

"Hush," she said.

They had reached the avenue of sphinxes leading to the propylon of the Temple of Sarapis. There was still no sign of dawn, and Derketaios' torch cast a radiance that was feeble at best. Heron had only a dim impression of the smooth stone flanks of the sphinxes, and the propylon's fluted pillars; then Cleopatra was banging on a pair of gilded doors and servants were ushering them in with profound bows and unctuous greetings.

"Wait here with Antony," Stella said. "The rest of us have work to do."

"Whatever you say, Charmion."

The non-males disappeared through a side door. Heron, along with Antony and the two guards, stayed where he was in the breezy forecourt. He felt sand underfoot and glimpsed the silhouettes of lotus-crowned pillars all around him. The scent of myrrh teased his nose, faint and mysterious, overlying the dry odor of stone. So this was Egypt. A smile spread across his face. Antony flicked him a glance as he settled into the sand.

"Once more the world waits on Cleopatra's pleasure," said the Roman, and curled up for a nap.

During the next half-hour the ordinary citizens of Alexandreia drifted into view around them, speaking quietly among themselves in twos and threes. Many carried offerings of fruit, flowers, or honeycake. By the time night's blackness had faded to indigo they numbered in the hundreds.

A figure appeared at the center of the far colonnade. With Nikias' insight he knew it was the Prophet of Isis, a tall old man with a shaven head, dressed only in a linen kilt so white it glowed. He lifted his arms and said, "Come, behold the glory of the One Who is All."

The crowd surged forward with a soft sigh. Derketaios roused Antony and led his party to the front of the congregation. They mounted three shallow steps and entered the pronaos.

Blue dawn streamed through clerestory windows, diluting the yellow warmth of the oil lamps, lighting the sanctuary's monumental interior. Massive pillars, painted with a bewildering array of figures, supported a coffered ceiling. A bright mosaic of river scenes covered the length and breadth of the floor, and at the far end of the hall, wrapped in umpteen yards of fringed linen, was a cult image at least four meters high.

The Prophet stood facing the image and began praying aloud in Greek. As he chanted, several dozen women entered from either side of the statue, all scantily dressed and carrying bronze sistra. At a pause in the invocation they lifted their instruments and, as one, launched into a swelling, full-throated hymn; the constant rattling of the sistra produced a metallic drone that surrounded the song like a halo. It seemed to be a catalog of the goddess's titles and epithets; its meaning was negligible, but its resonance raised the short hairs on Heron's neck.

While they sang, the Prophet fanned the embers resting on an altar of polished alabaster. Once flames appeared he lifted his arms dramatically, and the hymn shifted to a new key, full of triumph and joy. More young women appeared, carrying long slender poles; with these they disengaged the statue's linen wrappings, to reveal a standing figure of Isis, carved of the finest island marble, wearing the Hathor crown and long fringed robes. Her face embodied inhuman beauty.

The choir fell still; the rattle of the sistra ceased. Into the silence the Prophet intoned a prayer in the ancient language of the Pharaohs, an invocation as old as the pyramids, rich in fricatives and pharyngeals and stark as a desert wind. He was summoning the goddess to earth.

A trio of flautists piped a melody like the calling of doves. The choir shook their sistra gently, producing a soft tinkling note. From behind the statue Cleopatra appeared, adorned from head to toe in bright gold.

She who had impersonated a whore was now divine. Her face was as serene and beautiful as the marble image's. Her hands lifted like flowers in the sun, holding forth the symbols of resurrection. From Prophet to slave the entire congregation fell to its knees, rendering homage to the goddess incarnate.

"Kleopatra Basilissa," they cried. "Queen Cleopatra."

"Isis Neotera," they cried. "The New Isis."

She stood unmoved, shimmering in a garment of light. The horns and feathers of the Hathor crown lent half a meter to her height, so that she loomed larger than any mortal woman. There was no suggestion of age or excess flesh about her now. She was transfigured.

Behind her came Charmion and Mardion the eunuch, both

dressed in pure white linen. They held fresh palm branches overhead like the supplicants painted on the wall. As the flutes began a new ostinato they broke into song.

Their contraltos were as alike as a voice and its echo, blending in spine-tingling unison, rippling and shaking with ornamental quarter tones. They detailed the blessings of Isis, singing of her transcendent love: a love sufficient for the resurrection of the body in the heavenly kingdom.

"She is love, she is life, she is the love that conquers death. She is the One Who is All."

Many of the worshipers were weeping, caught in the ritual's illusion. Cleopatra set down her gilt ankh and electrum-plated staff and took up a large bowl, carved out of a single piece of rose quartz. Inside was holy water drawn from the Nile at Elephantine. She raised the vessel aloft, whispering a last prayer, and poured its contents into a trough before the cult statue. The choristers and musicians broke into wild ululations.

Now another detachment of priestesses entered bearing great armloads of jewelry—turquoise collars, carnelian necklaces, gold pectorals, ropes of pearls, pendants of emerald and lapis lazuli— all crafted on a heroic scale. With the aid of hooks and poles they loaded the statue with treasure, until the marble was almost completely hidden beneath massive gems.

Then, to the music of a final hymn, the celebrants filed out, the Queen leading, the Prophet bringing up the rear. Heron, Antony, and the two soldiers followed after them. They passed through a cedarwood door into the ordered confusion of the sacristy.

Heron's eyes lit up. Amid laughter and gossip, forty or fifty nubile young women were in the process of stripping off their sacred regalia and changing into street clothes. He scanned meter after meter of firm brown flesh, looking for Charmion, but she didn't seem to be around.

A half-naked young thing approached Antony with a bow. She gestured toward the curtained area at the far end of the room. "The Queen is there," she said, eyes sparkling. Antony chucked her under the chin and went to find his wife. Heron sat down on the floor to wait.

"Somebody has one hell of an imagination," he murmured. "I wonder if it's me."

7

The Seventh Wonder
of the World

The royal entourage left the Sarapeion in a small fleet of covered litters, sometime during the second hour. Mardion and Heron shared one palanquin, Antony and Cleopatra another; Charmion traveled alone.

Heron's fascination had given way to exhaustion. He slouched in a pile of cushions, on the edge of sleep but completely unable to cross the line. Mardion, however, simply draped his himation over his head and was snoring within minutes. Heron listened with a mixture of annoyance and envy.

At irregular intervals, as the chair jerked and bumped its way down clotted streets, he poked his nose through the curtains for a glimpse of the city. All he could see was white-hot sunlight glaring off whitish walls and brownish faces; all he could hear was a clamorous babble of conversation, conducted in varying proportions of Greek, Egyptian, Aramaic, Persian, and Arabic. At first its accents suggested low-class speakers, but as the entourage entered the city's northern zones, hints of refinement crept in, mingled with sarcastic witticisms and scraps of world-weary philosophy.

More than one passer-by attempted to guess the identity of the palanquins' occupants. Heron was amazed at how astute they could be.

"No doubt it's the Queen and her gigolo," said an acidic voice, "heading home after an all-night drunk."

"No doubt," replied its companion. "At least we can be thankful that Antony plays his tragedies in Rome, and saves his farces for Alexandreia."

"By Isis, that's an old line—so old it's out of date. Rome's tragedy has chased our Antony across the seas; very soon we'll see it miming and moaning outside the gates."

Many other early risers shared the same foreboding. For it was only two months ago that Octavius Caesar had launched his invasion of Egypt, and no one doubted that he would lay siege to Alexandreia. The city was suffering from a serious case of the jitters.

Heron himself knew almost nothing about ancient history, but Nikias kept abreast of current events, and MEQMAT, their cybernetic emcee, had the entire chronicle of humanity in active memory. So with a little concentration he could retrieve the brief and sorry tale of Antony and Cleopatra's gamble for an empire.

It was 30 B.C., or, to use local parlance, Kleopatra Thea Philopator's twenty-first regnal year. Elsewhere in the Greek-speaking world they were calling it the 186th Olympiad, while the Romans, in their miserable little town on the Tiber, insisted on *annus DCCXXIII ab urbe condita*. Julius Caesar had been assassinated fourteen years earlier in an abortive coup d'etat. His untimely death had wrecked Cleopatra's plans for Egyptian glory—which included moving the capital of the Roman Empire to Alexandreia, and instituting the mysteries of Isis throughout the Mediterranean—and reduced Caesar's hard-won peace to a family quarrel between sober Octavian and profligate Antony.

In search of new backing, Antony had joined forces with the Siren of the Nile, whereupon she hatched even more grandiose schemes. Everyone from Varro to Vergil began to worry that this god-intoxicated temptress might finally succeed. Antony's military expertise, backed by the fabulous wealth of Egypt, could scarcely fail to triumph over untried Octavian. Rome would fade into ruins; Alexandreia, last resting place of Alexander the Great, would rule the world.

Then came Aktion. East met West; Rome clashed with Hellenized Egypt; and Antony kissed away an empire. His navy was outmaneuvered, and in desperate retreat he surrendered his legions without a battle. That debacle was now almost a year old. Since then Antony and Cleopatra had waited in their dream-city for Octavian's inevitable siege, drinking and drugging and debauching themselves as never before.

A pivotal moment in history, Heron thought. Egypt's last gasp; Rome's iron dawn.

Nikias, lacking his perspective, merely saw it as one more phase in the long slow decline of the Ptolemies, one more opportunity for the wolf of Rome to take another bite of the world. Like the rest of Alexandreia, he was hoping that those fangs wouldn't sink too deep.

The chair halted abruptly and hit the ground with an unceremonious thud. Mardion's eyelids flew up; the palanquin's curtains flew open, and Charmion sang out, "Broucheion!"

Heron unfolded his limbs and stepped into bright daylight. Charmion was waiting for him, with Stella smiling out of her eyes.

"The Queen has assigned you a suite in this wing of the palace. It's a lot more convenient than going all the way to Lochias. Come and I'll show you the way."

She ran lightly up a marble staircase, looking as fresh as if she'd slept the night through. Heron followed her with somewhat less vigor through a monumental portico, as the palanquin lurched off again, carrying Mardion to his quarters by the harbor.

Inside, the palace was all fluted marble, particolored mosaic, ivory paneling, and agate inlay. A pair of servants met them in the entry hall, and at Stella's command conducted them to a spacious bedchamber, curtained against the heat with bolts of saffron-dyed linen.

"Sleep now, Nikias," she said. "Someone will come around to attend you in the afternoon, when the sun declines."

"And you, Charmion?"

"I'll be nearby. I have rooms here, too." She smiled once more and bowed in the Egyptian manner, bending from the waist till her hands touched her knees. Then she was gone.

He sniffed the breeze of her departure, smelling attar of roses and something fleshier, a womanish aroma that briefly made him forget his weariness. But only briefly. Then he turned to the lonesome bed—a lavish affair of ebony and malachite, cushioned with goose-down and supported by four recumbent sphinxes—and stripped off his chiton. A minute later he was asleep.

And caught in a vision of heaven.

A dream within a dream is one thing: all sensitive dreamers

know that experience of nested realities, of layer after lucid layer of unconscious delusion. But what name can we attach to a reverie that occurs within the logic-flow of a cybernetic fugue? Heron's skepticism remained intact, even through the artful branches of MEQMAT's code; he kept enough presence of mind to wonder just how complex a program and just how much storage was needed to fool him into thinking he was asleep and dreaming in ancient Egypt.

He kept looking for scan-lines. Sometimes he thought he found them.

He was on the observation deck of the *Kosmograd*, weightless and content. His jumpsuit had that old-socks smell of thirty days in space. He was looking through a bubble at the blue globe of Earth, three-quarters full and floating against a field of stars.

Someone whispered his name. It was Teofila, his first wife, snuggling against his left flank.

"What are you thinking, John?"

"About how far away we are. About how amazing it is that we can ever go back, that we can find our way across all those magnetic fields and gravitational gradients to the New City again."

She laughed, very softly. "Funny that you're thinking of home. I've been trying not to. I wouldn't be sorry if I never saw that town again."

He shrugged, the action pressing him a little tighter into the circle of her arms. "I'll be ready when the time comes. I'll be ready to come back up again, too."

"What if it's all different?"

"Different?"

"What if somehow we did lose our way, and went back to a different world?"

"Maybe it would be a better world. Maybe it *will* be a better world."

She mussed his hair, already the silver-gray it would be at forty-three. "Oh, John," she said.

Stella shook him again. "John." He opened his eyes and saw her leaning over him, long black hair shedding the scent of roses. Behind her were two Egyptian boys carrying ewers and lengths of linen. "Wake up," she said. "Let's not miss out on these last hours of daylight."

She withdrew several paces as he rose from the bed, all naked and clumsy. If he hadn't stopped them, the two boys would have moved in and started bathing him at once.

"Wait!" he shouted. "Don't Alexandreians pee in the morning, too?"

Charmion laughed. One of the boys pointed to a silver jug encrusted with garnets and sapphires. The lady politely turned her back; the gentleman noisily relieved himself. Only then did he begin his ablutions.

Midway through he caught a glimpse of himself in a bronze mirror. It was a few seconds before he realized that he looked exactly the way he usually did. It was John Heron—height 1.87 meters, weight eighty kilos, hair gray, eyes blue—looking back at him from those metallic depths, not some two-bit tutor of Greek rhetoric from 30 B.C. He blinked and looked again. Same eyes, same nose, but—maybe he *had* changed a little. The haircut wasn't right, and the teeth.

Stella noticed his self-scrutiny and said, "Give it a rest, pal. You're thinking too hard."

He raised an eyebrow and started pulling on his chiton.

When he was dressed, another pair of servants arrived with a tray of bread, olives, dates, wine, and water. Charmion joined him on a terrace that overlooked the green courtyard. Shaded by a striped awning, they shared breakfast.

"Sleep well?"

"Surprisingly well. What time is it?"

"Almost the eighth hour." The sun was more than halfway down the western sky; Alexandreia's rooftops shone bright orange. "I thought you might want to see a little of the city," said Charmion.

"But I—don't I live here? Don't I see it every day?"

She wrinkled her nose. "Silly. You know what I mean."

They rose together. "Do I?"

She took his arm and guided him along a covered walkway, saying nothing, though a grin played with her lips. They crossed a series of darkened rooms and emerged in a second courtyard, small and dusty and filled with lounging Egyptians. "Menches! Phibis!" she called. "Attend us." Two young men in white linen stood and fell in behind them. "People as important as we are never go out without an entourage," she said. So they left the palace in style.

In a sun-washed square just east of Broucheion, Charmion gave their companions a few instructions in Egyptian. They bowed and assumed the lead, clearing a path through the crowd on a northbound route.

"How is it that you can speak with the natives?" Heron asked.

"I can't."

"Charmion *is* a native," said Stella. "She's Egyptian through and through. Her real name is Nitokris; Charmion is just Cleopatra's nickname for her." It made sense; in koine the word was a diminutive of *Charme*, Joy. "She was a palace slave till Cleopatra took a fancy to her and made her one of her principal ladies-in-waiting. That's why she's the epitome of loyalty."

"Almost like a daughter, eh?"

"Yes, except that Cleopatra's own daughter is pampered like a baby goddess." She sniffed. "Charmion must be content with slightly humbler perquisites."

"I see." He noticed that "humble," at least in the Alexandreian sense, might still signify the wearing of Tyrian gowns and emerald collars. "By the way, where are we going?"

They had turned onto a broad avenue lined with ornate piles of marble. Here, as everywhere else, the crowds were dense and polyglot.

"See up ahead?" She pointed to a white tower on their right. "That's the Royal Tomb, the city's main attraction. You're getting the grand tour."

This vast mausoleum, better known as the Sema, was a Greco-Egyptian fantasy run wild. There were sphinxes and heroic marbles and massive double colonnades with capitals in the shape of palm leaves. There were monumental stairways, a dozen smoking altars, and a pediment depicting the conquest of Persia. Surmounting this splendid jumble was a steep pyramid of white limestone, inscribed with proclamations in Greek, hieroglyphics, and hieratic. Its apex—the highest point in all Alexandreia—flashed gold.

Beggars thronged the main entrance. At a nudge from Charmion, Phibis reached into his tunic and showered them with coins. They passed through the portico into a cool, echoing vault, where foreign tourists of every stripe spoke in awed whispers.

Charmion took Nikias by the hand and led him to the center of the chamber, directly beneath the pyramidal superstructure. At the sight of her rich garments, and also of the two brawny Egyptians, the common folk gave way. Heron found himself staring at an enormous sarcophagus of rock crystal. Filtered sunlight sparkled in its depths, surrounding the figure inside with a brilliant aura.

He was a young man, lying as if asleep. Though thin and wasted, his proportions hinted at an earlier, more robust physique. His hair fell in golden curls over a wide forehead; his face might have been the model for some Pheidian sculpture of Adonis. He was dressed in gilt armor, and a plumed helmet lay at his side.

"Three centuries he's rested here," Charmion said. "The art of Egypt's embalmers was never practiced to better effect."

A voice in the back of Heron's mind supplied the caption: Alexander of Macedon, called the Great, conqueror of the known world. He had died of fever in Babylon; his general, Ptolemy, had then conveyed his corpse to this world-seducing metropolis and placed him on display, so that future generations might look on him in wonder.

Heron was moved. From Nikias' memory he quoted a verse from the *Iliad*:

> Now you lie in the palace, handsome
and fresh with dew, in the likeness of one whom he of the silver bow, Apollo, has attacked and killed with gentle arrows.

Charmion smiled. "Well said, Nikias. How Alexandreia needs a Hektor, or better still, a new Alexander, to face this new crisis."

"But all MEQMAT sent was me."

"And me."

That was a new way of looking at things. "Are we a team, then?" he asked.

She shook her head and wouldn't reply. They turned away from the sarcophagus.

"Most of Cleopatra's ancestors are buried here too," she said, "but they're not as interesting as Alexander. I have other wonders to show you before the sun goes down."

They left the same way they had entered. From the mausoleum steps Charmion indicated another enormous complex across the avenue, a hodge-podge of pillars, fountains, and statuary in what Heron already recognized as the Alexandreian style.

"That's the Mouseion," she said. "We won't go there either; it would take days to explore. That's where the Library is, whose volumes outnumber the stars in the sky. It's also the place where Euclid wrote the *Elements of Geometry*, where Eratosthenes measured the earth's circumference, where Apollonios wrote his epic, where Herophilos and Erasistratos performed the first autopsies, and where Ktesibios built his clocks and pipe organs. There's never been so much scholarship concentrated in one place before."

They continued down the Avenue of the Sema to its intersection with Kanobos, passing temples, palaces, law courts, and gymnasia. Along with the crush of foot traffic there were hundreds of carriages and carrying-chairs, and now even a few four-horse chariots. Their pace diminished to a shuffle. Then, amid the human chaos, they stumbled upon a flock of long-legged birds, parked squarely across their path. They were pecking at the pavement, hunting out garbage, oblivious to the feet, hooves, and wheels all around them.

Heron tried walking into their midst, but the birds refused to budge. He was about to aim a kick at the nearest beak when Charmion caught his arm in horror.

"Nikias! Are you tired of living? These are white ibis. The Egyptians think they're sacred. They'd rip you to pieces if you hurt one."

Heron scowled. "Don't you think these people carry their religion too far? Sacred cows, sacred bulls, sacred crocodiles, sacred beetles, sacred fish—"

"You sound just like a tourist."

"Well, why shouldn't I? There must be worse things in the world, even in 30 B.C." But he made a careful detour all the same.

They were close to the harbor now. A temple to Isis loomed on their left; before them was a maze of warehouses and shops, the mighty Emporion itself, the funnel through which all the treasures of the East must pass. From the crowded square at its mouth rose a pair of obelisks, one sheathed in silver, the other in gold, flashing like twin deities of wealth.

"They were dedicated by Nektanebos, the last native ruler of Egypt," said Charmion. "One of the Ptolemies ferried them downriver to Alexandreia, and now, like everything else in the land, they proclaim Cleopatra's glory."

From the central square Phibis led them down a series of side streets that bypassed the marketplace and ended at the main wharf. Here they saw ships of all sizes and descriptions, lying at anchor or moored to the quay. Some were being loaded, to the accompaniment of shouts and curses; some were being unloaded, to equal vituperation; some merely rested in peace. There were biremes, triremes, and quinqueremes; there were feluccas, dhahabiyas, and papyrus rafts; there were bull-horned canoes from Libya and swan's-necked merchanters from Rome, rocking on the sun-flecked water, creaking in the Etesian wind. White seagulls glided overhead, as if in a separate zone of reality; brown men swarmed on the ground, like ants, like mice in cheese. Complex and cosmopolitan, luxurious and squalid, this Great Harbor was a fitting summation of Alexandreia.

With considerable effort Menches and Phibis shouldered a path through the crowd, bringing their party to a small pleasure-craft tied up at the nearer end of the wharf. Eight boatmen lounged nearby. They snapped to attention at the sight of their visitors.

"Lochias," said Charmion. "And quickly."

The boatmen bowed. All eight climbed aboard, followed by the contingent from Broucheion. A moment later they were rowing through chaos.

Screams and challenges greeted them; obscenities followed. After twenty minutes they emerged in more open waters, already halfway to the piled roofs and colonnades of Lochias. A westering sun cast its light over acres of marble and tile.

"Well?" said Charmion.

"I see it," said Heron.

"Are you speechless?"

"That's one way of putting it."

She didn't mean the water-palace. Off to port was a long, low-lying island, known to the Alexandreians as Pharos. It was joined to the mainland by a stone causeway adorned with the usual baroque statuary. But rising from its eastern tip was something unique: a three-tiered tower of white marble, almost two hundred meters high.

"Jesus," said Heron. "It's a skyscraper."

"It's more," said Charmion. She pointed to its uppermost terrace, where a bonfire burned, even in the light of day; huge mirrors of polished bronze amplified the blaze and reflected it out to sea.

"It's a lighthouse," she said. "The Greeks think it's as grand as the Pyramids and the Sphinx. They call it the seventh wonder of the world."

Heron looked a little longer, taking in the conical roof, the massive pillars, the golden statue of Zeus. "It does have a nice line," he conceded.

Charmion laughed. "That light hasn't failed in two centuries, and it will go on burning for a thousand years to come. It's a beacon to guide all men to this fertile ground where the learning of Egypt couples with the genius of the Greeks. Look around you, Nikias of Rhodos. Look at those palaces and temples, those libraries and public gardens. Look at those ships that carry half the wealth of the world. Think of Babylon and Thebes, of Athens and Pataliputra. As mighty and as wise as they once were, they could never rival Alexandreia. This city alone is the yardstick against which all future ages will be measured."

The boatmen's backs stretched and rippled; eight oars cut the water with sharp strokes; the Etesian winds played with Charmion's rose-colored mantle. Heron gazed out at the white tower of Pharos, remembering the black tower of his own city. He was, after all, in the presence of an original.

8

The Suicide Club

The royal palace at Lochias had its own harbor, which they entered through a colossal archway decorated with nautical motifs: frolicking tritons, leaping dolphins, and a languid Proteus with seaweed for hair. All were brightly colored in a manner both elegant and sensual. As they tied up at the green marble quay, alongside Cleopatra's pleasure barges and racing yachts, a choir of slaves hurried out scattering lotus petals. With clear childish voices they piped a song of welcome; the sun's last rays turned their dusky faces gold.

Statues of Dionysos and Aphrodite flanked the portico. These were antique bronzes, mellowed the same soft green as the quay, but even a glance told Heron that their features had been reworked to resemble Antony and Cleopatra. There seemed no limit to the Queen's vanity.

Lochias itself was every bit as splendid as its exterior, a monument to royal pretension, a sprawling cybernetic fantasia. Past its agate threshold dozens of hulking Nubian mercenaries saluted them with steel-shod spears. Babylonian slaves came next, ushering them down hallways of porphyry and alabaster, while wire-haired Lybians sprinkled rosewater at their feet. They followed one corridor for what seemed like a half-kilometer, passing scores of marble columns and flickering silver cressets, inhaling all the while the fragrance of myrrh. At the end was a wide drawing-room frescoed with scenes from the *Odyssey*.

"From here," said Charmion, "Menches will show you to the men's baths. I must go attend the Queen. I'll see you sometime during the banquet, if I can manage."

"Aren't you invited?"

She smiled. "Servants don't sit at table with the rulers of the world." Her bow held just the slightest hint of mockery; she walked off without a word.

The Lochian *thermai* occupied an entire wing of their own. Its entrance was a door ten cubits high, inlaid with hand-colored tortoise shell and chips of emerald. Menches motioned him through as if into a sanctuary. In the grand foyer more slaves undressed him, and led him to the first stage of the bathing process—a steam room so hot it made the Alexandreian afternoon seem chilly by comparison.

A minute or two was all he could stand. He staggered out and plunged into a pool of tepid water; every cell of his epidermis cried out in shock. He floated on his back for a while, gazing up at a dome painted with Apollo driving the chariot of the sun.

"Amyntas!" A male voice hailed him. "Amyntas! No time for daydreaming! The Queen's table is waiting."

Heron stroked to the lip of the pool, where a wrinkly old gentleman with an enormous belly was hunkering down, reaching out his jeweled hand. But as the distance between them closed, the old man jumped back.

"Oh, sir, do excuse me! I took you for my colleague. My eyesight isn't what it used to be."

"No harm done. My name is Nikias Rhodios."

The old man cocked his head to one side. "I don't believe we've met," he decided. "I'm Archibios, a native of the city."

Nikias knew the name—Archibios was a shipping magnate, a millionaire many times over. "This is my first visit to the palace," he confessed. "It's no surprise we haven't met."

Archibios smiled democratically. "The honor is all mine, sir. But do come along to the hot tub or we'll be late for dinner. It would be bad form to arrive after the Queen."

Heron followed him to an adjoining room, most of which was occupied by a bronze basin full of steaming water. They immersed themselves in slow stages, centimeter by scalding centimeter, till they were in up to their necks and rivaled the pigmentation of cooked lobsters.

"The older I get the better this feels," said Archibios, letting out a long sigh. "My physician recommends a good sweat every day;

it's kept me alive so far. But what an age my health has brought me to!"

"As apocalyptic as Troy under old Priam, or Babylon in the days of Belshazzar."

"Too apt, too apt!" Archibios laughed raggedly. "We won't say these things in Cleopatra's hearing, but by Herakles, it looks like the long madness of the Ptolemies is about to find its cure—in Roman steel." He wagged his beard. "You must remember Auletes, the Queen's father. If ever a man was touched by the gods, it was he. He preferred music and debauchery to the practice of statecraft, and played the pipes like Pan himself. I was no stranger to the palace in those days either. I've witnessed many an orgy where the king trilled and tootled on his flute with the frenzy of a demon, whipping his guests into Bacchic transports, urging them to the most unspeakable excesses. Shame had no place in the royal lexicon back then. Wine laced with opium was the favored beverage, adultery the nightly pastime."

He clambered out of the basin, streaming water like a whale, and emitted a low-pitched moan of relief. "I remember one drug-sodden banquet when Auletes was buggered by ten black slaves in succession, and in turn buggered ten of Egypt's most gently born maidens. Oh, he was a devil." He shook his head in a mixture of admiration and regret.

From the hot tub they passed to the *tepidarium*, cooling off gradually. "The only way Auletes kept his throne was by bribing whoever had the upper hand in Rome," said Archibios. "He bankrupted Egypt and still suffered exile at the hands of his own daughter, the Queen's older sister. Berenike—what a miserable harpy. Poisoned her mother, strangled her husband, would have done in her father too if she could have. I was glad to see her head roll. Compared to her, Cleopatra is a paragon of virtue."

Heron laughed. MEQMAT could give him a bare-bones historical narrative, but Archibios brought these delectable old scandals back to life.

They had reached the last chamber of the thermai, the cold plunge. Heron drove in like a dolphin, gasping and sputtering in delightful shock. Archibios declined to enter—"Bad for the heart," he said.

But sitting on the sidelines he continued his stream of reminiscences. "Cleopatra does have a certain taste for debauchery, however. We won't mention those nights when she dresses as a commoner and roams the streets of Rhakotis, or the mysterious deaths of her two brothers. The infamous days of the *Amimeto-bioi*, the Unparalleled Lives, were quite enough. You remember, don't you? That first winter with Antony—who can count the measures of gold and silver that they squandered in pleasure and folly?" Archibios gave a rumbling laugh. "And I was there from the start. We inscribed our names on tablets of lapis lazuli—the most daring, the most lighthearted, the most sophisticated of all Alexandreia's world-weary tribe, joined together in a society devoted to pure sensuality. Ah! Like youth and innocence, those days will never come again."

They had arrived at the massage tables. First a team of brawny masseurs took up strigils and scraped every inch of their skin, till they glowed like month-old babies. Then came the perfumed oils, worked in to the accompaniment of vigorous pounding.

"The Society of Unparalleled Lives was officially dissolved in the month of Phaophi," said Archibios, between gasps and grunts. "Now those of us as remain have become the *Synapotha-noumenoi*—the Partners in Death, or if you will, the Suicide Club. Perhaps you'll be inscribed tonight?"

"I don't know if I could hold my own in such aristocratic company."

"Have no fear on that account! We welcome parvenus with open arms. Isis knows how many have deserted Cleopatra's cause since Aktion, and especially since the skirmish with Arabia. The Queen needs all the friends she can find."

Back in the dressing room Heron found new clothes set out for him—a white tunic of tissue-thin linen and a mint-green chlamys with an embroidered hem. Archibios was even grander; his chiton was interwoven with gold threads, and his himation was deep Tyrian purple. More slaves dressed them and fussed with their hair.

"We're new men, eh?" Archibios admired himself in a tall mirror. "Though maybe I'm a bit overdressed." He laughed. "It's not good form for me to look too flush at the moment, since I owe the Queen two thousand talents. I'm practically the only man in town right now who can claim to be her debtor. Since Aktion she's been robbing tombs and temples, confiscating property, borrowing money right and left. It takes quite a fortune to wage war with Rome, you know."

"And a faultless strategy to win," said Heron. "Unfortunately even gold can't buy one of those."

Archibios winked. "By Athena, you're a dry one, Nikias. I can see why the Queen invited you."

It was a long walk to the dining room. By the time they arrived they were much better acquainted, and almost hungry enough for the feast that lay in wait. Slaves met them at the threshold to sponge their feet; then Mardion the eunuch appeared with a low bow and a formal welcome.

They entered a large square chamber with gilt rafters and a cedar ceiling, walled on three sides with Carian marble and open on the fourth to the Great Harbor. Four fluted pillars with acanthus-leaf capitals framed the harbor view; draped artfully between them were heavy tapestries rescued from the sack of Corinth. From various niches around the hall, pine torches shaded with colored glass provided a soft, even light.

All but the guests of honor were there before them, sampling hors d'oeuvres and exchanging gossip. Archibios' wife, Praxinoe—a grand dame with false hair, painted eyes, and a gown worth eight hundred tetradrachmai—scolded the old man for his tardiness. "Running your mouth as usual, I suppose, my love? Spouting hogwash at every chance-met stranger?"

He kissed her carefully, to avoid smearing the paint, and settled down on the couch next to her. "Volubility is the worst of my vices, darling. You can thank Sarapis for that."

Mardion showed Heron to his own place, next to Amyntas of Kyrenaika. This was the same man Archibios had mistaken him for: a youngish sea captain who specialized in the Indian route. His hair and beard were sun-bleached, his skin deep bronze and crosshatched with wrinkles, his Greek spiced with phrases from half a dozen Eastern tongues.

"I'm new to all this myself," he said softly. "I've been away from Egypt for three years, conducting Archibios' business in the markets of Taxila and Pattala. The Queen never considered me worthy of an invitation before, but the whole world has changed since Aktion."

"So they keep telling me," said Heron. He had already dipped into the appetizers—lotus bread, brine shrimp, and roast dormice glazed with honey and poppyseed. "Apparently there are quite a few vacancies at court."

"So much the better for us, eh?" Amyntas grinned and took a healthy swallow of beer.

"Maybe," said Heron. "But I think it pays to be cautious in the house of kings."

Amyntas pursed his lips. "I suppose you're right. There must be something behind all these defections from Cleopatra's cause."

"I've thought the same thing. But we'd do better to discuss this elsewhere."

Amyntas nodded and turned back to his plate.

Taking his cue from Archibios, Heron ate no more than a bite or two of each dish, and drank sparingly. Royal banquets were lavish affairs; it seemed wisest to move slowly and exercise restraint, in food as in all else. There was plenty more to come.

But the Queen and her lover still hadn't turned up when the first course officially arrived, carried in by Circassian slave girls to the music of harps and double pipes. There was a Spanish wine in abundance, red and hearty; bowls of green and black olives; skewers of orioles broiled in Indian pepper; roast goose garnished with fresh coriander; apples, damsons, and pomegranates; and a peculiar Egyptian side dish, consisting of lumps of pork fat floating in a marinade of cumin, radish oil, and juniper berries. Hungry as he was, it was hard to maintain his reserve; the orioles in particular were fantastic.

With a conscious effort he eased back on his couch and watched the rest of the party, who were mostly talking, giggling, and forcing tidbits down each other's throats. Leaning over Amyntas he asked Archibios for a quick review.

"Well, that plumpish gentleman with the blond curls is Phrasidamos, the famous tragedian," said the old man, lowering his voice to a stage whisper. "The woman next to him, oddly enough, is his wife Chloe, a dancer. Or ex-dancer, I should say; she's hardly kept her figure, has she. Next to them is Anaxenor, who's almost as rich as I am, though not half so well-mannered, and his half-breed mistress Euterpe; then there's Petosiris, a priest of Harpokrates, and Olympos, the Queen's physician, one of the most brilliant men in Egypt."

"Who are the two boys? Even the older of them barely has hair on his face."

"You *are* green, aren't you. The one on the left is Antony's eldest son, Antyllos. The one on the right is Ptolemy the Fifteenth, better known as Kaisarion: son of Cleopatra and Julius Caesar, Pharaoh of Egypt, scion of Amun-Re: a living god in his own right."

"Ah." Heron took a good look. Antyllos was curly-haired and athletic, as beautiful as a young Apollo; he resembled his father at the same age. But whatever character he might possess was a mystery. From this angle he looked like any other seventeen-year-old, licking fat from his fingers, drinking cup after cup of wine, punctuating inane asides with a belch or a wink.

His companion was another story. Kaisarion was fourteen and as sharp-eyed as a falcon. Neither of his parents was notable for good looks, and neither was he. His hair was fine and dark, clipped close to the skull, and his face was bony, dominated by a haughty Roman nose. His eating habits were fastidious, his expression thoughtful and circumspect. An Egyptian slave hovered at his side, tasting everything before he did; even at this age the boy could retain no illusions about his safety.

Once the remains of goose and oriole were cleared away, a round of light snacks appeared: tiny bowls of chickpeas and lotus seeds, seasoned with marjoram and dill; toasted almonds, lupines, and filberts; and young squids cooked in their own ink. This was all washed down with another Egyptian specialty: an exquisite beer called *zythos*, which had the flavor and bouquet of dry wine.

Heron was on his second cup when a commotion in the hallway announced the Queen's arrival. A jar smashed, Antony's voice cut off in mid-curse, and the two lovers stalked in, looking as if they had barely finished an argument.

"My friends! How good of you to wait for us!" Cleopatra spread her arms as the company flopped to its collective knees. "Once more we gather to celebrate the birthday of my dear husband, Mark Antony, born under the sign of the Twins. If memory serves me, this is the thirty-third banquet in thirty-six days that I have dedicated to his happy nativity, and in token of the boundless devotion I feel for him, we will continue to commemorate that date with the same liberality, until Rome falls, until his next birthday comes round, or until we all die—whichever happens first."

Her voice dripped sarcasm; uncertain applause accompanied her to her place at the head of the party. With stone-faced Antony beside her she stretched out on a couch that was all ebony, gilt, and lambswool.

Previously Heron had seen her as a streetwalker and a priestess; now she was Basilissa Basileon, the Queen of Kings, the Empress of the East. Her gown was pure silk, dyed a Tyrian purple of many soakings and encrusted all over with Indian pearls. Her hair was dressed in hundreds of tiny curls and encircled by a gold fillet inlaid with amethysts, emeralds, and quartz. From her ears dangled a pair of marvels: the two largest pearls ever seen west of the Indus. Gossips appraised them at twenty million sesterces apiece. On her left hand, among other ornaments, was an enormous amethyst ring engraved with the word METHE, drunkenness: not common alcoholic intoxication, but the mystical transport of Dionysos himself. This had been her father's favorite jewel, and she wore it constantly in his memory.

Cleopatra clapped her hands; the room fell silent. "I hereby call this meeting of the Suicide Club to order. These are my royal commands. Eat and drink to your hearts' content; take no thought of tomorrow. Though the barbarians may be skulking at the gate, true civilization still lives in Alexandreia-by-Egypt. Enjoy it while you may!"

There were cheers and toasts. The Queen was in high spirits, no doubt about it, while Antony was sinking into a drunken funk. He lounged darkly at her side and said nothing.

Archibios put his head next to Heron's. "It must be Thyrsos again. That's all they argue about anymore."

"Thyrsos?"

"That handsome freedman Octavian sent to negotiate with Cleopatra, a few months past. The Queen granted him so many private interviews that Antony went into a jealous rage and had him flogged."

Heron would have replied, but a new commotion prevented him. Five slaves trudged in wheeling a small wagon covered with artificial rocks. Upon them sat three bare-breasted women wrapped in spangled green fabric, so that they seemed to sport fish tails instead of legs. As they combed out long golden hair they sang a yearning melody in one of the Asiatic modes, using soprano voices as clear and true as bells.

"The Sirens!" said Cleopatra, to a round of applause. More slaves came along carrying an enormous krater depicting Odysseus tied to the mast of his ship, writhing in desperate ecstasy, while his comrades rowed stolidly onward with wax-filled ears. Nikias' eye recognized it as an antique, handed down from the days of Perikles: a minor masterpiece of classical art. One tall slave poured an amphora of Mareotic wine into the krater as another added water. "Not too much water!" Cleopatra cried. "It's my grandfather's vintage."

"I thought we finished that off last week," said Phrasidamos.

"Not quite," said the Queen. "Even Antony hasn't yet managed to exhaust the cellars of Lochias."

Antony rolled his eyes and kept quiet.

A wine steward came around to collect the silver drinking cups everyone had used till now, replacing them with fine kylikes of the same provenance as the krater. Heron's showed Nausikaa dancing with her maidens; Amyntas' had Telemachos toasting Helene and Menelaos.

The Sirens withdrew. Then, with a great roar, two men appeared wearing Cyclops masks, carrying trays laden with roast meat. There was a wild oryx basted in persea honey, a gazelle in a bed of lettuce so sweet and fresh that Adonis himself might have rested there, and a fat sow stuffed with apples, walnuts, and sweet Syrian dates.

After more applause the company settled down to serious eating, as harps played softly on the terrace. When the meat was accounted for there was an interlude of grapes, ripe figs, and melons. Conversation grew louder and sillier. Chloe threatened to sing; Phrasidamos stuffed her mouth with an apple. Anaxenor commented on the antiquity of the tableware; Cleopatra said, "There are whole rooms full of it in Broucheion. Antony uses a piece by Phintias to pee in."

Amyntas would have laughed, but Archibios poked him in the ribs. Antony kept drinking, saying nothing.

The fish course was carried in by a corps of mermen, brandishing tridents and wearing conches over their genitals. They offered swordfish swimming in a broth of parsley and leeks, sardines in olive oil, oysters and mussels in wine, octopus in mustard sauce, and hot buttered snails.

The Queen ordered a fresh vintage, delicate white wine shipped all the way from Attica. Then came soft cheese steeped in Cretan sherry, eggs in pastry, olives pickled in caraway, and broiled thrush all around. Every belly in the house was bulging.

Cleopatra, however, dined abstemiously. When she saw that her guests were relatively sated, she steered the conversation to more serious topics, asking each one in turn the state of his or her affairs, and adding some pithy observation of her own.

To Amyntas she said, "I've heard good news of your last voyage to India. King Maues received you warmly and repeated his friendly intentions toward Egypt. Tell us something of the state of things in the East."

So he did, much to the Alexandreians' delight. According to Amyntas, India was the richest and most densely populated country in the world, and its women were second only to those of Alexandreia in beauty. Among its wildlife were animals known nowhere else, such as striped panthers and double-humped camels, not to mention the Indic breed of elephant.

At the first pause in his narrative Kaisarion asked, "Is it true that there is a desert, east of the Indus, where the dunes are made of gold dust, and ants as big as foxes go about mining it?"

"That's just a fairy tale, Your Highness," said Amyntas.

"But Herodotos himself recorded it as fact." It was clear that the boy didn't like to be contradicted.

"Much nonsense has been written about the East, I'm afraid; even Herodotos nodded once or twice."

"What about this, then," said Euterpe. "I've heard that in India the postures of love are expounded and demonstrated in academies, in much the same way that music and rhetoric are taught in Athens."

Amyntas blushed. "I doubt that, madam, though I will confess that Indian courtesans are the most accomplished in the world."

"Then what about the Indian holy men," said Petosiris. "Onesikritos writes of a sect of Sophists who roam the countryside naked, living only off what they can beg, under oath never to kill even the tiniest insect."

"That much is certainly true," said Amyntas. "The Greeks have called Egypt the most religious of all nations, but India is even more deserving of the honor. We have our Apis bull, but the Indians consider every cow sacred, down to the oldest and scrawniest."

"That's been known since Alexander's time," said Olympos. "Ptolemy the First, our blessed Queen's ancestor, wrote that once while on campaign Alexander disturbed a group of Indian sages as they argued doctrine in a country lane. Observing the Macedonian army, they merely stamped their feet, and returned to their disputations. When Alexander asked them what they meant by this behavior, the oldest among them said, 'You seek to conquer the world, O King, but you fail to realize that no man, not even you, can own more of the earth's surface than the little piece he stands on.' The sage stamped his feet again in illustration, and continued, 'Moreover, when you are dead, you will own only as much as will bury you." Now, you might imagine that the proud, hot-tempered Alexander would be offended, but on the contrary, he was pleased, and thereupon offered to hire the old man as his tutor. But the Indian said, 'With all your wealth and power you can offer me nothing better than this sunny day, so why should I stir from my garden?' "

There was a scattering of polite laughter. Cleopatra, however, was not amused. "Alexander may have admired such sophistry," she said, "but it never convinced him to change his ways."

Olympos conceded the point. "Those who would rule the world end up being ruled by the world."

Cleopatra gave him a sharp look, but before she could speak Petosiris, oblivious to her pique, said, "That brings to mind the story of Kalanos, another of the Indian sophists. He was also invited to join Alexander's train, and unlike the previous sage, he agreed. But as soon as he left India his health failed. He took this as a sign from heaven that he had betrayed his calling, and so to make amends he had an enormous pyre built, in which he threw all the gifts that Alexander had given him—golden cups, precious oils, perfumes, and fine robes—and then, singing praises to the gods in his own language, he walked into the flames and was consumed. Alexander's soldiers hailed him as a hero, and even the elephants trumpeted his praise."

Now Cleopatra smiled. "At its best the human spirit can rival the gods themselves. In fact I have often reflected on Kalanos' sacrifice. The story is a familiar one in my family, since it was the first Ptolemy who built Kalanos' pyre. I myself will certainly choose death over degradation, if the choice ever becomes necessary. I trust that all of you here will follow me—as you have in fact sworn to do." Her eyes glittered like a cat's, and Olympos offered her a formal bow.

Once more the discourse lightened. Slaves appeared to sprinkle the floor with saffron, and the wine was mixed with warm water instead of cold. Young girls wearing garlands served pastries fresh out of the oven: pies in the shape of birds, with raisin and almond stuffing; birds' nests made of fine dough and pistachios, steeped in honey; rosewater puddings; Spanish oranges; and cardamom seeds to munch on. Heron was amazed that he could even think of eating another bite, but he did, while his head swam in a haze of Oriental spices.

In the midst of the comings and goings of the stewards and caterers a young black woman entered and went straight to Cleopatra. She was very beautiful, and dressed in the most elegant Alexandreian fashion: gilt sandals, a red silk peplos, and a hairdo of incredible complexity. She whispered something in the Queen's ear, then bowed and departed. Cleopatra merely studied her kylix and said nothing.

"That was Eiras, the Queen's hairdresser," murmured Archibios. "Next to Charmion she's Cleopatra's principal confidante. Something's afoot."

A moment later one of Antony's Roman bodyguard came in, saluted, and drew his master aside for another whispered exchange. Once the tale was told, Antony showed none of his mistress's constraint. For the first time that evening the hall rang with his best battlefield voice.

"Cleopatra!" he cried. "While we sit and trade fables about the furthest East, Octavian has tightened his noose around Egypt's throat. This very day Paraitonion fell to a surprise attack. Cornelius Gallus has taken command of the African legions, and he's no mouse, no Pinarius Scarpus. Our last battle is at hand."

There was a ghastly silence. Paraitonion guarded the western approach to the Delta, just as Pelousion guarded the east. Rome was in striking distance of the capital.

"So Octavian is a liar and an opportunist," Cleopatra said slowly.

"Did you ever doubt it?" Antony shouted. The threat of ruin had sobered him more thoroughly than a good night's sleep. Heron finally had a glimpse of the man who was Caesar's right hand. "You listened too long to the promises and flattery of that pretty-faced Thyrsos, my love. Octavian feels no filial devotion to his stepfather's mistress. Our moment has come. We must strike away his grasping fingers or die trying."

"Do we dig in for a siege, then?"

"That's coward's counsel. No! Antony may have been a fool, but a coward is he never! I'm on to Paraitonion with all the ships Alexandreia can spare. I'll turn this defeat into a victory, if Herakles still loves his most loyal son. I'll move so fast they'll never know I'm coming till my sails fly into Paraitonion's harbor."

From conquering general, Antony switched suddenly to courtly lover, kneeling at Cleopatra's feet and taking hold of her jewel-laden hand. "Give me your blessing, my love, as Andromache did to Hektor on the ramparts of Troy."

There was a shine in Cleopatra's eyes that neither Nikias nor Heron ever expected to see. "No, Antony, I won't go whining and pleading like the daughter of Eetion, who had so little faith in her husband's prowess that she mourned him while he lived and breathed. Instead let me give you my blessing as the New Isis."

They rose together and she folded him in her arms, as Isis had embraced Sarapis on the morning of his resurrection. "Go,

Antony, to victory! Noblest man of the age, boldest warrior, sweetest lover." They shared a long kiss, insensible to the party around them. So it had been in the great days of their passion.

They separated; Antony's smile was radiant. "Derketaios! Eros! Alexas!" he cried. "Attend me! We go forth for the glory of Egypt!" And with his bodyguard around him, gleaming in the torchlight like men of iron, he strode out of the room.

The company applauded furiously. Cleopatra beamed after her warriors like an actress at a curtain call, then raised her hands for silence.

"I'm afraid, my friends, that history has intruded on our fun, and this meeting of the Suicide Club must adjourn early. Each of you may take your cup along with you. They may not be gold or silver, but the workmanship in them is worth far more than their weight in precious metal. Let this be tonight's lesson: Life is short, art is long; the greatest artist is he whose life itself is his masterpiece, for his memory long survives the decay of the flesh." So saying, she made her own exit; Charmion and Eiras appeared out of nowhere to accompany her.

But between two pillars of black-veined marble she turned suddenly and said, "Nikias, you come with us also. I have a job for you tonight."

Eyebrows lifted all around the room. Heron scrambled to his feet and fell in behind them. Stella flicked a glance at him, secrets laughing from her eyes; Cleopatra led the way with head held high, a candle shining in the Egyptian night.

9

Through the Gate
of the Dead

In the uncertain light offered by two or three alabaster lamps, Heron could only guess at the opulence of Cleopatra's bedroom. She half-reclined on a couch, silent and withdrawn. Charmion, Eiras, and Heron himself sat around her on footstools.

He was expecting a conspiracy, but Cleopatra did no more than lie there with that abstracted look in her eyes. After a while she said, "Sing for me, Charmion."

Charmion produced a lyre out of the shadows. Strumming it once to check its tune, she said, "Sappho, my lady?" The Queen nodded. She closed her eyes and began.

> Eros again—he leaves me weak and trembling.
> O sweet-bitter, irresistible savage . . .

Her voice was as clear and taut as the lyre's strings. The two instruments found a perfect marriage in Sappho's verses; words and images gleamed out of the melody like jewels.

> You came, when I yearned for you;
> You cooled my heart, when I burned for you . . .

Heron's eyes lingered on Charmion's rouged lips, on the tip of her tongue, on the pillar of her throat as she threw her head back for a long, quavering note. All his yearning for Stella converged on this cybernetic stand-in. All his digitized hormones fired in answer to her song. Could she be unaware, or indifferent? It seemed impossible.

"Enough love," said the Queen. "Play that sad one."

Charmion returned her strings to the mixolydian mode and obliged her.

> Come, Hermes, friend to wandering spirits.
> Come, lord, guide my footsteps,
> For by hell's mistress I swear
> Being on this earth gives me no pleasure,
> And a longing has hold of me
> To die, and see the banks of Acheron—
> Choked by lotus blossoms,
> Heavy with dawn's tears.

Cleopatra kept time with her hand. A line of kohl streamed down her cheek; she whispered the names of old lovers, gone before her into dust.

When the song ended, Charmion stilled her strings' vibration with a finger. Cleopatra turned to Heron; her voice was a cracked whisper.

"All my planning and scheming seem on the verge of failure," she said. "In spite of his heroics, Antony will never turn back the legions of Rome. Sappho was right when she said, 'We can do nothing against fate.'" She closed her eyes and shook her head. "There were two dreams in my life. The first was to see myself on the throne of a strong and independent Egypt. The second was to see my son succeed me. For seventeen years that first dream has been reality, but I've begun to despair of the second. Octavian has made me many promises, promises which are now revealed as lies."

She sat up straight and stared deep into his eyes, like an actress in a cheap tragedy, like a two-obol fortune teller in the market-place. "One alternative remains, and you must help me realize it. Of all my allies only two kings in the furthest East have kept their oaths: Artavasdes of Media and Maues of India. For months now I've planned to send Kaisarion to one or the other of them, to be raised to manhood far from Octavian's grasp. He was to leave in the spring; the westerly monsoon would have carried him swiftly. As his guardian I chose his tutor Rhodon." She glanced at

Charmion. "But at the last moment this Rhodon was exposed as a traitor. Only Charmion's guile uncovered his perfidy, in the form of a secret correspondence with Rome, and after that I doubted everyone. I decided to wait and see what the summer would bring." She lowered her eyes and toyed with the amethyst ring. "Tonight we saw the folly of that choice."

Heron saw the direction she was taking, and would have spoken, but she silenced him with a gesture.

"There can be no more delay. My intuition, and Charmion's, tell me that you are a good man and an excellent teacher. Oh, we've made inquiries about you; even in one day the Queen's spies can uncover a great deal. Except for your penchant for *extremely* young girls your record is unblemished. And your espousal of the Mysteries speaks volumes in your favor. So this is what you must do. In two days' time you, Amyntas of Kyrenaika, and my son Kaisarion will set out from Alexandreia in the garb of common travelers. You will sail up the Nile to Koptos, and from there trek overland to Berenike, where Amyntas is well connected with shipowners. From Berenike you will secure passage to India. My letter of introduction will ensure your welcome at Maues' court. By then, barring a miracle, Egypt will have fallen and I will be dead."

Heron bowed his head, expressing submission and sorrow.

"Naturally you will be amply provided with funds, and the Indian king will shower you with honors. But even beyond the grave you owe me this debt: you must nurture and educate my son to suit his station in life, as heir to Caesar, Alexander, and the myriad noble kings of Egypt. You must never let him forget who he is, and you must always drive him to avenge me and oppose Octavian. Kaisarion is Julius Caesar's only son. He, not Octavian, is the rightful heir to the Principate. He has his partisans on the Tiber; if the gods are willing, he could one day rule the world. As I hoped and failed to do myself."

"I swear to fulfill everything you say, madam."

"That's good to hear," she said dryly. "But I require a stronger oath, Nikias, one we both learned in the House of the Two Goddesses."

Heron would have hesitated, but Nikias seemed eager to prove his loyalty. He swore to execute Cleopatra's will at the expense of his immortal soul, using all the most binding and terrible oaths of Eleusis. When he had finished she settled back on the couch and waved her hand in dismissal.

"Come to me tomorrow at the second hour," she said. "I will instruct you further."

Charmion rose to see him out. In the anteroom, as she was about to entrust him to one of the eunuchs, he caught her hand and said, "Charmion—Stella—stay with me. All this wine and song and eternal pledging have my brain spinning. You know so much more than I do about this craziness. Please talk to me."

"Isn't tomorrow soon enough?"

"No, no." He felt the sweat starting on his palm, felt the dry smoothness of hers. "I'll never sleep. Just talk to me, please."

She withdrew her hand. "Cleopatra expects me back."

"Make an excuse. I'll wait right here."

Her mouth twitched. "All right. But wait for me in the pantechnicon instead." She produced a key from the folds of her chiton, opened a door, and led him into a small room crowded with clothing and jewelry. He settled down on a bolt of linen; she stepped out, locking the door behind her.

He felt drunk and euphoric. His universe was a dark room full of treasures and anticipation, anticipation for Stella. All the rest was background—Cleopatra, history, the Two Goddesses, everything. His body shuddered with potential.

Ten minutes later he heard the key turn and glimpsed her silhouette moving against the shadows. He inhaled deeply, smelling her come nearer, savoring her scent. She sat next to him; he couldn't see her, she was a warm presence in the night, a cluster of flavors to taste, textures to feel.

"Okay, John, what's wrong? You're not losing it again, are you?"

"Stella," he said.

He drew her against him, gently, stroking the folds of silk that hid her thighs.

"Do you really want to do this now?" she whispered.

"Don't you?"

She said nothing, and his hands continued their journey over the fields of flesh. "Don't you, Stella?"

She let out a sigh; it sounded like regret, resignation, defeat. But her body was telling another story. She shifted position slightly, and their groins came into sweet and sudden contact. Her hands mimicked his, sliding under his clothing, tracing the contours of his body in a long slow caress. Their mouths found each other like two hungry animals. They fed, they feasted; Cleopatra's banquet had nothing to compare with this ambrosia, which tongues and teeth could nibble and suck forever, and never exhaust.

Silk fell away. Skin moistened, bodies warmed, dilating, sweating, sliding together in exquisite friction. Everything was easy and slow; there was no confusion, no insistence, no false moves or missed cues. She's everything I hoped she'd be, thought Heron, a fantasy made flesh.

Their breath quickened. Their hips moved together with greater urgency. Words of encouragement traded back and forth: signals, affirmations. Perception narrowed and intensified.

She cried out. He made a hoarser sound, arching over her like a bow. His climax was a bolt of fire.

He squeezed his eyes shut and saw purple flowers exploding in the dark. There was an instant of total disorientation; he couldn't tell up from down, and his heart pounded in something like fear. Voices babbled in his head; splinters of light pierced his eyelids. Then her hand was soothing him, stroking his face, cupping his chin.

"It's okay, John," she said.

She rolled away from him and lit an oil lamp, a bit of alabaster carved in the shape of a duck. His heart quieted; he touched her arm for reassurance, and found it. God, she was so good, so fine. Once someone told him that perfection existed only in the mind. But their love had been so perfect it was terrifying.

"Can we talk?"

"Just a little." She lay facing him, on her side with the lamp behind her. Tiny hairs caught a line of light along her jaw.

"When does this stop, Stella? Will I just wake up and see it all fade away?"

"No, no, John. It's real, we're real together."

"Then—what? What about Cleopatra? I've sworn away the rest of my life to that woman. Are we stuck here forever?"

"No. We can leave soon. Nikias and Charmion stay here, but you and I are allowed to go. Though we may return from time to time."

"Return?" He caught his breath. "I guess that's no disaster. Compared to Residencia Trece this place is a pretty cushy score."

"Compared to anything back home this place is a pretty cushy score." She laughed quietly. "In fact, I enjoy being Charmion. Especially when she sings. I'm an artist at last, John."

His smile was invisible in the shadows, but their kiss was perfectly tangible.

"Yes," he said. "There's a lot to like in Alexandreia. But I still have—I don't know—doubts. A creeping anxiety. Just what kind of an experiment are we involved in? What's really going on?"

"An adjustment." She laughed again. "We started out in the Bureau of Adjustment, remember?"

"Then what are we adjusting?"

"MEQMAT."

"But MEQMAT runs the Lottery. MEQMAT lives in a weird room in the twenty-first century. MEQMAT is a ghost in a machine. How can psychedelic sex in this ersatz version of ancient Egypt possibly relate to MEQMAT?"

"It's complicated. It'll all be explained when the dip is over."

"Oh, come on. I don't know anything about history, but I have a funny feeling about this."

"Ask MEQMAT."

He did, with another squeeze of the eyelids and another stab of light. All he got was a line of text read by a soundless, bodiless voice.

". . . reputed to be the son of Caesar the Dictator, was sent by his mother, with a great sum of money, through Aethiopia, to pass into India; but his tutor, a man named Rhodon, about as honest as Theodoros, persuaded him to turn back, for that Caesar designed to make him king. So, afterwards, when Cleopatra was dead, he was killed."

"I have a bad feeling about this, Stella," he said.

"Don't. It's really minimal." She stretched and rose to her feet, pulling the himation around her.

"You're not leaving . . ."

"I have to. I'm Cleopatra's personal maid. I sleep at her feet."

"Oh Stella . . ."

"Sorry, Nikias. It's Charmion again. And you'd better run along to that assigned bedroom yourself. You can't sleep in the royal wardrobe."

He gave in. After one last kiss, one last squeeze, he crawled into his chiton. An adolescent boy—or was it a eunuch?—showed him to his suite. He lay down on a coverlet of Indian cotton and slept soundly, without any dreams at all.

Cleopatra waited in her morning room with Kaisarion by her side. An army of secretaries and bureaucrats surrounded her, brandishing pens and scrolls. Amyntas of Kyrenaika stood by, shifting his weight anxiously from foot to foot. Olympos hovered darkly in the background.

"I trust you passed the night in comfort?" the Queen asked. Her voice was sharp; her eyes glittered like glass.

"Very comfortably, Your Highness," said Heron, bowing low.

"Good; because you have a long journey before you. I've moved your departure to this very day, at dusk. The news from Paraitonion is not good."

He did no more than nod.

"You will devote the morning to a conference with Amyntas and Kaisarion over what supplies to bring." She waved a hand. "Olympos will assist you."

Heron bowed again and Olympos ushered them into a side chamber, making quick gestures like a wooden doll.

"You have been allotted one donkey," he said. "That will scarcely suffice to carry the metal and jewels. Anything else must be carried on your backs."

Amyntas let out a sigh and started listing their necessities. Heron, with Nikias' passion for literature, thought longingly of books, of leather-bound volumes of history and rhetoric, of antique editions of the Ionic philosophers and the Aeolic lyricists. All superfluous, alas. At least they'd be allowed to bring a copy of *The Gallic War*, and perhaps Ptolemy's life of Alexander.

Kaisarion paced the room like a hunting dog. From time to time Olympos frowned at his agitation, but wisely refrained from comment. Heron could imagine the ill-mixed drives battling in the boy's heart: shame that he was fleeing, rage that he had no choice in the matter, curiosity over what lay ahead, elation at the prospect of foreign lands.

"You're about to go where even Alexander never ventured," he said. "Do you fancy being a prince in India?"

"Not half as much as I fancy being king in Egypt," Kaisarion said curtly. And in the uncertain pitch of his voice, Heron sensed another layer of emotion: fear. The natural and ill-disguised fear of a child whose life is on the line. This boy will be a difficult charge, he thought. He has too much pride to reveal his weakness.

Then a wave of confidence flowed out of Nikias the pedagogue. *He's no different from any other child*, it said. *I've handled far worse*. And Heron could see in his memories that this was true.

By noon their travel arrangements were set. A covered carriage took all four of them to the city's western district, where Archibios maintained a villa close by the harbor.

Praxinoe received them at the door with gracious words. She conducted them down marble halls to a table set with silver and fine crystal. Cleopatra was there before them, arrayed in emeralds, with Eiras and Charmion beside her.

At the sight of last night's lover Heron's groin went hot. She filled his vision like the sun filling a garden, and his senses strained toward her like leaves toward light. She held him with a look that said everything; in so much they were one.

Cleopatra missed none of it. Her brow furrowed briefly; a half-smile crossed her lips; and then she had dismissed it from her mind.

"Kaisarion," she said. "Are you ready?"

"Yes, mother. In my heart I'm already gone."

"Oh, not wholly gone! Some part of you—your heart, perhaps, or your spirit—must always stay here in Alexandreia to call you back."

"As you say, mother."

She smiled once more, this time sadly. "I doubt your companions will see you so docile again. What do you say, Nikias? Are you sorry to have such an arrogant brat on your hands?"

"Not at all, madam. King Ptolemy has a fine spirit and a brilliant mind. A teacher can ask for no better disciple."

She watched Kaisarion to see how he reacted to this flattery, and seemed satisfied. "Sit, then," she said.

They did. The meal that followed was modest only in comparison with the previous night's excesses. By mid-afternoon they presided over its remains, drinking well-watered wine.

When the krater ran dry Cleopatra drew her son aside and spoke with him at length. He listened obediently, never taking his eyes from her face. Heron and Stella withdrew for their own farewells.

"How far do I have to go with this?" he said, holding her hand in both of his. "Now that I've caught up with you, I don't want to lose you again. Let's get back to real life so we can stay together."

She grinned. "Don't be such a passionate boy, John. You know I'm a hard woman. I don't want to see you fall apart."

"But how much longer?"

"Soon," she said. "Soon."

The three travelers changed into dun-colored robes and went out to find the donkey, which waited patiently in the yard beside

Archibios' stables. Cleopatra and Charmion followed them; there were kisses and tears. From her son the Queen exacted a lock of fine black hair. To him she entrusted her ring, the enormous amethyst called METHE.

"You are the last Ptolemy," she said fiercely. "Let this ring remind you of your kinship with the gods." The boy knelt and kissed her hand, to more silent tears. Amyntas looked relieved when they finally crossed the threshold and began the first leg of this odyssey into the vastness of the East.

They took Kanobos through northern Rhakotis. Evidently Kaisarion had never before set foot in the city's ordinary streets; he dodged peddlers and mendicants with horror etched across his face. The world would be a better place, thought Heron, if all its kings had to confront the misery from which they profited.

Toward the eleventh hour Kanobos came to an end, amid crumbling row houses and stinking middens. They stood before an antique gate dating back to the second Ptolemy's reign. Above its broad arch was a frieze depicting Artemis enthroned within a crescent moon. Long hair streamed down her shoulders; a wolf and a lion crouched at her feet.

"Pyle Selenike," said Amyntas, reading the worn inscription. "The Moon Gate."

"Also known as the Gate of the Dead," said Heron.

It lay open and unguarded, a haunt for beggars and water-carriers. The westering sun shone through with a fierce orange light; gaunt shadows followed after them.

So the habitations of the living gave way to the mansions of the dead. Past a stretch of rubble lay a verdant district of fruit trees, thriving in soil made fertile by generations of corpses. There were date palms and vines, orange trees and lemons, casting shade over the quiet avenues of the Nekropolis. Proud mausolea gleamed with island marble and polychrome mosaic; commemorative obelisks towered higher even than the palms; simple headstones offered a line or two of verse. So Alexandreia's citizens, great and small, bore witness to lost lives.

They came to a canal cutting south, a brown channel angling toward Lake Mareotis. An old boatman waited in his bark.

"You've taken your time, gentlefolk," he said. "I've lingered since the tenth hour. And I don't know about that donkey."

"She's a sweet beast," said Amyntas. "She'll never capsize us."

In fact the donkey balked at the gunwale, and only determined persuasion saved the day. The boatman grumbled all the while. Amyntas finally handed him a few obols to ensure peace.

The sun had touched the horizon by the time they were under way, poling silently through acres of marble. Kaisarion sat gathered into himself, his lips a tight line. Heron watched the landscape glide by in shades of rust.

Little by little he began to feel lightheaded. When he raised his hands to massage his temples the motion went on forever. His body felt vague, rarefied, elongated; his neck seemed as tall as Nektanebos' obelisk, his feet as distant as the Nile. His vision dimmed and dulled. The panorama of palm trees and tombstones flattened out, became schematic, gridlike. Scan lines wove into place between his eyes and reality.

Amyntas turned and spoke. His face was a hasty sketch, color bleeding through the angles. His words were all tongue-flicked consonants and drawling vowels, thickening by the nanosecond, a stream of decelerating sound that carried no meaning whatsoever.

Heron had enough sensation left to feel profound nausea. The world grew darker and brighter, throbbing with his heartbeat, twitching and jiggling to the motion of his retinas. His gut heaved up into his throat. What was that roaring in his head, that foreign babble, those quick snapshots of unknown faces riffling along his optic nerve, that wave of narcosis invading his cerebrum?

Alexandreia dwindled and shrank. Alexandreia gasped and expired. Alexandreia faded into the background murmur of history, while a voice intoned, with bloodless accents,

". . . through Aethiopia, to pass into India and the court of King Maues; and his tutor, a man named Nikias, schooled him so carefully that when he grew to manhood he was a thorn in Caesar's flank, and instigated numerous insurrections in Parthia and Armenia. But all these things, and much else concerning his ill-starred life, are related elsewhere."

PART THREE

CITY SUMMER

10

An Unqualifed Success

Halfway through trying to sit up he realized he couldn't. His head was tied down somehow, and persistence would only result in a broken neck.

"Hey, John, take it easy."

A face swam into focus, young and plump. It was familiar but he couldn't think of its name. Something Russian.

The face sprouted hands that went to work on the things attached to his head, disconnecting sockets and loosening wires and finally slipping under his shoulders to bring him safely and comfortably upright.

It retreated a little and smiled a bland all-purpose smile. It was a young man's face. The name was coming. Grigori? Gregory? Grishka?

"So how are you feeling, John?"

"Not bad, I guess." He took in his surroundings. Spotlights, shadows. A second face. A woman. Something ran cold inside. This was all wrong.

"Is it you?" he whispered. "Is it really you? What the fuck is going on?"

Her mouth tightened and her eyes went hard. "It's happening again," she said quietly.

Grishka's smile didn't slip. "I think you're a little disoriented, John. Can you tell us the last thing you remember before waking up here?"

"I was in the boat, with Kaisarion and Amyntas and that cranky old geezer. We were poling through the graveyard on our way out of town."

"Excellent. What town was it?"

"Alexandreia." But how absurd that sounded. Alexandreia? Something had to be wrong.

"And how long were you there, John?"

"Two days. With a night in between."

"Excellent. What day does that make today?"

"I—" That was a tricky one. His brain was a mess. Light, light. Brighten up in there. "I entered the Tower around sunset on New Year's Day. A while later I was in Egypt, just before dawn. I left at dusk the next day. So it must be January third, right?" Grishka's expression told him nothing, and everything he was saying rang false. "Or was it all a dream that took place over the course of a few minutes, and it's still January first?"

Grishka and the woman exchanged glances. "You're a little off," he said, "but actually that's a good guess. Apparently you've had an extremely successful dip. Now please bear with me and we'll have you out of here in no time. Just tell me, in the minutest detail you can manage, exactly what you've seen and done since we first spoke."

Heron's mouth took over. For now, it didn't pay to examine anything too closely. But her face, her face, her face . . .

When he first noticed the clock it said 1950. When he wound up in the Nekropolis, a few cups of coffee later, it was up to 2138.

"Excellent, John, excellent." Grishka never sounded sincere, so it was impossible to gauge the degree of his enthusiasm. But even the woman (God, was it really her?) looked relaxed and pleased. "An unqualified success," Grishka said. "You can be proud."

He wasn't, though. He was just exhausted and on the brink of fear.

"Tired, John?" Smile smile. "I know this is hard, but we still have some more work to do. Would you like a stimulant?"

He accepted the red skinny and stuck it on his throat. Argument would get him nowhere.

"Now I'm going to show you a few pictures, and for each one I want you to tell me a story to go along with it. Be completely spontaneous. There are no right or wrong answers."

Uh-oh, he thought. The hell there aren't. He knew a thing or two about Adjustment Bureau bullshit.

The first picture showed two well-groomed young men, wearing suits twenty years out of style, standing in a Miami hotel lobby holding briefcases. Their names were Jemmy and Johnny, but Heron wasn't about to let on how he knew that. *Where the fuck had they ever gotten that photograph.* . . . But he didn't clam up. He started talking more nonsense than had passed his lips in at least a decade, anything he could think of except the truth.

Grishka gave him monosyllabic encouragement.

The next picture was much easier—a nondescript woman pushing a stroller through the Plaza de la Paz on a sunny summer day. He babbled on.

There were three more, none of them anywhere near as threatening as the first. At the end Grishka said, "Excellent!" for the fifty-eighth time and sat back with folded hands.

That was his colleague's cue to come forward. Her hips swung in a tight black skirt which did nothing to hide their size, and Heron's heart fell down an empty lift-shaft.

Same mass of jet-black hair, same blue eyes rimmed with sparkling kohl, same elegantly simple clothes. But not Stella, somehow. Not Stella.

She sat across from him. There was no warmth in her eyes, no trace of sympathy. She was doing her job.

"First of all," she said, "I don't just look like Stella Cranach. I am Stella Cranach. Second of all, yes, I have put on weight. It happens."

He wanted to wince, to cringe, to knock back a nice double shot of vodka. When she said weight she meant it, nine kilos worth at least. It wasn't a flattering transformation—but it couldn't possibly account for the way he wasn't feeling. On the woman he thought he knew, that extra flesh would still somehow manage to be voluptuous. He'd still get off on those melon tits, those soft Northern Renaissance arms, that big funky ass. But not this time, not her.

I don't believe any of this, he thought, and was about to say it when Stella cut him off.

"Don't speak." She pointed to a video screen a meter from his knee. The image flicked on. It was him, looking haggard. His mouth sagged open and said, "I don't believe any of this."

"I don't believe any of this," he said, and hung his head.

"You will." The screen went dark. She fixed him with a shrinky stare. "That tape was made six weeks ago, on the occasion of your last dip. I think it can do a better job of convincing you than I can."

"Okay," he said. "I'm convinced. Keep talking."

She smoothed her skirt, a typical Stella gesture. "I guess we've made it to point three. It isn't January first, or even January third. It's July twelfth. And no, you haven't been asleep for six months. You're suffering from a minor and temporary form of amnesia. You've had it the past three times you've emerged from a dip."

"The past three times?"

"You've done four. The breakthrough is that this time you're remembering the four separate dips as one continuous experience. You see, most subjects have a hard time sustaining the illusion. You were no exception. On that first dip, as soon as you found yourself in Alexandreia, you started questioning your own perceptions. So you popped right out. You remember it now as a brief moment of disorientation that hit you while you were exploring Rhakotis. When we sent you back down again we used Charmion, your anima construct, to ease you through the transition. But you popped out a second time when you fell asleep in Broucheion, and couldn't accept the fact that you were dreaming inside a dream; and then a third time when you copped that messy orgasm in the royal lumber room. Stress points. But ultimately—as of today— you've turned out to be our best subject ever."

"Anima construct?"

"Excuse me? Oh, you mean Charmion. Yes. She was designed as your ally, your confidante. We've found that dips are more productive if we program in an opposite-sex companion—or same-sex, depending on the subject's erotic orientation—to smooth over the rough parts. It certainly helped in your case."

"I see." His face burned. This supercilious cow was telling him that his most perfect lover had been nothing but a long series of codes, a colossal stroke fantasy. Shall we talk devastation? Shall we talk spiritual disembowelment? His mouth went as dry as the Egyptian desert and gaped as wide as the Nile in flood, just as it had done in the video. The phrase "rude awakening" couldn't begin to describe the way he felt, especially since he wasn't really awake yet. He was an amnesiac, a miserable, emasculated, abysmally disillusioned brain burn-out, and he was sitting face to face with the ultimate creature of nightmare: a fat smug perversion of the woman he'd mistakenly thought he loved.

"About this amnesia . . ."

"You should be over it in a day or two." She spoke blandly,

with a clinician's professional optimism. "Meanwhile you're free to do as you please until you're feeling more, shall we say, in time with yourself. We've designed a personally tailored program of medication for you, in case you need it."

Heron stood and rubbed his jaw. Scratchy; and no cherub-faced slave boys on hand with bronze mirrors and freshly stropped razors. "There's something I'm still missing," he said slowly. "You said my experience in Alexandreia, or in the belly of MEQMAT, or wherever I was, was an unqualified success. Why? Just what is the point of all this?"

Stella and Grishka regarded him benignly, as if he were a puppy who'd finally figured out where to pee. "That's your characteristic reaction at this point in the debriefing," Grishka explained, with a dash of ersatz empathy.

"You successfully completed the course of action." Stella tapped keys on a keyboard; obviously the session was ending. "You followed the script to its conclusion."

"Accomplishing what? My anima construct, as you called her, referred to a process of adjustment."

Stella shrugged. "I'm not responsible for what Charmion may have told you. As I explained to you at your induction, this is an experimental process with ramifications on many levels. At its simplest it's an attempt to perfect a method of reality simulation, via direct cybernetic interface. The Bureau hopes to exploit this process in various forms of behavior modification. I personally am involved as a researcher in another, more tangential area: the interdependence of memory and identity, which is my special interest." She favored him with a glance of bovine warmth. "As far as that goes, you're an extremely useful subject."

He ignored that. "Okay. So we're talking personality research, behavior modification. Then why history, why Antony and Cleopatra?"

"That's one of the ramifications Stella mentioned," Grishka said smoothly. "I'm telling you this in the strictest confidence, John. For several years the Bureau has been developing predictive models of human society. Theories that can project from the past into the future, theories that can accurately forecast the effects of discrete present-day events, whether political, social, economic, or environmental. You can see how crucial such theories would be to the Junta's policy decisions, now as never before. The New City occupies a delicate position in the current world political structure; in this period of hemisphere-wide upheaval, we New

Citizens can only hope to survive by our wits. The Bureau's goal is to provide the Junta with a means of foretelling the future."

Heron stifled the urge to laugh right in his face.

"Now, you may wonder what possible relevance ancient Alexandreia can have to the twenty-first century," he continued, charmingly oblivious. "In fact, MEQMAT is running hundreds of simulations on hundreds of different subjects, set in periods as diverse as the Umayyad Caliphate, the Aztec Empire, the Protestant Reformation, and the world conflicts of the last century. These simulations contain everything that is known or conjectured about the time and place in question. We position our subject, give him a 'script,' so to speak, set him in motion, and see what happens. This is the first time anyone anywhere has been able to do that: i.e., conduct laboratory investigations into human history—controllable, duplicable, completely scientific experiments. Our process has more potential than I know how to say."

Heron's bullshit meter was clicking wildly, but there was no mistaking the excitement in Grishka's face. Maybe this kid wasn't telling him everything, but you couldn't deny his dedication.

"I think I get it," he said. "Stella's covering the mind-fucks and you're covering the time-fucks."

Grishka emitted a quick high-pitched giggle. "I always enjoy your humor, John."

"Yes, ever the plain-spoken Middleman." Stella's tone dripped sarcasm, recalling—very fleetingly—the affectionate irony that had once disarmed him.

He planted his fists on his hips. "Then I guess the real significance of my computerized visit to the past was the part where I smuggled Cleopatra's son out of Egypt."

"Exactly." Grishka beamed. "That led in a direct causal sequence to one of the key events of the early Principate, namely the Parthian campaign that ended in Augustus' suicide and the accession of the boy-emperor Gaius. It was a nodal point in history, so to speak, and through your testimony we're able to examine it in detail. Eventually we'll repeat that same dip with another subject and see it from a different angle. Meanwhile MEQMAT collates and synthesizes all this data into a coherent model of the historical process."

"And here I am an absolute historical ignoramus." Heron shook his head. "So that wraps it up, does it? We're finished till next time?"

"That's right," said Stella. "I don't suppose you remember your address?"

He had "Residencia Trece, corner of Avenida Segunda," on the top of his tongue, but he caught himself just in time.

"No, I have no idea."

She offered him a printed card. It was heavy, good-quality paper, listing his name, his hex code, and his address: Suite 2772, Torre de la Raza. MEQMAT had transferred him to the Black Tower itself.

Grishka gave him a hearty handshake and handed him a small portfolio full of skinnies. "Give me a buzz tomorrow morning," he said. "We'll have a complete session on Friday—but don't worry, no dips! And if you have the least problem, don't hesitate to call either Stella or myself at any time."

He nodded politely and everyone smiled. That was the worst, seeing her smile at him like he was a stranger, a string of digits, a laboratory animal.

He had a series of armed escorts from the laboratory to his door. That generated a degree of paranoia, but when he asked the last grunt if there were any restrictions on his movements, she said, "No, sir!" and all but saluted. Apparently he was to be an honored guest of the Junta.

Or so his new apartment suggested. It was in a prime location, facing a light-well on the twenty-seventh floor, and it seemed so comfortable and lived-in that for a moment he wanted to believe all the shit they'd been slinging him. There were his clothes, his discs, his Pacheco print, and a pair of shoes he didn't recognize but which his own feet and nobody else's had obviously broken in. It was, indeed, home, or a brilliant facsimile thereof. It was also a considerably plusher set of digs than any he'd known in years. Kitchen, bedroom, living room, bathroom, foyer: an outrageous amount of space, with every last detail exactly the way he preferred it.

He shook his head and tried hard to like it; but he couldn't quite.

Though at the moment he felt incapable of liking anything. He felt off, out of phase, like he'd just flown in from another time zone and left his circadian rhythms behind. In spite of the hour he wasn't the least bit tired. In fact, after all the coffee and stimulants, his mind was racing.

This is so wrong and oh Charmion oh Stella those mindfuckers are *spieling such a line* of doubletalk I feel like I've been *squeezed* into somebody else's *skin* is maybe John Heron as arbitrary a host as old Nikias the Greek *except my head feels big enough to hold this whole goddamn tower* and empty enough too—

Yes, there it was: something was missing. Something major had faded away when the Nekropolis dissolved into its constituent units, back there in 30 B.C.: the intoxicating brew of pure knowledge in which his brain had been swimming, reveling, exhilarating. Now he had no more Homer, no more Alexandreian scandal, no more secret teachings of the Two Goddesses, no more Orphic rhapsodies, no more polished gems of Sapphic verse.

He was in a blank, two-tone world, and his foot hurt.

His foot hurt? He squatted down and took off his shoes and socks. If it really was July 12, his injury should have had seven months to heal. He felt along the metatarsal arch of his right foot, probing carefully for signs of damage. One spot twinged slightly under pressure, but otherwise the foot seemed as good as new. In fact, now that he was really concentrating, it didn't hurt at all.

He rose up on the balls of both feet. Nothing. He bounced a little. Still nothing. He hopped. No pain. Hmmm.

There was a mirror hanging over the bookcase that held all his favorite books. He studied the face it showed him. "Looks like me," he said aloud. "Looks like Nikias Rhodios too."

He shrugged. His body was trying to tell him something, but his mind wasn't sure it wanted to listen.

A quick search of the apartment revealed not even a drop of alcohol. That was odd; decidedly out of character. Had he gone on the wagon since January?

Jesus, he thought, here I go believing them.

He collapsed on the living room couch and pulled out the portfolio of skinnies that Grishka had provided. So many pretty colors. This one might do. "Aphypnone. For difficulty in sleeping. One before bedtime." They were a soft, rosy shade, calling up visions of lovey-dovey nurseries where mommies glided like ministering angels and tucked in little cranky boys. He wondered what would happen if he took ten at once.

But no, that wasn't what he needed. He just wanted to rest his brain. No doubt reality would present a more agreeable aspect in the morning.

In the deliciously fuzzy state that precedes full waking he had himself convinced that he was in his old bed at the Residencia Omega, that he was still thirty-seven and married and filling a slot at the Banco del Hemisferio. Then he woke up alone and middle-aged and it started all over again. "I'm a prisoner in the Black Tower," he thought, "and the woman I used to love has stolen six months of my life. Something must be done."

He climbed out of bed. Vertical, yes, that was an improvement. Then he saw the clock. Its digits looked like an entry in a mathematical table, a logarithm, maybe, or an irrational number. How could it be 1515.15? But it was. He'd slept almost sixteen hours. Last night's kidstuff impression of aphypnone had been seriously mistaken.

The living room window showed him afternoon sunlight gleaming on the blank black wall of the wing across the well. A new day, soon to be an old one. His screen flashed purple.

He turned on the audio. "Yes?"

"Well, good afternoon, John. It's Grigori Likhodeyev. So you're up at last."

"Yes, thank you. I'll talk to you later, Grishka."

"Whatever you say, John."

The screen went dead and Heron swore. That was no coincidence. He was under surveillance.

He considered calling someone like George Early and saying, "Hey, pal, can you fill me in on what I've been saying and doing for the last six months? I've got this little amnesia thing and it's making me paranoid as hell. . . ." But on second thought that didn't sound like the best way to resume relations with his oldest friends, and besides, it would just provide Grishka with more ammunition for whatever head-war he was waging. It made more sense to conduct his interviews on a face to face basis—outside the Tower.

He showered, careful not to spend too much time washing his genitals, just in case they were looking, and dressed in loose trousers and a singlet that said, "Life Is Cheap, Art Is Expensive." This was a slogan whose accuracy collectors from Tropicana to Pacifica would confirm, after only a quick look through the galleries along Libertad. It was also an old design of Ursula Schell's. He hadn't even realized he owned it. How many more surprises was this apartment hiding?

What he needed right now was a taste of the outer world. Coffee and tortillas in some café on Segunda sounded like the best solution. Just to make sure he could swing it, he checked his code in the scanner. The screen flashed a healthy balance.

"Then it's on to the streets," he said aloud. On to the open-air clubhouse, the improvisational theater, the roofless marketplace, the museum of the lost and found, the pulsing arteries of the New City.

11

Sighs Smell of Secrets

When he stepped from the cool dim atrium of the Tower into July's humid heat it was like putting on a heavy garment. Ten more steps and it was obvious that Alexandreia-by-Egypt had nothing on summer in the New City, at least when it came to sheer sweat-soaked oppression. Though hot, Alexandreia's air was also dry and clear, alive with breezes off the Mediterranean. The New City was hazy, grimy, and asphyxiatingly still.

Crossing the Plaza he kept to the shade of the big oaks, planted in long lines from the west portal to the avenue. It didn't help much. Everyone he saw—Chinese messengers with canvas shoulder bags, Latin matrons toting whimpering babies, polyracial trendies in tattoos and mesh—looked as miserable as he felt.

Was this normal? Were city summers always this hot? Had the planet maybe shifted on its axis, or was this just a regular old heat wave?

Clustered in the shade of the monumental statue of Chin Leung were five or six pedicab hacks, legs propped skyward. Heron peered narrowly at the one in the middle, a scruffy blond who seemed malnourished and ill. He looked an awful lot like Pacifico Ortiz.

He came closer. God, it was Pacifico, and he was down to skin and bones. "Hey," he said. "Pacifico! Remember me?"

The young man glanced up incuriously. "I'm not up," he said. "Talk to the guy on the left end."

"I'm not looking for a lift. I'm just saying hello."

Pacifico looked again. "Oh. I guess you're one of Ursula's friends."

"That's right. I'm John." He cracked a smile, but it was just as fake as one of Grishka's. Pacifico himself had introduced him to Ursula. The kid was so strung out he didn't know what was going on.

"Pacifico," he said. "Are you okay?"

Pacifico stared at his knees. "Get lost, man."

Heron's mouth opened and drifted shut again. Obviously Pacifico was in the middle of some pretty bad shit. There was no point in trying to talk to him now, but he'd ask around later and see what he could do. With a shrug and a wave he moved on.

He crossed 12 de Octubre, passed the familiar windows of the Librería de Tres Vidas, continued down Ninth Street to Primera, and saw Iris Mulvaney rounding the corner wearing a lightweight flowered dress and lugging a string sack full of this week's vodka ration. He smiled and said hi; she did the same. They weren't really friends, so there was no reason to stop and talk. But after Pacifico it was a relief to make real contact with someone. It strengthened his suspicion that he actually did exist, that this heat-hazy cityscape around him wasn't about to flicker out when someone in the Black Tower changed the channel.

He stopped short and whispered, "Did I really just think that?" An old lady in a sari and hoop earrings frowned at him. He frowned back and kept walking.

By the time he reached the Café de la Quinta Esencia on Segunda, even his eyebrows were dripping sweat, and his balls were crying for a quick plunge into a mound of talcum powder. He took a table in front of the oscillating fan and ordered iced coffee.

His waitress served him with the most honest smile he'd seen all day. "Hi, John," she said. "What's new?"

She was only dimly familiar. He thought fast. Had they worked that bank job together, or was she the painter who had co-curated that exhibition with Milagros Oquendo? Impossible to say. He gave her a fuzzy but sociable answer and turned the question around.

"Well," she said, "I'm still working with Max on staging *Saint Gertrude*, and we're still looking for a stuffed dog. You haven't turned anything up, have you? I didn't think so. Oh, and I had dinner with Aviva last night, and she asked about you. She just cleared the third funnel in the most recent drawing, so she'll be staying with the agency at least three more months. It's good for her."

"Wow," he said. "Great."

Another customer called for her attention, sparing Heron any further embarrassment. He hadn't connected with a word she said. Six months . . . Sometimes nothing seems to happen for a whole year, and sometimes your entire life can turn around in a matter of weeks. Exactly what had been transpiring in the day-to-day affairs of John Heron since that fateful January first? He had to find out soon.

The waitress (Jolanta? Or maybe Maureen?) stayed busy during the time it took him to drink two coffees and eat a plate of corncakes with black beans on the side. Over forkfuls of food he studied his fellow café socialites. Many were fixtures of the Segunda scene; he exchanged nods with everyone he recognized, and looked hard at the ones he didn't. Could that bearded old fogey with the yellow fingernails possibly be a newcomer to the scene? He was ensconced with a couple of indisputable old-timers, chatting garrulously, seeming as at home in the Quinta Esencia as Heron himself—yet Heron would swear he'd never set eyes on him before. It didn't sit right.

He finished his meal a little quicker than he might have and got up to go. As he did, the old man cocked an eyebrow in his direction, calling, "John! Too engrossed in the global crisis to greet a poor old drunkard like me?"

Heron forced a grin. "Forgive me, old sod. I have to go see a man about a horse." He walked out the door, avoiding the old guy's squint, cursing himself for not coming up with a better line than that.

Curiouser and curiouser, he thought. Now which childhood classic did that come from? Was it Dorothy wondering over the talking scarecrow in the *Wizard of Oz*, or was it Zelda's obnoxious trademark in *The Many Loves of Dobie Gillis*? One more mystery to bug him.

And it had to be solved. He had to talk to someone. But who? Fabio Pacheco? George Early? Sally Kuo? There was a callbox right over in the Correos; ten quick taps and he could be connected. But no, somehow he didn't want to try. Not yet. He felt too vulnerable.

So he did what he usually did when he had too much on his mind. He walked, and kept on walking. He followed Tenth Street past Tercera, past Libertad, glancing uptown at the graceful spire

of La Crísalis, the second tallest building in town, the only
skyscraper to survive the terror strikes of the last century. But he
kept his eyes on people more than on buildings. At every
passer-by, he thought, do I know you? Should I know you? Should
you know me? That woman with the tall topknot and the copper
bangles—had they made passionate love together in a cinder-
block dorm room on the night of March 17? That young boy on the
technicolor skateboard—had Heron promised to help him study
for the upcoming examinations in orbital habitat maintenance?
That gentleman in the straw hat and wispy mustache—had he
joined him for *aguardiente* one Liberation Day at the Puerta
Negra, and matched him glass for glass until the old man was
singing hamburger-throated tangos and Heron was puking under
the table? No way he could possibly know.

He skirted the vast red bulk of the Armory squatting between
Quinta and Hemisferio. From a residential window across the
street a disc sang down to him:

> El suspiro que yo oía—
> Los secretos que me decía,
> Mientras mi alma se moría.
>
> That one sigh I heard—
> Oh, the secrets it told me,
> While inside my soul was dying.

An old song, and a pretty one, with a pretty title: "Suspiros,"
Spanish for *Sighs*. He hummed its sad slow tune as he crossed
Hemisferio, flicking a glance at a big gasoline-fueled lorry
stopped before a traffic conductor's white-gloved hand. Just like
the one that pulled in the day Cymbal died. It already seemed so
long ago, and it was, at least by the calendars in the Black Tower.
Seven months . . .

Toward Suerte began the warehouse district, all vans and lorries
and sweaty truckers taking late-day *cervezas*. Ragged fliers
plastered every available wall. Although unauthorized notices
broke several of the New City's ground rules, the Guardia didn't
pay much attention to details over here where no tourists came.
They were pretty tame stuff anyway:

Lithographs by Yoshiko Kawada, Café de Dos Mundos
MEETING OF HOLOCAUST STUDY GROUP, 2 de Agosto

(New Members Welcome)
Available Now! Issue #3 of THE ADVENTURES OF CHI-CHI
BIG FAT BEAT Plays Parque Retiro: Tonight!

Nothing unusual, he decided, nothing that hadn't been there last year or last decade.

But at the corner of Del Río his assumptions suddenly changed. All at once he was seeing a different kind of notice, a closely printed square of coarse yellow paper whose top line said, "IS THE LOTTERY REALLY FAIR?" Underneath was a long political harangue: accusations that the Junta routinely rigged the drawings to maintain its position; several mysterious references to "the war," as if this were something everyone knew about; and a shrill conclusion—"Is the New City the City of Luck, or the City of Lies? WE WANT TO KNOW!"

Now this *was* something new. He walked a little farther and saw more of them; some looked like they'd been up for a while, some looked freshly posted. They could all be the work of a single crackpot, but whether they were the product of one lunatic or a hundred, they were forbidden, illegal, and dangerous. Two things, and two things only, the Junta would not tolerate: religion and politics. And this postering campaign certainly smacked of dissent, of political unrest, or revolutionary fervor.

The New City was a city of immigrants—by definition, people who were there because they wanted to be. Participation in the Lottery, therefore, was voluntary. If you didn't like the way things were going, you could leave on the next boat. Meanwhile you kept your mouth shut, followed the rules, and enjoyed more personal freedom and material comfort than eighty-five percent of the hemisphere. But as soon as you committed a criminal act—murder, falsification of data, religious evangelism, noncompliance with Lottery assignment, political agitation—you forfeited your rights and became subject to punishments ranging from deportation to forced labor.

And as much as players might grumble, Heron hadn't seen a single political movement arise in his two decades in the Lottery. Maybe this little gesture wouldn't amount to anything either, but it was suggestive of some deeper current of change. Once you started questioning the Junta's honesty, the whole structure was threatened.

He regretted not having read the current *Luz y Verdad*. Underneath the censorship and misinformation there was usually a germ of fact. Wait, hadn't he seen a copy lying on the chair beside him at the Quinta Esencia? Yes indeed—now what had that headline said? Something innocuous, something like NEW CITY WINS GREEN CONTRACT. Or maybe it wasn't so innocuous. That nasty little placard had just referred to "the war," and he remembered the hostility brewing between Texas and Tropicana back in December. Had it boiled over? Was Green using the New City as a think-tank again, looking for strategies to avoid being sucked in? Was this a return to the bad old days of Dr. Jeremiah Brown, the Man Who Loved To Hate? He had to talk to somebody.

Funny how embarrassing amnesia could be.

He was in sight of the river now, a broad quivering expanse of sun-flecked wavelets that looked inviting till you recalled how toxic it was. The hills and ruins of Contracosta floated beyond like a cloud of green smoke, stretching along the western horizon to the limit of vision. Out on the water, a little to the south, he could see three barges, a tall passenger ship, a couple of river patrols, and a huge ugly vessel flying the flag of Texas.

He crossed to the edge of the esplanade, oblivious to the old men playing chess and the vendors hawking *mavi* and *helados*. Was that a destroyer or was that a destroyer? Long, low to the water, painted a grimly uniform gray, she sported a squat conning tower and a dozen or more massive gun turrets. Black letters spelled out her name: *The Prince of Peace*. No doubt about it. This was one of the oleocrats' floating death machines, a brutal leviathan charged with supporting Texan arrogance. And she was just lying at anchor, half a klick off the waterfront, as if she belonged there.

Heron broke down and took a seltzer from the nearest vendor. "Some ugly motherfucker out there, huh?"

The vendor was a dark, slender woman of about fifty. She pulled down the corners of her mouth, raised her eyebrows, and half-closed her eyes. "Nothing in the rules says you have to look at it, citizen."

"True, true, but now that I've seen it, it won't go away. How long has it been there, anyway?"

"A week, maybe less. Don't you read the paper?"

"I've been away—uh, working out on the Island. My brigade was pretty isolated."

She made a dismissive gesture. "Some delegation came here from Texas to talk with the big shots. Convoy, I guess you call it.

There's one more destroyer and a bunch of other ships waiting out past the Battery. All because of this damn war."

Just hearing the word *Texas* tickled John Heron's paranoia. "That's a new one," he said. "The New City snuggling up to Joe Bob Lewis and company? I'd sooner believe a coyote and a rattlesnake were sharing the same hole."

"Now, if I only knew what coyotes and rattlesnakes were, I might be able to talk to you." The vendor pointedly turned her back. A crèche jobber tugging three toddlers on a long leash had just come up to bother her anyway. Heron shrugged and set off down the esplanade, keeping the river wall on his right.

Food for thought indeed, he reflected, an intellectual glutton's paradise. And all in just six months. Six months that had changed every aspect of everything in his world.

People he didn't know who knew him (definitely). A rigged Lottery (maybe). The Junta wheeling and dealing with born-again Fascists (probably). His ideal woman exposed as a psycho-pornographic short subject, a quick steamy eyelid movie in a monumental jerk-off session. (And could there be any doubt?)

Yes, there could, and he was most actively doubting. If everything he used to think was true no longer was, what would prevent the things that seemed true now from proving equally false in the very near future? His mind did a quick cha-cha over a field of quicksand. He sank back into his suspicions of the night before. To wit: A man who believed he was really John Heron had inhabited the persona of a man who believed he was really Nikias of Rhodos. Now that same man was solidly replanted in the persona of John Heron, but who could guarantee the authenticity of any of it? A smooth-talking bureaucrat? A ball-busting cow? A machine?

And another thing. What was the story with that photograph Grishka had flashed, the one that showed him and good old Jemmy on their way to committing the crime of the decade? To his knowledge no such picture had ever existed—because if it had, he himself probably wouldn't. So was it a fake? Was it the Adjustment Bureau's way of saying, "We know all about you, John Heron, all about how you helped rub out three Texan politicos back before you came to town, and if you make one wrong move we're sending your head to Dallas on a silver platter"? Or was it simply another article of anachronic debris?

He felt in his pockets for the portfolio of skinnies he'd brought along just in case. Here it was, the lavender sheet: "Propapaverium. For stress." He peeled off two at once, applied both, and waited for the rush.

But there was nothing. Disappointed, he fingered a third before deciding against it. You never knew with unfamiliar drugs. Best to hold off a bit before trying more.

Jesus, he thought, I can't even trust their prescriptions.

He'd had enough of the river view. He'd had enough of walking, too, but he had to keep at it at least until he made it to the Avenida Segunda. He followed Seventh Street's long diagonal back toward the east side.

Somewhere past Hemisferio he heard music, a monotonous jangle of guitars on top of a contagious drumbeat. It didn't seem to be a recording; it had that full-spectrum sound of the real thing. As he tuned into its precise acoustical nuances he realized he was high. The drug had taken effect.

He was abruptly and completely devoid of curiosity. Incriminating photographs; political intrigue, whether in 30 B.C. or the twenty-first century; a fat Stella or a svelte Stella; none of it made much difference. All the confusion that had been bouncing off the inside walls of his cranium was still there, but it just didn't touch him anymore.

Nice. Grishka did know his stuff. When it came to drugs that boy sure could deliver.

Heron felt fifty kilos lighter. His mouth, especially, seemed to have shed its burdens, and it twitched up, up, curving into a certified 100% shit-eating grin.

There was a parade coming down Quinta. That was where the music was coming from. A ragged crowd had spread out along the avenue to watch and listen, and Heron elbowed his way to the front, where he fell into an explosion of movement and color.

A huge banner proclaimed the Ticotuco School of Samba's Annual Celebration of Liberty and Love. Men and women, mostly black, high-stepped and shuffled and spun their way down the avenue, dressed without exception in outrageously brilliant costumes. Sequins, satins, spangles, glitter, huge flaring skirts, embroidered vests, towering crowns of gold foil and glass, velvet slippers with turned-up toes: the effect was of kings and queens who had escaped from a deck of cards to frolic in the street. One man in rhinestones and white satin sported a peacock's tail, twice as tall as he was and three times as wide. A whole corps of bare-chested men in harem pants banged on drums and tambourines. A few dozen more pulled the float carrying the singers and guitarists, who played and sang exactly the same phrases over and over again in a mad, mesmerizing incantation. There was no one who wasn't smiling, no one who wasn't dancing, no one who wasn't drenched in oceans of sweat.

And what could be more out of place and disorienting than an old-time Brazilian carnival winding down the streets of the New City? What offered better evidence that the whole universe had gone insane?

Any number of things. Actually the Ticotuco's celebration was a downtown institution with a respectable history, a party John Heron had been dropping in on most Julys for years and years. The Junta smiled on such pluralistic fiestas, as long as they steered clear of religious taint. Now with the propapaverium sloshing through his brain cells and the samba melody teasing his feet into a little side-stepping jig, Heron began to suspect that maybe everything was right with the cosmos after all.

12

The Boy With My Nose

"Toma, toma!" A fat sweaty man addressed him in broad Portuguese, holding out a bottle of clear liquid with something mysterious floating at the bottom. "Have some! It's real *cachaça* from Salvador."

"Don't mind if I do," said Heron, and he took a mouthful. The guy wasn't kidding; this was the real thing, wet fire with an aftertaste of cane. He took another swig just to show how much he liked it, winking at his benefactor down the length of the bottle. *"Obrigado!"*

The fat man skipped off; the parade kept coming. A little cluster of belly dancers shimmied past, an Arabian Nights fantasy of hot wet skin in coffee, cinnamon, honey, and cream. Cream—that blonde with the paste ruby in her navel and the sequins glued to her breasts—was she familiar, or was he drunk already? "Ursula!" he shouted. But she just kept dancing, pale eyes drugged and unfocused, while her body curved and coiled in figure eights, as if infinity itself were writing its signature in plump Teutonic flesh.

Heron hopped off the sidewalk and into the midst of the dancers, shuffling a samba so he could more easily thread the maze of moist arms and torsos. Of course it was Ursula; no other natural blonde in the New City could shake it like that. He planted himself right in front of her, nose to nose, mirroring her moves with shoulders and hips. "Ursula," he said. "It's me, John."

Her arms rippled, her fingers fluttered like hummingbirds. Her

114

eyes gazed off somewhere beyond the rooftops, beyond the soiled blue afternoon sky. "I know," she said. "I know." And she just kept dancing.

Apparently she wasn't in a sociable mood. He dodged back through the bodies, as crestfallen as the drug would let him feel. At least she'd recognized him, or pretended to.

It wasn't a very long parade. A few minutes more and the last parasol dancers had bounced away, the last jangles of the guitars had faded, leaving Heron alone on the corner of Quinta and Ninth in a little pile of spangles, peacock feathers, and broken glass. He could have followed after, as most of the crowd had done, but he figured he was better off on his own side of town. He kicked a bottle and headed east, grinning again in the rush of propapaverium.

Sidewalks, garbage bins, doorways, steps, overarching trees, ivy-covered walls, old ladies hanging from upper windows, young men passing with bouquets of flowers, kids playing hopscotch, hacks cruising by in three-wheeled pedicabs, street sweepers leaning on brooms, trading banter in four different languages: it was a typical afternoon on an ordinary July day in the most extraordinary city in the world. Already the heat was easing, and as the sun relented, little by little, it picked out patches of red gold on brickwork, and green gold on ivy, sinking heavily towards the river.

He strolled along with no more on his mind than the passing scenery. Or maybe the tiniest, the most infinitesimal bit of anticipation: east, night, Avenida Segunda, bars, vodka, friends. And after friends? Information. And then? Insight. Into what? History.

History. Now that was a funny word, almost a painful word, all sharp edges and confusion. Even though the drug kept such things at a distance, common sense recommended saving history for later. Just as a precaution he slapped on another skinny and let its wave of nothingness carry him to the boundaries of the Barrio Violado.

As he crossed Libertad the clock over the Xin-Xi Polyclinic said 1848. When he reached Fourth and Segunda, time had regressed somewhat, to 1844, but this was no prodigy, as downtown clocks rarely agreed. By any measure, another hour of daylight remained. He was deciding how to kill it when his eyes chanced on a woman rounding the corner of Third. Pale skin, crazy black hair, sleeveless black dress, forthright stride: it had to be her.

Without even thinking about it he was halfway down the block. She kept her eyes straight ahead, completely oblivious. The gap narrowed. He tried not to run. He was within reach, ready to thrust his face at hers, about to speak. She noticed him. She looked sideways and frowned.

"Stella," he whispered. The word died on his lips. His eyes, or possibly his mind, had played him false. She was a stranger.

He whispered an apology; the woman walked off, saying nothing.

Much more slowly he retraced his steps to the corner of Fourth. Of course, there must be at least five hundred black-haired, white-skinned women between the ages of twenty-five and thirty-five living east of Libertad. And of course, on any given day at least fifty of them would choose to wear a black dress. That didn't transform a single one of them into Stella Cranach.

Especially since the real Stella spent twenty-three hours out of every twenty-four in the Black Tower, and could by no misfiring of the imagination be confused with the Stella of his dreams.

He walked into the dim front room of the Café-Bar El Rincón and took a corner table. The crowd was small, low-key, appropriate to the hour; he didn't recognize anyone. He ordered a vodka and picked up an abandoned *Luz y Verdad*.

He hadn't gotten past the headline when a hearty voice called out, "John! What a surprise!"

He looked up into Alberto Favaloro's grinning beard. Okay, reality, he said to himself. Do your worst.

They shook hands with the warmth of a fifteen-year-old friendship. "So then, Alberto," he said. "How have I been doing lately?"

Alberto laughed. "You have a head start on me, pal." He clinked glasses and downed his drink in one swallow. "Run that by me again."

"I'm serious. This isn't something I would ask just anyone. How has my life been going lately, as far as you can tell?"

Alberto's cheerfulness faded several notches. "I guess the program is getting to you again."

"Yes?"

"You made a big mistake when you got involved with that vampire woman, John."

"Yes?"

"Just how much do you remember this time?"

Heron sighed. "Have we had this conversation before?"

"We certainly have."

"You didn't make a videotape, by any chance, did you?"

"Huh? No. Oh, I see. That sounds like Miss Brainrape's style. No, there are no records. Unless—last time I told you to keep a diary. Maybe it's lying around your flat somewhere."

What a fantastic idea. Heron resisted the urge to jump out of his seat and hurry back to the Tower.

"When I get back home I'll look for it," he said. "Meanwhile here we are. Just for old times' sake, just to help out an old friend, could you give me a quick overview of everything that's happened to me since New Year's Day?"

Alberto could. In fact he seemed to have the speech all prepared. It didn't take long to deliver.

During his first month at the Bureau of Adjustment, Heron had dropped out of sight. He was taking classes at the Universidad del Siglo 22, studying a lot and staying on the wagon. Apparently he was also fending off the advances of Stella Cranach; yes, it came as a shock, but that was how it went. Her recent coldness immediately made more sense. Then, in his second month, he began an affair with Ursula Schell. "Another mistake," according to Alberto. He slacked off at school and got into the Segunda scene in the worst way.

"Seeing Ursula also made you enemies with Pacifico Ortiz," Alberto said.

"Why in the world . . ."

"Simple jealousy, man."

"But Pacifico's gay."

Alberto stared. "No he's not."

Heron was about to argue, but he caught himself. More anachronic debris. At least it explained Pacifico's attitude earlier on in the Plaza.

The thing with Ursula lasted three months and ended badly. Apparently she had cradled his head through one of his bouts of amnesia and it had led to an argument, or a series of arguments; Alberto didn't know why. Once it was over, Heron had straightened out again and reapplied himself to higher learning.

And that was that. No gruesome revelations. No unspeakable crimes. Just a few damaged relationships.

Heron rubbed his chin, sipped his third vodka, and said,

"Huh." Then he took another sip and said, "None of that really sounds like me."

"You said that the last time too."

Heron's eyes opened wider.

"That's why I keep telling you to get the hell out of the Bureau of Adjustment. It's no good for you, John. It might sound like a cushy score but it's not. What it's doing to your head is insidious. It's slow and treacherous and all wrong."

"Do I have any choice in the matter?"

"As a matter of fact, you do. You told me just the other day. You have the right to terminate the assignment any time after six months and go back into the pool. You could quit tomorrow."

"You know, Alberto, I think I will." In spite of the fuzzy cottony swaddling-clothes effect of propapaverium plus vodka, his course was absolutely clear. Miss Brainrape and friends could just fuck off. John Heron, for the umpty-umpth time in his life, would put his fate in the hands of fortune.

Alberto's grin resurfaced. "This calls for another drink! On you, of course."

They downed their celebratory shots and headed for the door. The Rincón was filling up; time to move a little closer to the heart of things.

Night had fallen, the soft tropical night of July. Gold neon outlined the distant tower of La Crísalis. Neighborhood folks moved out onto the sidewalks, luxuriating in cool darkness, making swarms of firefly-lights with the glowing tips of their joints and cigarettes.

It was standing room only at the Siete Pecados Mortales. Since the hour was young, and since there was so much competition, Heron and Favaloro decided to slow up a bit and mix some tonic with their vodka. It went down like pop. They leaned against a comfortable pillar, cracking jokes about the Texas-Tropicana War (Alberto had brought him up to date in slightly over a minute) and looking down their noses at a group of West Coast tourists who had somehow wandered in, no doubt after a strenuous hike up the Black Tower.

"Pastels," said John. "What is it with Pacifica and pastels?"

Some mutual acquaintances drifted by; there were greetings, hugs, kisses. Heron felt the most perfect alcoholic exhilaration, that lively stage of the drunk when your body sings with youth and energy, no matter how old you are, and no problem looks insurmountable, no matter how colossal it may be; and tomorrow seems as far away as the next millennium. His paranoia turned into a cloud of pink balloons and vanished into heaven.

"Hey, Alberto," he said, cresting on a wave of bonhomie. "You know who I'd love to see this very second? You know who'd make the ideal third musketeer at this party?"

"Who?"

"George Early."

"Who?"

"George Early!"

But even as he spoke, he understood. Alberto had no idea who he was talking about. And the only, only way that could be so would be if none of this was real. None of it, not a molecule, not a nanosecond.

It felt like the universe, or maybe MEQMAT, had landed a punch to his solar plexus. The core of his being was under assault. But he didn't cave in, no, he didn't dissolve into shivers and sweat; his mind chased after the insight and worried it till it yielded some kind of sense. There were two possibilities. Either he was still enmeshed in a computer-generated scenario or he'd landed in another reality altogether. The second alternative was strictly imponderable, but the first—the first was actually kind of appealing. Why not go with it? Why not assume that this was just another of the Adjustment Bureau's chronodynamic obstacle courses, and keep playing along? The drugs were free, the liquor was cheap, and the company was good.

"John?" Alberto looked suspicious. "Who's George Early?"

Heron shrugged. "I forgot, you don't know him. Someone I used to work with at the Almacén." Alberto still had a funny look on his face. "Don't worry, pal. My brain hasn't turned to marshmallows yet. I bet you've heard me mention strangers before, right, dropped names you never heard of and swore they were old friends of yours?"

Alberto nodded.

"Well, don't bother your head about it. It's just another one of those nasty side effects of the Adjustment process. And that's all behind me, right?"

So he said. But as the words slid off his tongue it became obvious that there was no way he could back out of the program now. Stella and Grishka and MEQMAT had him by the prefrontal lobes. If he ever wanted to get home again he'd have to play their game to the end.

He finished his drink and wormed his way over to the men's

room. In a smelly stall liberally decorated with erotica he took another look at his skinnies. There were lots of the lavender ones left, lots of the propapaverium, but at the moment he was interested in those funny yellow ones. "Eumenidol," said the label. "For depression."

Though he wasn't depressed yet, he wanted to take a few precautions. Three, to be exact. Just in case. They kicked in like skyrockets on Liberation Day.

He landed at Alberto's side. "Come on, man," he said. "Time for a change of venue. Onward and upward."

They tooled up Segunda to the Puerta Negra. A woman Heron had never laid eyes on greeted them both like brothers and stood them two drinks each. Everything she said was funny. Heron soared on wings of mirth. It was a splendid time.

Meanwhile, fugitives from the Ticotuco celebration straggled in, still decked out in Carnival finery, adding the most delicious air of fantasy. And why not, thought John, laughing at the stranger-woman's jokes. Why shouldn't we all indulge our fantasies? If this is just a dream, anything can happen, and should.

That fat oily guy with the long hair and the glittering cape—wasn't he the living image of Mardion the Alexandreian eunuch? And wasn't he winking over his beer in Heron's direction, as if to say he caught on too? And that black girl with the big tits—wasn't she Eiras, Cleopatra's hairdresser? And if those two were here, could the fake Charmion, the real Stella, be very far behind? He laughed again, closing his eyes in blissful expectation.

"But listen," said Jasmine, his stranger-friend, taking hold of his arm. "We don't want to be late for the show at the Lagarto. Lola Achebe is singing. You're a fan of hers, aren't you, John?"

Of course he was. In fact Lola was George Early's old girlfriend. He wondered if she missed him.

"But the Lagarto?" said Alberto. "That's a foreign currency only place. We could never swing it."

"Of course we can," said Jasmine. "One friend of mine works the door, and another one tends bar."

So off they went, arm in arm in arm.

They whisked by the Lagarto's red velvet ropes and let a tuxedoed waiter usher them to a good table. Jasmine ordered a magnum of Argentine champagne. Alberto paled slightly at the notion, but once the bottle arrived, poking its gilded neck out of an ice bucket, he brightened up and downed a toast in exemplary form.

Dancing lights swept over their faces. A saxophone sang a yearning melody. The drummer brushed his high hat, and Lola Achebe stepped up to the microphone.

El suspiro que yo oía—
Oh, los secretos que me decía,
Mientras mi alma se moría.

Her dusky tone, the bruised edges of her phrasing, that perfect opening song—oh, Lola was a dream singer, and MEQMAT was a wizard of hope and desire. Heron sipped his champagne and basked in glory.

Ensconced at the tables around him was an unlikely collection of potato-faced foreigners: a clutch of Middle industrialists, a Texan ambassador, a Green senator, a crime czar from Tropicana. Heron's party was conspicuous in its raffish underdress. But then they *were* on the Avenida Segunda, where scroungy artist types were as much a part of the landscape as pedicab hacks and officers of the Guardia Civil. We're just supplying atmosphere, Heron thought; no doubt the tourists figure we were hired to complete the décor.

He studied their bland, empty faces, looking for a woman with jet-black hair and knowing eyes. Would he find her here, or would it be the next club on the circuit, the Faro or the Faraón or the Dos Mundos? Let it be soon, MEQMAT, he whispered. Let it be soon.

Lola meanwhile moved effortlessly from Spanish to English, from *danzón* and *cumbia* to jazz and blues, her expression always uncompromisingly real. Between songs she exchanged small talk with some admirers at the first ring of tables, who had a more New City air than the rest of the clientele. Heron paid close attention. Among them there were lots of black dresses and kohl-rimmed eyes—could Stella maybe have changed her haircolor, could she have disguised herself as a blonde or a redhead, could she have reverted to her boringly natural brown? Anything was possible.

Then, as he looked, one of the looked-upon looked back, with an oddly wistful curiosity. He was a young man with short curly hair, black as the Egyptian night. He had smooth olive skin and solid, regular features. He was familiar in a frustratingly tip-of-the-mind way. Oh God, thought Heron, oh Isis and Osiris, what if the computer has turned Stella into a boy?

He jerked his eyes away and stared blindly into his drink,

struggling against this new anxiety. But biochemistry came to the rescue; as his pulse surged, so did the eumenidol, and in seconds he was calm again, his mind once more a chuckling kaleidoscope of good humor. When he looked back the boy was deep in conversation with his left-hand neighbor, making incisive gestures and displaying a rugged profile.

Good-looking kid, thought Heron. Sensible kind of face. A credit to his generation. And as if he felt Heron's attention, the boy glanced over again, smiling shyly.

Heron nudged Jasmine. "Do you know him?"

"Who?"

"That Egyptian-looking guy with the nice nose."

"Oh." Jasmine squinted and then broke into grinning recognition, nodding to the elegant young man. "Of course I know him. His name is Mario, or Marco, or Manuel, and he's a poet or a sculptor. Or possibly a choreographer. Typical Segunda material, in any case." She looked closely at Heron. "Um, do you want me to introduce you? I mean, are you—interested?"

"Oh, no, no, it's just that he looks so familiar, so unexplainably familiar."

"I see. Because I don't think you'd have a chance anyway. He seems to be Lola Achebe's new boyfriend."

"Come on, Jasmine, you didn't really think—"

She silenced him with her knee. Mario, or Manuel, had materialized at Heron's elbow, eyes bright and eager. He looked very modish in his dark evening clothes, stylishly young and handsome.

"John?" he said, holding out his hand. "Do you remember me? I know it's been a while."

Heron took the offered hand automatically, racking his brains. So familiar—a memory of love—Stella somehow?

"I—" he said.

"It's me, Marco. Marco Herrero."

Realization and mortification arrived together. Heron struggled to his feet and the two men embraced. They were exactly the same height.

Turning back to his companions he said, "Alberto, Jasmine, let me introduce Marco Herrero, my son."

Jasmine laughed loudly and Alberto slapped the kid's shoulder. "I knew you all along," he said. "I was just waiting for your dad to come back down to earth and remember that he knew you too."

Marco shrugged. "Well, we haven't seen each other in four years, and I've grown up a lot."

"While your father has grown old! And forgetful."

They were cheerful together. Marco invited them back to his table, and the enlarged party was boisterous indeed. Lola joined them after her set. She was friendly and polite when Marco introduced her to his father, but it was plain she had no memory of meeting him before.

"You know what, Marco?" she said. "You've got his nose."

Marco also had, or rather shared, a sizable flat on Twenty-third and Segunda, where a celebration had been organized in honor of Lola's gig. Toward 1100 the whole lot of them trooped up the avenue and joined a noisy crowd in the front parlor. Light sculptures glimmered in five corners of the room; Marco was in fact a scenic designer, not a poet or choreographer. His creations cast shifting, multicolored illumination across the faces of his guests, and Heron, pupils dilated like a pair of black holes, found that the vagaries of his inner world had met their match.

On the way over, of course, he'd tried another skinny. Bored with the lavender, glutted with the yellow, he had impulsively peeled off a green one without even reading the label.

And now he felt—elongated. Thin and tall and twisted, bent and warped and inside out. The raw noise of the roomful of talk was a roar that ebbed and flowed in his ears, and the colors of the revolving lights were a tangible stream, dripping and splattering across densely packed bodies. As for the heat . . . what was 98.6 times sixty? Certainly something that could rival the temperature at the core of Sirius or Fomalhaut. He thought of hiding in the bathroom and bathing his face in cool water, but the prospect of waiting in line (and naturally there was a line, multitudinous and logorrheic) dissuaded him. So he stayed propped against the wall, watching colors surge across the ceiling in incandescent waves, feeling blood course through his veins like rivers of lava.

Faces rippled past him, self-luminous, metamorphic; sometimes they resurrected characters from childhood cartoons (Milton the Moose, Sneaky Snake, Pretty Patty Pig), sometimes they were mere abstract agglomerations of ears and chins and eyebrows. Every few minutes he glimpsed an old friend from Alexandreia: Derketaios in studded vinyl, Olympos in drill shorts and army boots, Archibios in shredded jeans. It made him want to laugh out loud, but he kept it down to a smile.

She smiled back in that irksome way she had. As if she knew better than he did what was on his mind, and wouldn't dream of telling. No, she stood there grinning, fist on hip, cocktail akimbo, kohl glittering darkly round bloodshot eyes.

"It's about time," said Heron.

"Oh? Have you been waiting?"

"Like a dead man waits on Acheron's shore for the ferryman to row him over to the Fields of the Blessed."

Champagne sputtered from scarlet lips. "Did you really just say that?"

"No, it was an echo from another present era. I'm eternity's sounding board."

"You're fucked up is what you are. But you're awfully articulate for a guy who can barely stay on his feet."

"I'll show you stay on his feet!" He stepped away from the wall, waving his arms. "See? No hands!"

She caught him around the waist before he could fall. He steadied himself, resting his hands on her shoulders. "Okay, I give up, you're right. Just get me out of here."

She shrugged gamely and walked him down a short hallway leading off the parlor. The first door was shut tight; the second opened into a tiny room, just big enough for a bed. At its edge Heron performed a convenient stumble that brought them both bouncing onto the mattress.

"Wait a minute!" she shrieked, but his expression was wide-eyed and innocent.

She subsided; they half-reclined, facing each other. "But you know," she said, "I'm not sure if you should lie down or not. Are you just drunk, or are you on chemicals too?"

"It's all prescription medication." He fumbled through his pockets for the sheet of skinnies, but in that position it was impossible to pull them out. "Anyway, don't worry. Now that you're here everything's okay."

"You sure know how to talk shit." She relaxed a little more. "But I finally figured out who you are. Marco has your photograph on the bathroom wall, posing with his mother and his aunt Lidia. You're all dressed up like an astronaut. It's obviously an old picture, but you haven't changed that much. Also you look a lot like him."

He humphed. "So to you I'm just the kid's old man, eh? Then who are you impersonating at the moment? His girlfriend?"

"Lola's his girlfriend, stupid. I'm one of his seven lucky roommates. This is my own room, as a matter of fact."

"What's your alias?"

She frowned. "Maybe I should get Marco. You're making less sense than you used to."

"Sorry. It seems like every time I wake up it's a new set of rules. So far I haven't figured out the current crop." He lay back, hands clasped behind his head. "I just wanted to know your name."

"Esther. Esther Sullivan."

Esther, Ishtar, Astarte, Ashtoreth, ladies of the morning star, of the *stella matutinalis*. A tidy symmetry. "I'm John Heron. Marco took his mother's name."

"Well, I guess I'm pleased to meet you." She leaned closer. Her eyes were very blue and attentive. Her jet-black hair tumbled in untidy clumps around a pale, perfect face. "Are you better now?"

"Only if you keep talking to me."

"Now don't get tiresome." But playfulness tweaked her lips. "Whatever made you get so drugged out?"

"A sudden apprehension of life's deceptions."

"Aren't you kind of old for insights like that?"

"As hardened as I get, there's always some new shock sharp enough to penetrate the barriers. Just wait, you'll see."

"Was it a woman?"

"Only a woman would ask that question." His face turned to lead. "No, it was—everything, this bind I'm in, the fear I'd never find—someone important—again. I'm not so scared now—" He looked at her appraisingly. "But things are still pretty twisted."

"Things? What do you mean, John?"

"I mean everything. Matter, memory. The shape of time."

Her face wrinkled in mixed concern and distaste. "This is way beyond me. I hate to say it—God, you seem so reasonable in what you're saying, but—maybe you should be talking to some Adjustment Pro, not a total stranger like me."

She was sitting up, back straight, brow contracted, hands clenched against her knees. The room revolved around her in a wreath of shadows, through which tiny sparks flitted like comets. With her black flowing dress and vivid coloring she seemed a painted image of a goddess, an ancient icon from Greece or Anatolia—Hekate, maybe, or hellbound Persephone. And yet, at the same time, she was just as surely Stella Cranach, Esther

Sullivan, and Charmion of Alexandreia, a three-faced pawn in the game of the New City.

"You've got to listen to me," he said. "You've got to understand."

She took his shoulders and held him tight. "I am listening, John, I am."

But in her eyes she was afraid. He saw that and was infected. What could she know that he didn't? Paranoia quivered and swelled in his belly, spreading outward, deadening his muscles, making him ill. His head throbbed and his stomach pitched and rolled. His hands trembled with a horrible electric flux. When he tried to stand he couldn't. Esther caught his arm and they fell together, wedging in a jumble of knees and elbows into the little space between the bed and the door.

Together they made unhappy noises, wordless groans and whimpers. In a moment a new face appeared at the door.

"Marco! Thank God you're here."

Heron looked up and very dimly perceived the straight sturdy figure of this kid who was supposed to be his son. His son! The idea made him rage. How had he been taken in by that insipid mixture of charm and noses? He and Teofila never had any children. It was just another lie, and he shivered at its monstrosity, he trembled, he quaked.

They were pulling at him, hauling him by main strength to an unwelcome vertical. "Your dad's fucked up," said Stella. "I think he needs a doctor."

"Dad," said the boy with his nose.

"No," he said. "No. You goddamn little bastard. You're in cahoots with them too." He raised his fist and looked for someplace to aim it. But the pain and the shivering hit him first, and he folded inward like an empty suit of clothes.

13

Schizogenesis

They made a ring around the white bed: Marco, Esther, Grishka, and Stella Cranach. Everyone smiled except Stella.

"Okay, I'm sorry," said Heron. "And thanks. Now please go."

But first Marco took his hand in a dry warm grip. His eyes said everything: it's all right, you did nothing wrong, I love you. Then it was Esther's turn. Her palm was moist, her eyes moister still. She was a gawky twenty-year-old with no sign of the worldliness he had imagined earlier.

"If you ever need anything," she said.

They left like a pair of ghosts. Grishka closed the white door behind them while Stella pulled up two chairs. Heron fidgeted in his cocoon of sheets, saying "Must we?" Stella's nostrils twitched in rebuke.

"You're a very lucky man," said Grishka, sinking into his seat. "And I'm a very shamefaced one. It was my fault, all mine, for turning you loose with that particular array of drugs. I didn't foresee the possibility that you'd take them all at once. The synergistic effect could have killed you."

"Shall I lodge a citizen's complaint?"

"Uh, I'm hoping we can persuade you that that's not in your best interest." Grishka's eyes were as wide as windows, and his apple-cheeked optimism seemed on the verge of slipping.

"And what in your opinion *is* my best interest?"

"Frankly, John," said Stella, "that's for you to define. We're at your service."

Potential was a black emptiness gaping before him and a blacker pain stabbing from behind. Heron winced and touched his brow. Stella gave a quick signal; Grishka disappeared without a word.

She leaned closer. Heron smelled roses. "There are two things you have to learn," she said fiercely, her voice little more than a whisper. "One is that *this is real*. Believing otherwise almost got you killed. Reality is a hard ground that will dash your brains out if you pretend it isn't there and try leaping into the void.

"The other is that I and no one else am Stella Cranach. Your delusions are perfectly understandable, eminently pardonable, but the sooner you abandon them the better off you'll be. I am, was, and will be the flesh and blood woman upon whom you briefly constructed a crazy romantic fantasy. These things happen, and when the context is a client-therapist relationship like the one we have, they become dauntingly complex. But they are by no means intractable.

"I care about you, John. I want to help you. I was the one who got you into this, and your participation in this experiment could well be the foundation of a brilliant career. For me, that is. I acknowledge my debt to you, and I thank you humbly. I'll do anything in my power to make things come out right for you. Just cooperate with me. Don't shut me out. Have respect for both of us."

And inside himself Heron said, God, what a beautiful shade of blue her eyes are. Would that be cornflower, or cerulean? And she doesn't look so bad today, even wearing that tentlike gown. She's really a brilliant actress. I almost believe her.

"Okay, Stella, I'm trying," he said. "But I feel pretty spent. Do you—if I—does your Bureau maintain some kind of rest home somewhere, off on a tropical island, maybe, in one of those Caribbean possessions? Somewhere you farm out old fogeys who've served honorably? Because I feel like I need a holiday. Would that be possible, if I were very, very good?"

She seemed surprised, even relieved. "I don't see why not. If that's really what you want, I mean. Would you like to go soon?"

"I think so. But don't you need me for the project?"

"As I said, it's all up to you. To be honest, though, I wonder if your effectiveness as a subject hasn't been compromised. Your outlook has been contaminated, so to speak."

He grinned. "Too suspicious, am I? Too eager to peek behind the stage setting?"

Her eyebrows drew together. "I wouldn't put it that way. You've simply lost your innocence."

"Whatever you say." He sighed and burrowed deeper into his pillows. "What time is it?"

"It's 0600. Are you exhausted?"

"Yes. I'd like to sleep a couple hours and then go home."

"That can be arranged. I'll notify the head nurse. Someone will be here when you wake up, to escort you back."

"Fine. And Stella? I think we need to talk some more. In a professional setting."

"Certainly. At your convenience."

They traded glances. Citizen Cranach was baffled. Citizen Heron was feeling remarkably better.

Predictably enough, his escort was Grishka. They took a pedicab from the hospital on Thirty-third and dodged potholes all the way down Tercera, on a zigzag course through the wilting crowds of noon. The heat was deadly and the traffic maddening, but Grishka remained completely unfazed, a marvel of cheerful concern; he practically held Heron's hand. And he never sweat a drop.

They turned onto Tenth and made it as far as Primera before running up against a stout barricade manned by a dozen officers of the Guardia Civil. Grishka dismissed the cab and took Heron by the arm. There was surprising force in those blunt Slavic fingers. "I hope you don't mind walking?" he asked, with charming irrelevance.

At the checkpoint Grishka had only to flash his ID to secure the utmost cooperation. The *sargento*, murmuring, "Yes, Citizen Likhodeyev, at once, Citizen Likhodeyev," delegated two of his grunts to escort them. Both carried submachine guns. And so, in spite of the crowds, they made brisk time down the block between Primera and 2 de Octubre; pros and players alike gave them a wide berth.

Once in the Plaza their pace slowed considerably, for a very good reason. The entire area between the avenue and the Tower was carpeted with human beings, bare-armed, streaming sweat, dressed in city-issued uniforms of gray, black, and olive drab. Except for their hive-swarming density, and the crude placards they carried, they might have been Tower employees catching some sun on a lunch break; though there was a rather more purposeful air about them than you would expect from any random crowd of players. Purpose or not, they recoiled at the sight of the submachine guns, shuffling and stumbling backwards into ever denser knots.

Heron had kept quiet all along Tenth Street. Obviously something major was in the works, but with Grishka emitting his smokescreen of jovial innocence, there seemed no point in trying to find out what it was. Now those hand-printed signs waving overhead told him everything.

They said:

> WHO'S FIXING THE LOTTERY?
> *QUIEN HA CORROMPIDO LA LOTERIA?*
> WE WANT JUSTICE! WE WANT THE TRUTH!
> *QUEREMOS LA JUSTICIA! QUEREMOS LA VERDAD!*
> WE WANT TO KNOW!

He heard shouted slogans as well, scattered and incomprehensible. Even as he listened they solidified into a chant: "Foresight is slavery! Fortune sets us free!" Powered by five thousand pairs of lungs, it echoed around the Plaza like the voice of the apocalypse.

Heron thought of the crude fliers he'd seen the day before, and remembered his feeble speculations. Clearly there was a great deal more to this movement than one crackpot working by himself.

"Grishka," he said. "Can't we stick around and see what happens?"

"With all due respect," Grishka replied, not even shortening his stride, "after last night's brush with death I think you'd better take it easy today, John. Things may get nasty; there's no telling. You're much safer relaxing in your own rooms and watching this on video. I'm sure it will be broadcast."

He did have a point. Besides, Heron decided, this wasn't really his issue. At the moment he had other bones to pick with the Junta.

Especially since, as he now discovered, the entire eastern quadrant of the Plaza was occupied by a detachment of Guardias, at least five hundred strong. In their ceramic riot helmets and opaque visors they suggested an army of robots, faceless and menacing. The first three lines gripped interlocking bulletproof shields in a twenty-first century version of Alexander's phalanx;

all the rest were armed with tangleguns, tear-gas rifles, and hardwood truncheons. A few even carried handguns.

By hugging the edge of the Plaza, they reached the militarized zone in under twenty minutes. A new detail hustled them through the Tower's front door, saluted smartly, and quickstepped back to the confrontation.

Inside the great hall it was business as usual; heat, dissidence, and outrage were effectively barred from this locus of power. And just to make sure it stayed that way, Grishka accompanied Heron all the way to his suite before bidding him farewell.

"Now take it easy, John," he said. "Remember I'm only a call code away."

Once alone Heron clicked through all the broadcast channels. But even the news reports were innocent of social unrest; as far as the media were concerned, this was just another summer day in Utopia. He swore and blanked his screen, collapsing back onto the couch.

A second later he was up again, punching Stella Cranach's access code. Her image swirled into focus.

"You're back; that's good." Her voice was carefully neutral, her face expressionless. "What can I do for you?"

"About that appointment I mentioned . . ."

"Yes?"

"Are you free this afternoon at 1500?"

"It can be arranged. Come to the lab."

"Fine. I'll see you then."

They signed off in unison.

He spent the next hour trying to find the diary Alberto had mentioned, without success.

An armed guard came for him at 1445. As they traversed the maze of corridors and lifts, Heron reflected—for at least the second time—that he had no idea where in the Tower's monstrous bulk MEQMAT's laboratory might be located. It could be in the highest tier or the deepest subbasement; he didn't have a clue, because some of the lifts he rode went up, others went down, and none of them indicated level. It was plain that he was being deliberately confused. And not just him. In the process of going to or from he always had three different guards, each one taking him a set portion of the route. Conceivably, only one of the three knew his destination.

So the Simulation and Modification lab was a big secret, a secret to which both Stella and Grishka were privy; which said a great deal about Stella and Grishka. Especially Grishka, who, in spite of his nerdliness, was the one Stella always referred to as the person "in charge" of the lab. Yes indeed, that rosy-cheeked boy must be someone of consequence in the arcane hierarchy of pros. Even the Guardia Civil seemed to agree.

Curiouser and curiouser.

Stella was waiting for him on the other side of the door marked "M." Her makeup needed freshening and her hair was a mess. She said, "I'm glad you're here," and led him through a second door he'd never noticed before.

Inside was a cozy little salon with antique furniture and art on the walls. A picture window offered a panorama of the New City skyline, looking west; it was a hologram. They sat in armchairs facing the view.

"Have you heard any news of the demonstration?" Heron asked.

"What demonstration?" she said.

"Never mind. I guess I shouldn't confuse the issue. We're really here to talk about me, aren't we?"

She smiled and gave a quick nod.

"Okay. So listen. In spite of the sensible advice you gave me earlier today—Stella, I just can't convince myself that this"—he waved his hands at the universe in general—"is really real. Or no, that's not quite it. I can't convince myself that this is the *same* reality I was inhabiting last Christmas."

She replied with a stream of syllables in a language that sounded like Spanish spoken with a French accent, but wasn't; Heron had the brief sensation of being shocked by moderate voltage.

It passed. Stella had just spoken Greek; he knew that much, and the meaning behind the words teased at his brain. He had almost, almost understood her, as if they were back in Alexandreia-by-Egypt having a little philosophical discussion before dinner.

"Come again?" he said.

"Herakleitos of Ephesos, circa 504 B.C. 'You may not descend twice into the same stream, for other and still other waters flow.' The classic formulation of temporal flux."

"Yeah, well, that's not what I mean. I don't mean the ordinary changes of six months. I mean that since I, uh—woke up?—the other day, I've had the feeling that this—world, this situation, this New City—just isn't the world I was born into. That time and space and reality and all that crucial shit have shifted in some fundamental way."

"Hmm," she said. "What makes you think so?"

"People. People I used to know behaving as if I were a total stranger. My friends acting out of character. My best friend, my very oldest friend in the New City, suddenly no longer existing."

Stella frowned. "Which friend is that?"

"George Early, a soft-spoken black man with great big eyes."

"Didn't I meet him at Minoru Fukunaga's Christmas party, the same night I met you?"

"Sure, but—you remember that?"

"Certainly."

This wasn't going quite right. "Then why did Alberto Favaloro claim he'd never heard of him?"

"I guess you'll have to ask Alberto that."

His argument was slipping away like sand from the top half of an hourglass. He held his head for a second before realizing he shouldn't. He didn't want Stella to see him crumble. She had to take this seriously.

He sat straight and faced her squarely. "Okay, I confess that my evidence is subjective. But the feeling remains. After all, MEQ-MAT sent me back to Egypt, right, and had me tamper with history, right? So that means the present has to be different."

"Can you elaborate?"

"Well, it's obvious. Change then and you change now. Like that video, God, I must have seen it in Third Form, way back in Middle. You city kids must have watched it too. The one where this guy gets in a time machine and goes dinosaur-hunting in two zillion B.C. He's only supposed to stay on the floating antigravity path and kill special preselected dinosaurs but he fucks up, he falls off the path and squashes a bug. One bug. So when he comes back it's a different world, with a new language and a fascist dictator, a real nightmare."

"And you—"

"And that's what happened to me. I smuggled Cleopatra's son out of Alexandreia and changed the course of time."

"Actually it was Nikias of Rhodos who smuggled Kaisarion out of Egypt, John; you were just riding his persona."

"Same difference. Either he or I or both of us changed history."

"Exactly how do you mean, changed history?"

"I mean that Kaisarion was supposed to be liquidated—or

rather, he *was* liquidated, until old Nikias and I came along and saved him."

"But the story of Kaisarion's narrow escape from Octavian, and his flight from Egypt, is in all the history books. It always has been."

"That's just the history books of *this* reality. In the world I came from it was different."

"But I thought you knew absolutely nothing about ancient history, John."

"I knew that much. I read it in a book once." He didn't want to admit that his information had come courtesy of MEQMAT.

"Huh." Stella nodded once and gave him a level look. "Okay." She folded her hands. "You know, this is fascinating. A completely unexpected development. Now let's clarify a few things. Does all this"—she waved her hands just as he had done—"seem somehow *unreal* to you?"

"Well, no." He banged his armchair. "It does seem real, perfectly real, but it's not the *same* reality as I used to know."

"Meaning that reality has different properties here? I mean, would water freeze at a different temperature, for example, or would light travel at a new velocity?"

"Not that I know of, no. Those aren't the kind of changes I mean. All I'm talking about is historical change."

"Such as the change in me."

He winced. "Yes."

"Okay. So you've somehow jumped from one version of history to another, via Alexandreia in the time of Cleopatra." He nodded solemnly. "Such a transition would involve what's called a causality violation, which actually is a perfectly respectable concept in theoretical physics. For that matter, so are time travel and time machines. An eminent physicist went so far as to design a time machine, sometime during the last century when there was more leisure and funding for things like that. His colleagues took him seriously; in fact, his idea hasn't been faulted in all the years since. But wait, it's not as simple as you might think. As I recall, his design involved an enormous rotating cylinder, something with a mass on the order of a neutron star. We're talking huge—astronomically huge. You can trust me when I say that Grishka and I don't have any such device tucked away in the next room."

Heron fidgeted. "So now you're going to make fun of me?"

"Oh, no, no!" Her eyebrows flew up, her lips pouted. "I'm just giving your scenario the attention it deserves. Because you are claiming, aren't you, that you were somehow present in the real Alexandreia of 30 B.C.?"

He avoided her eyes. "About that I'm not sure."

She brightened. "Then my suggestion is that in fact you weren't. Because I watched you with my own eyes during every one of your dips into digital fantasia, and you never once moved from your couch."

He tried not to scowl. "Then maybe my mind did the traveling."

"An interesting thought; unfortunately it presupposes a theory of mind beyond my powers to formulate."

"Beyond MEQMAT's too?"

She shrugged. "That I wouldn't know. MEQMAT, like any other complex intelligence, is at a certain level both incomprehensible and unpredictable. We still aren't sure just what he's capable of."

With a sudden inward smile she picked up a keyboard from the table at her right and started typing. After a few prompts and a few responses she glanced back at Heron, saying, "If you're really curious about what MEQMAT can and can't do, why not ask him yourself, John? We have enough core available to run a slightly slower and stupider version of the full-scale program—which is more than enough to simulate ordinary human intelligence."

"MEQMAT would talk to me?" It scarcely seemed credible.

"He would indeed—or rather, she would. The program's operating in a feminine mode at the moment; she likes to switch back and forth. So are you game? It's a rare treat."

"I guess so," he answered slowly. "But before we start anything—Stella, do you believe me?"

"Believe—"

"You know what I mean."

"Then, yes. I believe you're sincere. I believe something strange has happened. I don't necessarily put much stock in your own explanation of what it was, but I don't for an instant doubt your integrity. Or your sanity."

That made him feel glad, even though he didn't want to, even though he'd rather think of this Junoesque creature as a changeling and an adversary rather than a friend and counselor. But somehow it did matter that, whoever she was, she had faith in him.

"Okay, then," he said. "I'm ready."

She gestured at the wall behind them. What had appeared to be an abstract print in a gilt-edged frame was rapidly dissolving and re-forming into a high-resolution video display. As they rearranged their chairs for better viewing, the face of a young girl materialized in living color.

"Hi," she said. "It's so nice to see you."

MEQMAT was apparently an ethnic Chinese of about twelve, a plump shiny-eyed child with sleek pigtails, dimpled cheeks, and a pink Valentine mouth. Everything in her face and voice suggested good-natured competence. If she were a flesh and blood human being she would no doubt be a whiz at calculus, speak two or three languages, play a mean *Goldberg Variations*, and be in the midst of deciding whether to become a neurosurgeon or a career diplomat.

"MEQMAT," said Stella, "this is John Heron. I'm sure you're familiar with his case."

"Oh, yes! I'm pleased to meet you, John."

"Likewise."

"John would like to explore some topics in ontology with you today."

MEQMAT giggled. "Well, I'll see what I can do. What in particular did you want to talk about, John?"

Heron blushed scarlet. He was actually falling for this laser-generated construct's earnest pose. He caught himself imagining her budding breasts and smooth peach-colored belly, even though the image went no further than her neck. It was scary. Had Nikias Rhodios' pedophilic urges spilled over into the sanctity of his own true self?

She waited expectantly. "Oh—" he said. "Uh—have I—is it possible for someone to stumble into the wrong universe?"

"Wow!" Her sugarplum lips couldn't have rounded into a cuter smile. "Just how metaphorically do you mean that?"

"Is there more than one version of now?"

She shook her head in wonder. "When Stella said ontology she did mean ontology! But first, John, we need to find some common ground. When you talk about 'more than one version of now,' I immediately think of how each individual human being constantly experiences his or her own personal reality. So in a psychological sense, then certainly, there are as many versions of the present as there are discrete perceptive intelligences to inhabit it."

"Okay, sure. But I mean—something more like a hall of mirrors. A house with ten thousand rooms."

"Oh, I get it!" What a piercing little-girl voice she had. "The multiverse! Schizogenesis."

"Schizo what?" The word evoked unfriendly overtones.

"Schizogenesis. It means 'reproduction by splitting.' It's a biological term, really, but it also provides quite a nice description of the ontological process of becoming, as described in the Many Worlds Interpretation of quantum mechanics. Would you mind a little lecture?"

"Not at all."

She beamed. "Then here goes! Of course you have some familiarity with quantum theory, with the Uncertainty Principle, with the paradox of Schrödinger's Cat?" He nodded. "Great. You're aware, then, that the physical basis of reality can't be precisely determined, that it can only be defined in terms of probabilities, and that an observer is ultimately required for such a definition. Okay, so let's say we've got a system that can exist in one of two possible states. Without going into the reasons—you've heard it before, right, it's a fairy-tale classic anyway—we'll say our system is a box with a cat and some other stuff inside, and the two possible states are that A, the cat is alive, or B, the cat is dead. Quantum theory suggests that until we observe, until we look inside, the system is in an indeterminate state. In other words the cat's got a fifty-fifty chance. But when we take a look, we've got to see either A or B."

"But not both?"

"But not both. So you're with me so far?"

"Uh-huh."

"Okay. Then what if, at the instant of observation, the universe split in two? What if in universe X the observer saw a live cat licking its paw, while in universe Y he saw a dead cat stretched out all stiff and bedraggled? Pretty cool idea, huh? And that's schizogenesis. Where there had been one observer there would now be two. Where there had been one cat-box there would now be two. Where there had been one universe—one reality, if that's what you want to call it—there would now be two. Two time-lines which would carry on without any further reference to each other. Now, according to the Many Worlds Interpretation, that's what happens every time there is a change of state—thousands, millions of times a second. The universe splits."

Heron nodded eagerly. "That's what I'm talking about. There are different realities, different paths leading from the past into the future, and they're constantly forking. It's a maze, a puzzle, a labyrinth. You can lose your way at any moment; you can miss your destination. You can end up in the wrong place entirely! That's what I think happened to me. I'm not supposed to be here." He pointed his finger at an oblique angle, sighting along it like it was the barrel of a gun. "I'm supposed to be out there somewhere, a whole universe away."

MEQMAT studied him, wide-eyed. "You poor guy!"

"But you can help me! Or at least, maybe you can."

"How, John?" It was Stella speaking, very coolly and quietly and reasonably, and somehow she deflated him the way a pin does a balloon.

"Send me back," he said softly.

She glanced at MEQMAT. "What do you think?"

"I'm not sure." The twelve-year-old brow puckered in high-resolution display. "Let's talk a little more."

Stella nodded. "Before you arrived we were discussing the mind, and whether it can travel separately from the body. What are your thoughts?"

MEQMAT grinned. "You're giving my neural networks quite a workout today, aren't you! First we need to define *mind*. Thomas Aquinas can help us; he once called *soul* 'the form of activity of the body.' Building on his concept, we can substitute mind for soul and say mind is 'the form of activity of the brain.' In other words, it's a recursive algorithm"—her eyes twinkled mischievously—"just as I, by which I mean the 'essential I,' or 'MEQMAT,' am a recursive algorithm. So in theory, why of course the mind can travel separately from the body. It only requires a means of recording it, and then a means of transmitting it to some new apparatus capable of sustaining it. To my knowledge, however—and my knowledge *is* quite extensive, if I do say so myself—human technology is not presently capable of performing those operations on any mind of organic origin. Does that shed some light on your question?"

"I guess—" Heron struggled. "So you're saying that I'm talking nonsense, that my idea of what's happened to me must be wrong."

"Not wrong," said Stella. "Just incomplete."

Now he did hold his head, and he didn't care what Stella thought.

"Thank you for your time, MEQMAT," she said.

"Wow, sure. It was good to meet you, John. I'm sure we'll talk again." The little-girl image faded, and the abstract picture returned.

John and Stella faced each other. Seconds blinked by in silence. Outside the window brilliant sunshine played over the glazed imaginary towers of the New City. Beyond the narrow sky, across the manifold universe, systems great and small proceeded in schizomorphic discontinuity. Galaxies shuddered and pulsed. Present time fractured into past and future.

"So, John?"

"So, Stella?"

"What will you do?"

"Has this all been recorded?"

"Certainly."

He took a deep breath. "Then let me do another dip, as soon as possible, and let me see this video as soon as I come back." She looked alarmed, but he plowed on. "If things still don't make sense to me after all that, I'm in your hands. I'll concede that my mental state is not what it should be, and that I need whatever therapy the Bureau of Adjustment deems appropriate."

Her face darkened. "I hesitate to say yes."

"Why? Because you think I still have amnesia, because you think I'm not in the right condition to make decisions of this magnitude?"

"More or less. You see, this is the longest your amnesia has ever lasted, and we've never before let anyone dip until they had reestablished their temporal continuity, so to speak."

"But I'm willing to take the chance. You should be, too. Just this once."

She didn't speak; instead her fingers clicked over the keyboard. She studied whatever the display showed her for a frustratingly long time before looking up.

"There's a dip coming up at 2000," she said slowly. "I could cancel the scheduled subject, and put you in his place."

"You'd send me back to Alexandreia? Back to 30 B.C.?"

"Whatever scenario you prefer. The limiting factor is core. Once we have enough of that, we can run any simulation you want."

"Then do it! Please. Send me back to that same summer. I guess I couldn't be Nikias again, because he's already left town, but there must be some other persona I could use."

"Male, I presume? Or would you maybe settle for a eunuch?" His face twisted; she laughed. "Don't worry, I wasn't serious.

Just testing." She tapped in a few commands, sat back, and said, "Done."

Heron was sweating, that cold musty sweat of tension. He stood clumsily and offered Stella his hand. She accepted.

"You should go back to your suite now," she said, "and take it easy for the next few hours. I'll have someone collect you at 1930."

"Thanks, Stella." He couldn't help smiling. "Thanks."

She accompanied him to the outer door, where the same armed guard was waiting.

Alone in his room he tried calling everyone whose call code he could remember—George Early, Alberto, Fabio, Ursula, even Sally—and every time the box said, "We are experiencing temporary technical difficulties. We cannot complete your call." Swearing and shouting didn't improve matters, either.

The news channel mentioned an earthquake in Ecuador, an art opening in Dallas, a political rally in Portland, and finally, finally, a sixty-second spot covering the "confrontation" that afternoon between "a small group of demonstrators" and the Guardia Civil, just outside the Black Tower. There were a few quick shots of grim Guardias carrying dazed and battered-looking players into a paddy wagon; there was a hurried reference to the "dozen or so" agitators who had been charged with noncompliance with the Lottery. Then it was on to a speech by Citizen Zhang, number five in the Junta, urging all members of the labor force to greater diligence and more inspired strategies and more harmonious cooperation and so on and so forth until ninety-nine out of every hundred viewers would have switched to the New Music channel. But after Zhang's big yawn there was a tidy little statement to the effect that, because of an "exposed power cable" on Twelfth Street, a curfew would apply from 1900 to 700 throughout the Barrio Violado.

"What the fuck is going on!" Heron shouted. But the box wouldn't say.

For the next two hours he ate tortilla chips, tried to call his friends again, and searched through his personal file for something that looked even remotely like a diary. All he managed to do was bring on a headache and a case of heartburn.

When the grunt came by to pick him up she wasn't an instant too soon. It was an effort not to go skipping ahead of her; that big blue door had never looked so inviting.

But just as Grishka was positioning the electrodes, just as the aphypnone was sending its pink glow through his body, he remembered someone he'd forgotten. In fact it was someone he'd remembered and forgotten a few times already—namely Marco, his son. Except that, as he'd already realized once in the past twenty-four hours, he didn't have a son. Nor was he childless, as he'd told himself this morning. He had a daughter: his daughter by Sally Kuo, a plump Eurasian beauty of about thirteen who looked a lot like MEQMAT. And remembering her he realized how little he really understood of what was happening to him.

Obviously he couldn't trust anybody anymore, especially not himself.

PART FOUR

MESORE IN BROUCHEION

14

A Snake Dripping Venom

At first he fell softly, like a leaf in a soft breeze, and the breeze was a voice that knew everything and denied nothing, speaking cool, soothing words. *In the same stream we go and we don't go, we are and we aren't.* Puzzle words, play words, silly words, guiding his long descent, *merrily merrily merrily.* The *go* pushed him in and the *don't go* pulled him out; the *are* turned him on and the *aren't* turned him off; all of them together made a shuddering, a vibration, a friction that heated him, kindled him, *merrily merrily merrily.*

The voice was warmer now, and the stream was a river of fire. He fell and he burned.

"There he is! God, this heat."

"There's not a dent in his armor. Not a mark on any of them."

"Well, you've heard the tale."

"But to see it."

"Yes, to see it. Enter Chorus for last act."

The sea and sky were a continuous blaze of light, devoid of color; the shore was a riot of flesh, fabric, and iron, a sponge for the heat and a dazzle for the eyes. Heron blinked and caught the other man's arm.

"What, Diomedes! Evening liquor and morning sun a poor partnership, eh? A bit unsteady in your balance?"

He shaded his eyes; his brows dripped sweat. "It's passing."

The other man was stout and gray. His broad open face stirred

145

pleasant memories. Archibios, yes, the capitalist, the raconteur, friend to the Queen and her father before her. A smoother transition this time, a more immediate recognition.

But who was this Diomedes?

"They're almost close enough to speak. Come, come."

Three warships rode at anchor between the rocks of Antirrhodos and the smooth marble quay of Lochias. A squad of Roman spearmen lined the lowest tier, impassive in polished casques and glinting breastplates. Their general had already reached the top step, with his bodyguards at either hand: Antony, victor at Philippi, conqueror of Parthia, quondam lord of the East. His face was ruddy with wine and anger.

"Cleopatra." He halted three cubits from where she waited. "Cleopatra." His eyes were bluer than the waters off Crete, crueler than the British straits. "Cleopatra." He pitched his voice low, sparing her the trumpeting of his battle cry. "Cleopatra! My mistress, my wife, my queen. Mother of my children, keeper of my heart, goddess of Egypt's earthly paradise. Cleopatra! *What have you done!*"

Disdaining for once the habit of Isis, the Queen wore a voluminous purple gown of Koan silk, girdled with pale amethysts; pearls netted the heavy hair that coiled at the nape of her neck. The Delta's golden cobra, Wadjet of the Sorceries, arched above her brow, poised as if to strike.

"Antony," she said, "you will not accuse me."

"Oh, won't I? Here I come in ignominious flight from the walls of Paraitonion, where I lost two ships and two hundred men in honest battle, only to find that Pelousion is surrendered to Caesar Octavian, without a fight—indeed, with your own connivance!"

"I see." Cleopatra was a statue of herself, cool and unyielding. "You believe your enemy's paid informers, but not your own wife's word. Yes, it's all very clear to me. I've fallen at last to the miserable state of my predecessors, Fulvia and Octavia, those women you used and abandoned: the first to her death and the second to a loneliness worse than death. Revile me, then, noble Antony, accuse me of every imaginable crime—after I've given you half my throne and all my heart, after I've poured the wealth of Egypt into your cause."

"Oh, you artist, you player! You toy with words the way a harpist plays a harp, plucking pretty fancies out of air to beguile the whores and panders of Alexandreia." He spread his arms to include her entire court. "How dare you compare yourself to the women I put aside for you? It passes all decency! Your tongue is a snake dripping venom."

Her eyes narrowed till they seemed twin slivers of diorite. "You push me to the limit, Antony. I, at least, have never deserted a man, and never cuckolded a husband. Oh, how much better my lovers have fared than yours! Two men, two men in all the world have ever shared my bed: to the first I stayed faithful till the hour of his death, and to the second I can only pray to be as true. But how sorely he tries my resolve!"

Antony's lip curled, and he would have replied, but Cleopatra cried, "Enough!" For a long moment there was silence on the green marble steps of Lochias, while the two antagonists took each other's measure. Abruptly the Queen summoned her guard; eight or ten lithe Egyptians came forward, herding a wretched-looking woman with two children, a boy and a girl just short of adolescence.

"You will judge," said Cleopatra. "Seleukos Kanobios held Pelousion in my name. It was he who handed over the fortress to Octavian. These are his wife and children, the only heirs of his body; they were left with me as insurance for his loyalty. Their fate is yours to decide."

Seeing her last hope of salvation, the woman emitted a piercing wail and threw herself at Antony's feet, her chains clanging on stone. The two children wept pitifully. Cleopatra leveled basilisk eyes on her long-time lover.

The Roman was unmoved. "Take them away and kill them," he said, and the Queen smiled in triumph. With this bloodshed Antony absolved her of treason.

Though Seleukos' family redoubled their cries, the royal pair had already dismissed them from consideration. The Egyptians hustled them into the depths of Lochias, while courtiers gaped and whispered.

"Henceforth I trust we can save our enmity for Octavian," said the Queen. Antony nodded silently.

"But even as we stand here," he said, "Octavian's army sets up camp outside the Kanobic Gate, weary and footsore after a forced march. He never dreamed that I'd return so quickly from Paraitonion. He never expected an attack at this uniquely vulnerable moment." Antony raised his voice, conscious of his audience. "But that is precisely what he'll get! We have fresh cavalry waiting in Alpha Sector; I'll lead them forth in a sally before the day is half-spent."

"Excellent, my love!" Cleopatra clasped her hands, miming admiration and relief. "Young Caesar has never withstood us on land; now he'll see what good generalship is."

With a proud salute Antony strode off at the head of his iron-clad Romans. The Alexandreians cheered and tossed lotus blossoms in his path. Never mind that he had slandered their morals only minutes earlier; memories are short when kingdoms teeter on the brink. A hero was needed. Since Antony was all that was available, he'd have to do.

"So the farce continues," muttered Archibios, turning away. "You might expect Alexandreia's fall to be a subject worthy of Homer, or even Apollonios; but no—we watch it unfold in the manner of Menandros' lighter work."

Heron would have replied, but Diomedes was quicker. "Given the choice, who would pick a tragic life over a comic one? You have little cause for complaint, old man."

Archibios shrugged. "Yet there will be tears before the end."

Neither Heron nor his alter ego could dispute that.

After a few more pleasantries Archibios bade him farewell, leaving him alone in the gaudy crowd of eunuchs and hangers-on. Part of his mind urged him to hurry off and find the Queen, for reasons that were still a bit murky; another part insisted on a few solitary minutes simply to collect his senses and formulate a plan. The second part won. He slipped through a double colonnade, hurried down a hallway paved with jasper, and paused in an empty courtyard, cooled and enlivened by a fountain bubbling in a basin of polished porphyry.

Alexandreia again, the swankest scene in the world. And who was he this time? Only ask and be answered. Diomedes the Lykian, born a slave in Ionia, imported into Egypt at age six, trained in reading and writing, manumitted at thirteen, apprenticed to a clerk in the great Library of the Mouseion, presented at the royal court, retained by Queen Cleopatra. Another bookish type: soft hands, nearsighted eyes. He studied his forearms, felt underneath his chiton, and discovered a slender, supple body, in spite of his sedentary habits; but of course Cleopatra chose her staff partly on the basis of looks, so he couldn't be too unpresentable. This time he was actually young, no more then twenty-four: a boyish-faced Asiatic Greek who rather resembled John Heron at the same age. Not the worst mask to wear, in a time and place that valued appearances at least as much as his own did.

He poked around a little more. Again he experienced that

delight in pure knowledge that he had felt earlier with Nikias the rhetorician, the heady sensation of exploring a treasure house of poetry and philosophy. Though young Diomedes lacked the vast erudition of his first host, he was still a cultured man with a fine sense of language and a prodigious memory for literature. He had to be, yes, there it was, because he was private secretary to the Queen herself. At least two hours of every day he spent attending Cleopatra, jotting down her pronouncements and reminding her of appointments. The rest of the time he wrote letters, ran errands, and carried out special assignments, such as—he had to smile— spying on Archibios, and various other worthies of Alexandreia.

Obviously he must work in tandem with Charmion, the Queen's principal lady. And what could be more perfect? Eagerly he searched the archives of recall, seeking testimony of their contact, their intimacy. But what he saw puzzled him. Instead of affection, there was a chill between the two of them that amounted almost to rivalry. Diomedes saw Charmion as haughty and vain, full of spite toward anyone who intruded on her bond with Cleopatra. He felt a scornful amusement at her clandestine love affairs, which seemed rather frequent. He even remembered that particularly laughable night she'd spent with Nikias of Rhodos, the dirty old pedagogue. He'd been teasing her ever since.

Some changes appeared to be in order.

He sprang from his seat and once more entered the palace. Cleopatra would no doubt be holding forth in the Andromeda Room (so named for its frescoes of the Perseid saga), and her disposition was more likely to resemble that of a Gorgon or a sea monster than a blameless Aethiopian princess.

He wasn't mistaken. The Queen sat stiffly in an ebony chair trimmed with silver, surrounded by nervous courtiers. "So, Diomedes, arrived at last." She flicked him a glance from kohl-sparkling eyes. "Detained in the garden by some pretty-faced boy?"

Pretty-faced boy? But of course: first a pederast and now a homophile! Was this MEQMAT's idea of a joke?

"No, madam. I was speaking with Archibios."

"And what did Archibios have to say?"

"Oh, that life imitates art, among other things."

"You'll tell me more later. Meanwhile, on account of your tardiness, you've missed a pleasant charge. I would have had you organize this evening's triumphal banquet."

Diomedes tried not to smile. How like Cleopatra. Battle not even joined, and already she was celebrating victory.

"Mardion has the task instead. You, my child, will undertake a more interesting and more manly assignment. Collect a few quick-footed boys—I trust you know where to find them—and fly to the rampart overlooking the Hippodrome. There you will have an uninterrupted view of Antony's battlefield. I want you to send me dispatches on the progress of the fighting, written in your own fine hand, twice an hour if need be. Omit nothing. Understood?"

"Yes, madam."

"Then go!"

He did, commandeering a horse from the stables and four wiry Egyptian lads as runners. The ride down Kanobos thrilled Diomedes' blood. This was what he loved best, scurrying the length and breadth of Alexandreia on the Queen's business, poking his nose into the affairs of the great and the not so great, borrowing authority and purpose from his royal mistress.

John Heron, meanwhile, felt overwhelmed. Rather than governing and guiding a fusion of two minds, he was all but impotent. He was foundering, he was sinking beneath the information and emotion that flooded the young secretary's conscious mind; he was swept along by the force of the other man's personality, in which he seemed no more than a helpless intruder. It wasn't at all like the other time. Then he, the twenty-first century man, had worn Nikias' persona as little more than an outward shell. Now he was reduced to the role of spectator, while Diomedes acted out his life's own drama.

As Cleopatra predicted, the crumbling battlements of Ptolemy Soter's ancient wall afforded an excellent view of the cavalry skirmish. Diomedes spent hours there in the blazing sun, studying the shifting line of battle, cheering when Antony drove back Octavian's charge, chewing his knuckles when young Caesar gained ground. His pen scratched madly across papyrus, his little messengers flew to and fro like earthly versions of wing-footed Hermes, back and forth from Cleopatra's headquarters in the heart of the Broucheion. In his ears echoed the distant ringing of *spatha* on *scutum*, and the screams of men and horses dying beneath the palm trees were an anthem raised to Ares, cruel drinker of honest blood.

By the ninth hour Antony had beaten Octavian's cavalry back to an entrenched position east of the Hippodrome, and, well satisfied with this small achievement, he returned toward the city with trumpets blaring. Diomedes likewise took to horse in hopes of being the first to bring these happy tidings to the Queen.

It was still mid-afternoon. The great avenue was thronged with the idle and the anxious, for all business had been suspended in anticipation of the battle's outcome. As he plowed through these multitudes, many tried to detain him, saying, "What news? What news?" And when he answered, "Good news!" a cheer rose up around him that transformed his return to the palace into a progress worthy of an Olympic victor.

Great fun, all of it. Though empires might hang in the balance, Diomedes would have his moment of glory.

He delivered his report to Cleopatra and accepted a handsome gift of gold. But when Heron strove to make contact with Charmion, smiling in her direction, addressing bantering words to her, she completely ignored him. And Diomedes was content to let it be so. However strongly Heron willed him to linger in the royal presence, to delay his visit to the baths and the massage table, Diomedes brushed off his efforts as a child brushes off a pestering fly. The young secretary took leave of the Queen with a low bow and strolled cheerfully out the door.

Heron struggled. In despair he recalled what Stella had said about his last dip, about the way disbelief could break the illusion. He stared at the painted walls and imagined them as printed circuits. He studied the face of a Libyan slave and reduced it to an alphanumeric sequence. He strained against his digitized hypnosis, he ordered his senses to interrupt the bright flow of the world around him, to expose its ontological contradictions to the scrutiny of reason; and nothing happened. Nothing would stop the river.

"Diomedes, are you well?" An Arab slave frowned and peered into his eyes.

"Oh, well enough. I was just remembering one of the atrocities I witnessed today."

The slave made a gesture to avert demons and disappeared down a branching corridor.

After bathing, Diomedes looked in on the banqueting hall that Mardion and a host of servants were preparing for the impending revels. Satisfied that it would rival any extravagance the Queen had ever committed, he retired to a side chamber and amused himself chatting with Potheinos the Syrian until the banquet should begin.

Ninety-eight guests were served that evening in Broucheion's grandest hall. Olympos, the Queen's adviser in spiritual matters, arrived at this auspicious number by adding seven times seven to itself. These lucky hedonists, all the remaining members of the Suicide Club, dined off gold plate and drank the last of Auletes' vintage from golden flagons set with lapis lazuli. Larks, peacocks, Persian fowl, force-fed geese; oryx; antelopes, wild boar, new-born calves; swordfish, octopus, prawns, and squid: Cleopatra's chefs scoured every element but fire to find victims worthy of the feast, and offered them up in a zoo of gustatory delights.

Alexandreia's foremost musicians provided incidental music, plucking antique harps and lyres, sounding honey-toned oboes and flutes. Singers with voices clearer than silver bells sang the praises of brave Antony and divine Cleopatra, using every language of their fallen empire, every serpentine mode of the East. And when the last course was delivered, by slaves dressed as the Olympian gods, the hall's ivory ceiling parted to release a shower of red roses, a murmuring cloud of snow-white doves, and a rain of gold coins stamped with the portrait of Cleopatra Thea Philopator.

From his post in an alcove Heron observed everything through Diomedes' admiring eyes, and was disgusted, with a Middleman's plain-living disgust. People were people; food was food. These Alexandreians had made a cult of pleasure and driven themselves insane.

He slipped through the fog of incense to a terrace just off the hall. An old moon showed him a panorama of tiled roofs and marble colonnades spread out below; further on, a hundred ships rocked in the Great Harbor, each one carrying torches fore and aft, so that the whole area flickered like a vast constellation. Further still, the great bonfire of Pharos burned steadily against the open sea.

The stillness and simple grandeur of the scene refreshed both Heron and Diomedes. The Alexandreian's focus relaxed and wandered freely; he had drunk cup after cup of wine, and now his will began loosening its grip.

Finally. Heron turned back; he remembered seeing Charmion standing over by the Queen, and he was determined to confront her. But before he could leave the terrace he heard a man's familiar voice, close at hand. He was reciting some sort of litany over the cityscape. Peering closely into the shadows Heron saw grave Olympos leaning over the balustrade, speaking in ringing tones while Charmion the Egyptian listened with a mournful air.

"City of legends," (said the old physician)
". . . rich of gold, flashing with the spoils
of many vanquished kings, crossed by avenues whose temples
and colossi loom far grander than any of white-walled
Memphis, or Thebes of the hundred gates: Alexandreia,
wise as Athens, cruel as Carthage, glorious
as high-towered Ilion, and as doomed; for while you keep
your treasure of metal and jewels, your heroes
have betrayed you, save for one. And though our Antony have
the courage of an African lion and the noble blood
of Herakles the demigod, no man can hold a city
singlehanded. Even Hektor fought beside the tall sons
of Priam, and Argive Achilleus. . . ."

Heron laughed out loud, and stage-whispered, "If only Archibios could hear this! Epic dignity at last!"

Charmion frowned. "Any sort of dignity at all would be preferable to your adolescent boorishness, Diomedes. I hope you'll apologize to Master Olympos before running off."

"Why, certainly. Please pardon my levity, sir, and accept my praise. For whereas wine turns ordinary men into babbling fools, it coaxes grand hexameters from the tongue of noble Olympos!"

The physician studiously ignored him, but Charmion's annoyance redoubled. "Will you leave us in peace, or must we leave you?"

He lingered, wrestling with indecision. He had to speak with her, and this was the first opportunity he'd seen, however awkwardly it was progressing. Perhaps it behooved him to adopt a more serious tone.

"Forgive me," he said, hand on heart. "The times are so heavy that in protest I've assumed a frivolous air. Certainly I meant you no insult, Lord Olympos. But Charmion—the Queen sent me to consult you in private." He bowed to Olympos. "Do forgive this intrusion. We won't be a moment."

Olympos sketched a shallower bow and returned to the fevered lamplight of the banquet. Charmion waited with arms folded and face hard.

"Charmion?" he said. "Stella?"

"I don't speak Latin," she said crossly.

"Oh, neither do I. I just, ah, wanted to call you by a new name."

"Whatever for? Come, Diomedes. No more silliness. Let's have the Queen's words and be done."

Standing close to her like this he could smell the subtle perfume of roses he remembered so well, rising in waves from her hair. Her eyes were as clear as gemstones, innocent of wine or debauch, fixed on him now in the most becoming anger. This was, this had to be the woman who had called him across the gap of centuries.

"The Queen wants to know," he said carefully, "whether you're acquainted with a man called Heron."

She considered. "I'm sure I've met any number of men by that name over the years, but none in particular stands out."

So cagey, this exquisite lady. "But don't you realize that my own name is Heron, that it was Heron everyone called me before I entered the Queen's service?"

"No, and I can't see what possible significance it has."

"Stella, please, don't be cruel. I've suffered through a great deal to find you again."

Her mouth twisted. "Who is this Stella? What kind of madness are you feigning? Secret names, long-suffering desires? I won't be mocked this way, Diomedes."

It wasn't working. It was all wrong again. "We knew each other before," he said, as reasonably as he could, "in a different place. We meant something to one another."

She drew back, throwing a corner of her crimson peplos across her shoulder. "You're drunk, or mad, or both. I refuse to listen any further." She turned toward the banqueting hall in high disdain, and he was left alone in darkness, sick to the core of his being.

15

Distant Music

That night Antony drank even more heavily than usual, for, as he said several times, the next day might see him stumble into the kingdom of shadows, where he would never taste wine again. Both he and Cleopatra poured so many libations to the vine-god that the Queen herself grew drunk. Without the magic amulet METHE she had no defense against Dionysian wizardry.

But Heron touched no more wine. After his futile interview nothing seemed to matter; he had no reason to keep Diomedes submerged, because now, alas, he had no agenda of his own. In the midst of the revels he stole away, to sleep in Diomedes' bed and dream Diomedes' dreams.

He closed his eyes on MEQMAT's vast constructions, and reopened them, just past the threshold of sleep, on the colors of nightmare.

It wasn't like before. No memories of *Kosmograd* or Miami reared up to haunt him, no automatic pistols or multistage rockets. These were alien dreams, Ptolemaic dreams, teeming with sphinxes and demigods, foundering ships and screaming horses, rotting lepers and wretched women who begged for mercy while they rattled iron chains. Nothing here had any bearing on the world he used to know. These were visions of an archaic universe, a place even crueler and more capricious than his own century, a place where John Heron had no business at all.

He woke and cried out. It was the stillest hour of the night. He rose naked from his couch and stood shivering at the casement, gazing over the city as it slumbered in blue oblivion beneath the moon. Slowly his two-sided mind grew calmer; the throbbing in his ears quieted. A new sound stole out of the air. Off to the west he heard strange music, pipes and tambourines and shrill voices calling, as if born of invisible hands and throats. He could hardly believe his senses. The witchy music floated over Alexandreia's rooftops and traveled along Kanobos Avenue to the eastern gate. As it passed the Hippodrome, where Rome's legions were encamped, it swelled suddenly in volume, until it seemed that an army of dancing maenads had gathered in the sky to celebrate the Mysteries over Octavian's dreaming host. And then it faded. Silence returned, a silence so profound that he could hear the whispering of the distant sea.

Both Heron and Diomedes wept then, troubled by things beyond their understanding.

Before dawn Diomedes attended Cleopatra in the Hall of Appearances. Courtiers spoke of nothing but the eerie portents of midnight. Everyone had his own explanation, each one more farfetched than the one before it, and no two in agreement. Within earshot of Cleopatra, however, conversation turned to less ominous matters.

Antony arrived in due time, fully armed. His eyes were as red as the tip of his nose. He and the Queen exchanged the usual bombast and basked in the usual applause. But once he had ridden off with what was left of his army, so hung over that he could barely sit his horse—and still promising victory before the setting sun—Olympos turned to the Queen and said, "The god has deserted him, madam. Last night's auguries were plain. Dionysos will no longer hold his revels in Alexandreia."

Cleopatra gave no sign that she had heard. Instead she rose from her golden seat and signaled impatiently. "Quickly now, Olympos, and help me into my tomb."

But the Queen had no intention of dying, not just yet. Months before, with Octavian's assault impending, she had prepared a monument adjoining the Sema, where Alexander lay in state. It was a marble tomb as big as a house and as stout as a fortress, richly decorated in the Egyptian style. Inside she had laid by a comfortable store of food and water, not to mention the better portion of her treasury. Here she now repaired with Charmion, Eiras, and Mardion the eunuch following close behind.

"As for you, Diomedes," she said in passing, "take up the same position as yesterday, and report to me every move that Antony and Octavian make."

So back they rode, this ill-assorted pair, to the broken summit of Soter's wall, bringing along the same team of runners as before. By the fourth hour Diomedes had sent two dispatches, but when he looked for someone to carry a third, he realized he was all alone. Desertion, apparently, was the order of the day.

Antony had marched with shrunken forces. From twilight to dawn, troubled by the same portents as the rest of Alexandreia, hundreds of his men had defected—including many decorated for valor just the day before. So in spite of all the plumed helmets and tall spears, the blood-horses and the waving banners, it was an unimpressive army that assembled on the high ground east of the city. Octavian, accordingly, detailed only a portion of his strength to engage them. There followed an interlude of swinging swords and jabbing spears; but very few men seemed to take wounds, and the battle lines stayed fixed. To Diomedes, watching from above, it looked like a poorly acted stage play.

Frustrated with Octavian's shyness, Antony eventually ordered a cavalry charge. Trumpets flourished, along with some rather anemic battle cries, and then his entire body of horses cantered over to Octavian's line, saluted, and closed ranks with the enemy. As if that were a signal, the Egyptian fleet, drawn up in battle array opposite the Romans, raised its oars in token of surrender and fell in with Octavian's navy.

This was treason on a grander scale than even Diomedes could have conceived. He chewed his thumb thoughtfully. He prided himself on being privy to every one of Cleopatra's schemes, but for the first time he was in the dark. However deeply the Queen must be implicated in this betrayal, she had concealed her trail very cleverly, both from him and from Antony. Which left the question: Was it now his turn to defect?

And as his host pondered, so did Heron, along different lines but with the same anxiety. MEQMAT had sent him here for a reason. There was a node point coming up, a fork in the road; MEQMAT (or Grishka or Stella, it didn't seem to matter which) wanted him to observe and perhaps to act. But did he serve his own interests by serving MEQMAT's? When the line split he wanted to be on the right track. He wanted the world he had lost. Should he passively follow the script, or was it time to start improvising?

Two separate wills in identical confusion: the outcome was no decision at all. With the small force remaining to him, Antony was already falling back toward the city, with Octavian pursuing at a distance—like a cat who knows the mouse has nowhere left to hide. It would be disastrous to be caught in Antony's rout. West was the only direction open to him, and that meant Cleopatra.

He scrambled down the broken wall. His horse had disappeared, stolen no doubt by the boy in whose care he'd left it. He set out at a fast walk that shortly became a jog.

Along Kanobos he encountered almost no one. The defection of Egypt's navy had been plainly visible to anyone watching from the harborside, and word must have traveled quickly. Alexandreians both great and small were shut up in their houses, anticipating the worst. Even the temples were deserted, their choirs silent, their altars cold; no deity would intervene for Egypt now.

But Helios the sun god bestowed his rays as generously as on any other day, so that Heron felt half-dead by the time he reached Cleopatra's tomb. Sweat-soaked, footsore, his lungs burning to rival Pharos itself, he called out hoarsely: "O Queen! Hear the outcome of Antony's defense!"

The tomb's entrance was closed with a massive block of stone. Painted marble, still encumbered with scaffolding, rose to a point just beneath the pediment, where the builders had purposely left a gap so that men and materials could pass through. A head appeared.

"Come closer, Diomedes, so I don't have to shout."

It was Charmion. He did as she ordered, moving so close to the scaffold that he had to crane his neck to see her. Satisfied, she said, in a softly ominous voice, "The Queen is dead! Dead by her own hand. She left this message for Antony, and in her blessed memory I charge you to deliver it."

She dropped a scroll; he caught it. It was sealed in perfumed beeswax stamped with the royal seal of the Ptolemies.

"Return to me with his orders for the disposition of her remains."

Diomedes agreed and headed back the way he came. He knew Charmion was lying. He recognized all this as still another of Cleopatra's schemes, and he even had an idea what she intended. Cruel, clever woman. She might yet succeed.

Was this the node, wondered Heron. Should he participate in the lie?

For the first time since his return to Alexandreia, that cool bloodless voice spoke inside his mind. *Just try otherwise and see what happens.*

To get Antony's attention all he had to do was stay in plain sight. He sat on the broad stairway leading up to Broucheion's monumental entrance, alone in what was ..ormally a crossroads for the Alexandreian elite. Staring out across the bleak marble vistas he had the feeling that he was watching the end of the world.

Then a clatter of hooves sounded on the paving stones, and there was Antony, surrounded by his bodyguard. Catching sight of Diomedes, the Roman wheeled his horse around and shouted his name.

Diomedes skipped down the steps and handed up the scroll. Before breaking the seal Antony paused; in spite of his great broadsword and shining armor, untouched in battle, he had the look of a loser, a victim. His face betrayed his confusion and pain. An ox has that look at the moment of sacrifice.

Antony read the words, and cried in horror. The scroll tumbled from his fingers; he smote his own brow. "Now, Antony, why delay longer? Fate has snatched away your only pretext for living." He dismounted, almost falling, and his men closed in around him.

Heron pressed forward. "But she lives, noble Antony. She's playing a game with you."

"You've seen her alive?" Antony's pale eyes were half mad.

"Yes," he lied. "She spoke to me from her tomb."

Several emotions fought for control of the Roman's face. Suddenly rage won out, and he struck Heron across the mouth with a forearm ringed in metal. Heron saw stars, sat down heavily, and spit out a broken tooth.

"You surround me in a net of treason," Antony bellowed, "all you vicious creatures of Alexandreia! Today my ruin is complete! Whether she lives or dies I am lost." He covered his face and sobbed heavily. His men stood like stones.

When at last Antony looked up again he was much calmer, and he said, "Come, all of you, and watch how a Roman resolves the contradictions of his life."

One of his men grabbed Heron to make sure he didn't slip away. All together they entered the palace, whose bronze doors stood unguarded. Apparently Cleopatra's entire staff had gone into hiding. Like a sleepwalker Antony led them into a spacious salon off the main hall, where he halted and, without a word, began loosening his armor.

Derketaios and Eros immediately stepped in to help. They took his tall plumed helmet, his chlamys, his leather baldric, his wrist guards, his greaves, and his magnificent breastplate, decorated with the head of the Nemean lion. When he was stripped down to a linen tunic, he turned to Eros and said, "You will recall the promise you made on the day I left the Timoneion. You swore then that whenever I asked, you would set me free from this prison of flesh."

Eros, a likely youth of eighteen or nineteen, merely groaned and hid his eyes. "Come, my friend," said Antony. His voice was steady. "Do me this one last service."

Eros drew his heavy gladius from its scabbard and gripped it firmly in both hands. Antony braced himself, back straight, legs wide. His face was more serene than Heron or Diomedes had ever seen it. Eros was utterly miserable. *"Vale, imperator,"* he said, and on his Greek tongue the Latin words were sweet. Then, in a quick, smooth movement that would be the envy of far more experienced swordsmen, he turned his back on Antony and drove the sword into his own body, entering just below the ribs and angling upward in a vicious thrust. He moaned once, vomited blood, and fell down dead.

Antony expelled a noisy breath. "Even better, Eros. You've reminded me how a brave man dies." And taking his own sword he butted its pommel against the wall and threw all his weight against the blade.

But he wasn't as deft as Eros. At the last instant the point veered sideways. He toppled over in a spreading puddle of blood, swearing lustily, still very much alive.

"Help me," he said, blood and saliva gurgling down his chin. Heron stared at him in horror. "Take me to Cleopatra, let me see her one last time, whether she's alive or dead."

Derketaios stepped gingerly over to his side and drew out the sword. A rush of blood followed, and Antony moaned; but it was plain that the wound wasn't deep. Derketaios backed toward the door, never taking his eyes off Antony, and at the threshold he turned and ran.

Heron glanced right and left. Antony's third bodyguard had also disappeared, leaving him alone with this shambles. He could just as easily escape—Diomedes had no objections—but now he felt caught up in the melodrama. How would it end? He bent down and with great difficulty raised the Roman to his feet, supporting practically all his weight. Half dragging, half carrying him, he staggered out into the vaulted corridor and shouted for help. "In the name of the Queen!" he said, over and over.

Shortly a sturdy boy of fourteen or fifteen appeared, a household slave known to Diomedes. His name was Paris and he was confused and frightened. "Good lad!" said Heron, calling on all Diomedes' charm. "Cleopatra will reward you in gold."

They put Antony in a chair. He had fainted when Heron raised him, but now his bleeding had almost stopped, and from his regular breathing it seemed he might last a while longer. Heron and Paris hoisted the chair and carried him down the broad staircase. They came close to dropping him more than once. A group of slaves and freedmen had gathered in front of the palace, huddled together in a buzz of anxious speculation. When they saw Antony's chalk-white face and bloody limbs they hurried over for a better look.

Ignoring them, Heron and Paris trudged onward to Cleopatra's tomb. Again it was Charmion who answered his shout. She took one look and disappeared, to be replaced by Cleopatra.

"O my love!" The Queen stretched forth her arms, letting out a wail to rival the entire chorus of Trojan Women at the climax of Eurpides' tragedy. "Diomedes, bring him to me! Quickly, while he still breathes."

The crowd of onlookers was vastly entertained. This would be a tale to tell their grandchildren.

But lifting a large disabled man thirty feet in the air is easier described than done. The slaves yelled all sorts of advice; in the end Paris and Heron had to climb the scaffold themselves, throw down a rope, and pull Antony up hand over hand.

So, with a great deal of sweating, swearing, and straining, and some incidental help from Mardion and Cleopatra herself, the job was put in motion. Halfway up Antony regained consciousness. His eyelids fluttered; recognizing Cleopatra, he croaked her name, calling her his mistress and his love. Heron wanted to laugh and cry at once. Here was the woman who had calculated the man's death, and he was reaching up his arms to her like a child to its mother.

Nothing more pathetic had been seen in all the history of Alexandreia.

16

The End of the Soul

Heron and Mardion carried the dying man to a gilded couch. Cleopatra climbed up next to him, embracing his gory chest, weeping and wailing in a convincing display of wifely grief. Charmion and Eiras did what they could to bathe the wound; but all the while they dabbed and sponged, Antony and the Queen kept up an impassioned dialogue on love, luck, and the fate of empires.

Heron minded his own business at the other end of the chamber, drinking Mareotic wine. A climax was brewing, he was sure, yet he had no idea what his role would be. The Queen's tomb seemed as good a place as any to wait for his cue.

His split lip and swollen jaw reminded him how stupid it was to try anything else.

Here inside it was cool and dim. The only light came from the break in the wall. His first impression had been of a jumbled mess, of shadows and silhouettes, but now that his eyes were adjusting he saw wonderful things.

All around the room were statues of the Egyptian gods, some of painted stone, others of gold. He saw female deities with the heads of cats and cows, and male deities with the heads of birds, their eyes outlined in turquoise and inlaid with crystal. He saw the image of a pregnant hippopotamus in precious blue faience, and the sinister figure of Anubis the death-dog in black granite. Apparently Cleopatra hadn't scrupled to commit that crime most abhorred by Greeks and Egyptians alike: the plundering of consecrated temples.

Nor had she spared the tombs of her own predecessors. There were three or four mummiform coffins dating back to the Nineteenth Dynasty, each cast in solid gold and so heavy that six men couldn't budge them. There were thrones, footstools, chests, and couches, all of the costliest materials, most of such elegance that their like would never be seen again. There were harps and pipes inscribed with the names of gods; there were gilded chariots, silver ships, electrum-plated swords and ceremonial maces; there were coffers overflowing with earrings, finger-rings, necklaces, anklets, and bracelets, some of them worn by royal women dead two thousand years.

And that was only part of it. Scattered among the works of art were treasures in the raw: stacks of gold and silver ingots, tusk ivory piled man-high, bags of cinnamon and myrrh, bundles of ostrich feathers, bolts of undyed silk, boxes stuffed with uncut emeralds and Indian pearls. The odor of spices pervaded the entire space, stimulating the nose just as the flash of gold excited the eye.

And as a jewel has its setting, so did this imperial hoard. Over, under, and around the priceless objects was a trail of kindling, dry as old bones and waiting for the tiniest spark to explode into flames. This firewood represented Cleopatra's last hope of winning the contest with Octavian. Since, above all, Rome wanted Egypt's fabulous wealth intact, she planned to bargain fiercely, ready at any setback to turn her treasury into a crematorium.

Antony called for wine. Heron started from his reverie and went to the wounded man's side, bringing the cup he had just poured for himself. He held Antony's head; the Roman sipped, celebrating one last communion with Dionysos. He sipped again, choked, and croaked out a word or two. Cleopatra bent close to hear him. He gripped her hands in a last spasm of strength, murmured her name, and died.

Cleopatra screamed. It was a ritual utterance, a dirge-singer's professional cry. It was echoed by Mardion and the two serving women in voices equally shrill. Heron wanted to cover his ears, but decorum prevailed; he endured their ululations with stoic correctness. At length, after a good half-hour, the mourners subsided, and the three servants attended to the corpse, stripping him, bathing him, arranging his limbs, and wrapping him in layers of fine linen and myrrh.

When daylight faded, Eiras set lamps around the bier. Shadows gathered by the monstrous images of the gods. In fact as well as in name, the chamber had become a tomb.

"Mother Isis, how long will our vigil be?" Cleopatra's voice was rough with overuse, and she sighed piteously. "I suppose Octavian will secure the city before he turns his attention to me. He'll have no trouble finding us here. By now all Alexandreia knows where I am, and whose corpse I guard."

She looked like the Queen of the Dead. Tears had streaked her face with rouge and antimony. Her hair was loose and disheveled, her robe bloodied and torn. Heron raised his cup to her, with a little more irony than respect, and drank deep.

"Cleopatra!" Charmion's voice held a note of panic. "Someone is climbing up the wall."

Cleopatra rose, immediately in control of the situation. "Eiras, ready the fire. Mardion, bring the serpents." She hurried over to the opening and leaned out. "You there!" she cried hoarsely. "Stay where you are or face the direst consequences."

Heron went to her side, compelled by Diomedes' curiosity. He saw a scaling ladder lodged against the wall, and a man with a Roman toga tucked up around his waist, halfway to the top.

"Greetings to Cleopatra the Queen from Gaius Proculeius!" In spite of his position the Roman was cheerful and composed, though his Greek was barbarous.

"Antony praised this man to me in his last words," said Cleopatra, "saying he was worthy of my trust. And the fact that he still calls me Queen recommends him further." In a louder voice she said, "What is your business, Proculeius?"

"I bring salutations from Caesar, and condolences on the death of noble Antony."

"Pretty words from a man who creeps up on me like a thief in the night."

"Caesar assures you that you have no reason to barricade yourself in this grim monument. He will honor all his former promises."

"What of the ones he's already broken?"

"Please, madam. Caesar wishes you well. He invites you to return to your palace and resume your state."

"I'll have that in writing, if you please, over Octavian's own seal. And more: I want his solemn oath, sworn by Capitoline Jupiter, proclaimed in the presence of all his men, that my son

Kaisarion, the only son of Gaius Julius Caesar, will reign after me as Pharaoh of Egypt."

"I'll bring your words to my lord, and return with his answer."

"And one more thing! Tell Octavian, tell all the Romans, that at the smallest hint of treachery I will destroy all the treasures in this monument, and take my own life. Never doubt that I have the means to do it."

"As you say, my lady." Proculeius' cheer faded considerably, but he still saluted her in the Roman manner before climbing back down. Heron pushed the ladder after him.

"So! The first move is made." Cleopatra turned back toward the death chamber, immensely pleased. "Now we'll see how young Octavian behaves. Many times he's told me that if I would only hand over Antony's dead body there was no favor he wouldn't grant me." She signaled to the two women and, withdrawing to a corner of the room, she had them bathe her, change her clothing, and arrange her hair. As they worked she hummed lightly.

"Mardion," she called, half-dressed. "Show Diomedes our friends. See if he finds them as darling as I do."

Mardion held out a delicate vase of multicolored glass. "Look carefully," he said, "and mind your fingers."

Heron took the vessel. Holding it near a lamp, he peeked inside and saw three or four tiny snakes curled up in a nest of moist leaves.

"Asps," said the eunuch. "Each one could kill six men, more quickly and painlessly than any poison. This we learned after thorough investigation."

He handed them back. "Sweet little things."

When the Queen's toilet was finished she rejoined him, offering him figs from the dish of fruit she nibbled. "No other food will pass my mouth," she said, "until my dear Antony is buried." The ghost of a smile brushed her lips. "Poor Antony. Although I tricked him, I did save his honor. Suicide was the only course left to him, but he was too fainthearted to do it by himself. So I helped him along. Now history can report that the only man capable of toppling Antony was Antony himself."

"Certainly that's how he would have wanted it," said Heron, with a healthy dose of Diomedes' courtliness. "Do you suppose his spirit lingers somewhere close by, waiting to hear the verdict of time?"

She hugged her knees, and turned her head sideways. "I'm not sure how quickly the soul flees once its prison has been breached.

The wise are in disagreement. At Memphis and Abydos the priests teach many arcane doctrines, most of them conflicting. Some say that a person has six different souls, each requiring its own spells and offerings, and each with a separate journey to make after death. One is a bird with a human face, one is a miniature man, one is a shadow."

Heron shook his head. "The Egyptians delight in obscurity. I prefer the clear *logos* of the Greeks. Consider Plato and his elegant myth-making in the *Phaidros*. For him the soul is a creature with wings, whose home is outside the vault of heaven in the universe of forms. Through weakness, through failure of vision, it can lose its wings, whereupon it falls to earth. There it is incarnated in human form, to wander through life and death for ten thousand years, until its wings grow back and it can return to the place beyond the sky. What could be simpler and more beautiful?"

"You're right, of course." She smiled dreamily. "In Plato's view, if I've understood correctly, Antony's fall would constitute only one small episode in the long history of his spirit. Such doctrine removes the guilt from my own head, don't you think?"

"Well . . . I'm not certain what Plato would have said about the career of Queen Cleopatra. But I suspect he might withhold praise."

She laughed. "How fitting, to speak of the wanderings of the human soul here in this cold mausoleum, beside a fresh corpse. Please, Diomedes, tell me more."

"But Cleopatra," he said, "you yourself are a distinguished student of the ancients. Choose a text and we'll dispute it."

Her strange eyes glittered. "Not all the Greeks delighted in clarity. Perhaps we might discuss Herakleitos the Ephesian, who dispensed his wisdom in riddles."

Not Herakleitos again. Not that one about the river . . .

But she quoted, " 'You will not find the end of the soul, though you travel over every path.' "

However unfamiliar the words might be, they made a disturbing kind of sense. "Every . . . path?" he whispered. All at once it was difficult to breathe. His ears rang; his throat tightened; his tongue obeyed him only stubbornly. "What sort of path did he mean?"

"That's part of the riddle," she said.

The lamplight and shadow played a game, painting bizarre pictures in her carefully made-up face. He looked, and he looked again, and he knew her.

"How many paths?" he asked softly. "How many bad dreams and bloody corpses?"

"Ah, but that's more of the riddle."

"Where have you been?"

"It doesn't work that way." The regret in her voice matched anything he'd suffered. "If we tried to compare notes we'd probably discover we're not who we think we are. Hints and inklings will have to be enough."

"Oh Stella." He reached for her, but she pulled away.

"We're not alone, John. To those people watching us we still have to be Diomedes and Cleopatra."

"But where will you be when this is over? I don't want to lose you again. No, that's not it, please don't think I'm a mushy fool. I just don't want to lose *myself* again. And you seem so closely connected with—everything I was. When you're not there something essential is missing."

Half her mouth smiled. "That's what I've been thinking too; that's the way it's been for me. You and I have a bond. Maybe you don't realize it, but I've done this a lot more than you have. Not just Egypt. I've dipped into twentieth-century America, into eighteenth-century France. Every time the scenario fell flat. It never amounted to anything more than that tame experiment in memory I told you about last New Year's Day." She moistened her lips. "Until it changed."

"So that wasn't you, in July? You weren't that coldhearted bureaucrat?"

"John, don't." She was frightened. "Don't tell me about the between part. It might break the sequence. And if we don't follow this to the end, there's no hope at all."

"Oh Stella, Stella, you don't know how happy you're making me!"

"Happy? John, if you're not absolutely terrified, then you haven't understood anything."

"Tell me, then, tell me! Make me understand!"

Charmion looked up sharply at the sound of their voices. She plainly resented this sudden intimacy. "Cool down," said Stella. "I'll talk, but we've got to stay in character."

"Okay, fine, whatever you say. Just talk to me."

She drank some wine and smiled nervously. "You just figured some of it out without realizing it, when you talked about the wanderings of the soul. Our predicament does have a lot to do with reincarnation. But whereas all the ancient philosophers, from

Buddha to Pythagoras, taught that the soul is only free to migrate when the body dies, twenty-first century physics has opened the possibility of soul-transfer before death."

"MEQMAT told me that wasn't feasible."

"Really? Maybe MEQMAT was having a little fun at your expense. Or maybe there was some confusion over terms. Because this isn't really reincarnation, or astral projection, or any of those items of modern mythology. It's more like . . . sympathetic vibration. Like when one tuning fork hits a particular note, and a second tuning fork, tuned to the same note, starts vibrating all by itself."

"Who are the two tuning forks? John Heron and Diomedes the Greek?"

"No. They're both John Heron."

"You mean there's more than one of me?"

" 'You will not find the end of the soul.' "

His mind—spirit? soul?—made a quantum leap. "Then I'm not so stupid after all! We did get close to an answer, that afternoon in the Black Tower. Sorry—I won't mention it again. But one way or another, this old dog has learned a few new tricks. Listen. I assume you're no stranger to the idea that the universe splits, right, so that there are many, many worlds existing side by side, each one a little different from the next?" It gave him a powerful satisfaction to explain these things to her. "If that's all true, there must be many different versions of John Heron, and many different versions of Stella Cranach."

"Well done, John. You're catching on more quickly than I expected. But what you're saying also implies that there are even more worlds where you or I or both of us *don't* exist, or where we exist in such radically altered forms that we'd never recognize ourselves. Where the tuning fork wouldn't arouse any sympathetic vibrations. And all that, fortunately, puts a limit on how far we can stray."

She picked up an ankh sheathed in gold and covered with hieroglyphics. "Those Egyptian sages Diomedes is so fond of maligning actually intuited something like this. You know how obsessed they are with mummifying the dead. Well, isn't mummification simply a process that lets the physical body survive indefinitely, while still keeping the same shape it had in life?"

"I guess so."

"Of course it is. And do you know why? It's because, according to the Egyptians, the spirit wanders—but it also returns. When it does, it must be able to recognize its proper home."

He tried to remember what MEQMAT had said. Something about recursive algorithms, and apparati capable of sustaining them. The words took on a new resonance beside these icons of Sekhmet and Thoth.

"How do we wander, anyway?"

She smiled a real smile, antimony and all. "That's the crux of the matter. Where would you say we are? Don't think; just answer."

"In Cleopatra's tomb."

"But we're not. We're just remembering being here."

"Then this is all a dream? We're just lying side by side on couches in Grishka's laboratory, mumbling in our sleep?"

"More or less, except that we're not side by side, and that's our problem. We're in two different universes. That time when you were Nikias and I was Charmion we left the sequence separately, so we reached separate destinations."

"I've lost you again."

"Exactly. Just listen. All you've ever heard about the so-called experiment in history is true. The tricky part is that this process can backfire. Once a subject, such as yourself, has successfully pursued a given sequence, a fundamental change occurs—not in the past or the present, or anything like that, but in the subject's *relationship* to the past and the present. He has established new possibilities. He's made himself vulnerable to new vibrations. For one instant his soul—his mind, his individual algorithm—is free to wander."

"He jumps across the gap?"

"That's right."

"To a suitable receiving apparatus, to a body his soul can recognize?"

"Uh-huh."

"So if we want to end up together, we've got to jump together?"

"Right again, amigo."

"How?"

"Look inside."

He attempted the little shift in perspective that would take him to MEQMAT's level, the same shift he'd tried and failed to achieve several times since erupting into the persona of Diomedes the Lykian. But this time it worked.

He heard no cool voices. Instead there was a steady hum, the mechanical equivalent of a cat's purr. MEQMAT was busy working, performing computations, making connections, exploring new lines of inorganic logic. Neural arrays throbbed in theta rhythm. A picture wobbled into focus. His viewpoint hovered over a vast intersection, one of those heroic complexes of lanes, levels, cloverleafs, overpasses, and access ramps that the old folks used to build, and that survived only in ruins. Except that this complex was in pristine condition. He was looking down on a hundred thousand *automobiles* moving in parallel streams, heading toward each of the cardinal points and everywhere in between. It was night, and their lights flashed brighter even than Cleopatra's jewels.

"Yes," said Stella. "See how they weave in and out and shift from stream to stream?"

He looked longer and the picture changed slightly; or maybe he had misinterpreted it the first time. Now he saw beads moving on wires, and the wire matrix was on an even higher order of complexity than he had imagined earlier, because rather than clinging to a plane surface it extended outward in three dimensions. The beads whizzed by like bugs or bullets, or planets coursing in impossible orbits.

"This gives me vertigo," he said.

But despite him, the image progressed to a further level of abstraction, to the point where it was mere form and color in motion. Just as the second version had opened into a new order, so did this one, a complexity so evolved that his senses had no means of perceiving it and his mind no clue to comprehending it.

"Just try," said Stella. "It cost me some effort too. Find your own line."

So he tried, and after a little disembodied squinting and sweating, he managed to pick out one stream of color and light that seemed more central, more immediate than the others. Running almost parallel to it was another line, equally bright but colored differently.

"There we are," she said. "Now you begin to see. When the time comes, we'll return to this point of view, and use it as a map."

"But how will we know when the time comes?"

A trio of shouts broke their concentration. Color and form refocused into the somber grandeur of Cleopatra's tomb. Charmion was crouched next to the unfinished wall, struggling against two armed men. Two others scrambled past her into the room, and Heron recognized one of them as Gaius Proculeius. Mardion, grimacing like the mask of tragedy, reached for his asps. Eiras hovered over a pile of kindling, torch in hand.

"Miserable Cleopatra," cried Charmion, her arms pinioned behind her back. "You are betrayed!"

"Light the bonfire!" she commanded.

Eiras dropped her torch, and flames licked along a recumbent sphinx. In the same moment Mardion let out a heavy sigh and crumpled over a gold mummy case. A tiny serpent wriggled out of his fingers. Heron lunged barehanded at one of the Romans, aiming clumsily for the man's throat; but another soldier clubbed him over the head with the hilt of his sword, so that for the second time that day he saw stars. Cleopatra, unable to reach the asps, pulled a dagger from the folds of her himation.

"Shame, Cleopatra!" Proculeius leaped to her side and went for the dagger. "You wrong both yourself and Caesar."

"I'll die a Queen," she sobbed, beating him about the head with her free hand. But she was disarmed in short order. Heron could do nothing to help her; he lay flat on his back with a Roman sword pointing at his throat. Another of the band was smothering the fire. All three women wept.

"Come, my friends," said Proculeius, dabbing at the cuts Cleopatra had inflicted. "I regret this unfortunate incident. But Caesar has invited you to the palace, and it wouldn't do to spurn his hospitality. He's eager to show you how merciful he really is."

Heron sat up and rubbed his aching head. Olympos was right; the party was all over now.

17

Cheating Rome

Antony's funeral was as lavish as Cleopatra's fortune could make
it. Octavian allowed her this much. It pleased him to appear
magnanimous toward these two enemies he had so thoroughly
crushed.

The fallen imperator was laid to rest in the same tomb where he
had died. A dozen priests of Sarapis and Harpokrates officiated,
and several choirs sang hymns and threnodies in the Egyptian
manner. When the mourners finally made ready to leave, Cleopatra let loose an earsplitting shriek and abandoned herself to the
most histrionic excesses of grief. Arrayed in the guise of Isis, she
called on the gods of Egypt and Greece alike, begging forgiveness
of Antony's ghost, even lacerating her bare breasts with sharpened
fingernails. She clung so tightly to her lover's coffin that in the
end Olympos and Diomedes had to carry her bodily away.

In such moments there was no trace of Stella Cranach about her.
In fact, this became the normal state of affairs, and Heron had no
trouble accepting it—primarily since Diomedes also remained
ascendant over his own persona, during the days following the
debacle at the tomb.

Alexandreia became a dream observed secondhand. The opu-
lent colors and textures, the melodious flow of demotic Greek, the
shifting passions, the doubts and complications—all these things
washed around him like Herakleitos' mutable stream, touching
him only at great remove. In those first days of Roman occupation

life continued more or less unchanged. Diomedes retained his quarters in Broucheion and kept up his interviews with the Queen; he was even allowed the freedom of the city, though Cleopatra remained under house arrest. Heron rode in his accustomed place behind Diomedes' eyes and concerned himself with nothing they saw.

It was the month of Mesore, and the Nile was in flood. Cool breezes blew over Lake Mareotis, though Heron never felt them. Rumors came and went, but Heron paid them no mind. Antyllos, Antony's oldest son, had been beheaded; his tutor had been crucified . . . or perhaps they had merely fled together into Aethiopia. Octavian planned to exhibit Cleopatra in Rome, bound in golden shackles, and have her publicly strangled . . . or perhaps he intended no such thing, and would let her live on in Alexandreia as a private citizen, with Cornelius Gallus ruling in his name. Anxiety lurked in every heart, doubt on every tongue.

Still there came rare moments when Stella managed to put aside Cleopatra's persona and speak to him in private. Those were the most perfect times. Then, in spite of the sense of things apocalyptic hovering over all possible futures, Heron was happier dreaming in MEQMAT's maze than he had ever been knocking around the more substantial and more disappointing streets of the New City.

But on the third day after Antony's funeral, as he was crossing one of Broucheion's flowery courtyards, Olympos called to him from the shade of a stoa. While Heron dozed Diomedes wondered what new development had made the man forget his animosity. He doubted it was anything good.

Indeed, the physician's face was grimmer than usual. "Diomedes," he said flatly. "The Queen is ill."

"How ill?"

"She has refused food since Antony's death. This morning she woke in a fever. Just now as I left her she alternated between raving and lamenting, completely out of her head. From time to time she called your name."

Diomedes was concerned; Heron was appalled. "What's your prognosis, Lord Olympos?"

"Cleopatra has a fierce will—but death, as we know too well, would be a mercy."

Heron bolted into the palace without another word.

She lay in an upper room, half-naked on a silk-upholstered couch. Her hair was a damp tangle in which the gray threatened to overwhelm the black. Charmion sat by her side, pressing cool cloths to her forehead.

"He mangles every quality," said the Queen, "and motivates all tears. His engorged dominion . . . encroaches on God and Cleopatra." Her dilated pupils fixed on the painted ceiling; she muttered several more phrases, too softly to be understood. Then, louder, "Once he lives he has always lived, and who can escape his tyranny? O Antony! What should I stay . . ."

Her skin was flushed and glistening; there were great hollows around her eyes. She did seem on death's doorstep, and that, to put it mildly, dismayed him.

Charmion read his face. "But it would be better, Diomedes," she whispered. "There's nothing left to keep her in the light."

Yet it tore his vitals to watch the vessel of his love in such misery. Racking his brain for some means to comfort her, he remembered those verses of Sappho that Charmion had sung only a week or two earlier.

"Where is your *kithara*, Charmion? Perhaps you could soothe her with a song."

Charmion nodded quickly, infected by his eagerness, and went to fetch her instrument. The moment she·was gone the Queen turned to him and said, quite lucidly, "Don't worry your head over me, old friend. I'll live as long as I have to. Our moment is very near." Heron was elated. He put his hand next to hers and she squeezed it, closing her eyes in feline satisfaction. Her game was far from done.

While gossips whispered that she was already dead Cleopatra made a swift recovery. Octavian had sent his personal physician to attend her—not because he distrusted Olympos' skill, but because he wanted to ensure she didn't starve herself, or otherwise contrive a premature end. He also reminded her of a pertinent factor: although Kaisarion had escaped safely, Octavian still held Cleopatra's other children. He made it clear that if she died inconveniently they would suffer.

Eight days after the city's fall, and more or less restored to health, Cleopatra sent a message in Diomedes' hand to Octavian. The secretary found him closeted in a remote corner of Broucheion with the philosopher Areios, his constant companion.

The unchallenged master of the entire world was a youngish man of thirty-one. His features in repose were regular and even handsome; at a more frivolous age, he had once impersonated

Apollo himself at a memorably outrageous banquet. In conversation, however, he was inclined to wear a puzzled expression, and his mouth tended to gape. This by no means implied stupidity; but his wit was labored, and his conversation the opposite of scintillating. His oversized ears, which flapped outwards like little wings, added nothing in his favor. Antony had frequently mentioned his resemblance to a sheep, not in detail but in overall dullness.

He took the scroll and perused it for several minutes. Areios cocked his head curiously, but Octavian kept his own counsel. Finally he nodded, and said, "Your lady begs the privilege of an interview. Tell her that Caesar himself will come to her . . ." and he considered a moment—"today at the tenth hour."

Diomedes bowed low and hurried off to warn the Queen.

At the appointed time Octavian arrived in a spacious salon in the west wing of Broucheion. Two guards attended him, but these he instructed to wait in an antechamber, along with the freedman Epaphroditos, in whose charge he had placed the Queen.

Even for Broucheion the room was grand. Its floor was of tessellated marble in six colors, nine-tenths hidden by an enormous rug depicting the obeisance of Persia to Alexander the Great. Its walls gave the illusion of opening into a Babylonian garden, so realistic were their murals of trees, flowers, and floating clouds. Its ceiling glowed softly with a coating of gold leaf. Overstuffed cushions, likewise embroidered in gold, lay in particolored heaps on chairs and couches crafted in the Corinthian style, arranged throughout the room in intimate groupings. A painting by Apelles (Aphrodite rising from the waves off Cyprus, appraised at a thousand talents) rested casually in a rosewood easel.

But all this was merely background for the principal ornament of the room: a series of busts of Julius Caesar, modeled from life by Alexandreia's most gifted sculptors. Each one captured a different side of the man. Each was placed so that the westering sun caught it at its most expressive angle. Each seemed to gaze moodily toward the door at whoever should enter.

This, then, was the first sight to greet Octavian when he came calling on the Queen—the wealth and taste of the Ptolemies framing the sharp features of his own stepfather, in whose name he had risen to power.

With his second glance he took in Cleopatra herself.

She waited on a low couch, wearing nothing but a linen shift of gauzy fineness. Her hair (freshly stained with black henna) hung loose and unadorned. A powdering of fine white clay emphasized the pallor of her face, so recently ravaged by illness. Indeed, her eyes still burned with the memory of fevers, deep-set and dark.

She jumped up as he entered, and ran lightly to meet him, dropping to her knees in homage. "Hail, Caesar," she said. "Heaven has granted you the scepter of Egypt."

Octavian drew back, embarrassed. "Please, madam, no Oriental abasement. You are an anointed Queen; I am merely a temporary representative of the Senate and the Roman people. On your feet, I beg you."

She offered him her hand, and with his help she rose, regarding him through the fringe of her eyelashes. She led him to an ebony chair and reclined once more on the couch. The slender diet she had followed recently had trimmed off all her excess flesh, so that the limbs she arranged on the tapestried cushions were as lean and shapely as any twenty-year-old's.

Once they had exchanged a few pleasantries, Charmion appeared with a tray of sweets and a flagon of wine. She tasted everything before offering it, first to Octavian and then to the Queen. But when the Roman raised his cup he merely wetted his lips; clearly he was ill at ease accepting Cleopatra's hospitality.

"Please pardon me my slovenly attire," she said, over the lip of her kylix. "In my illness I've lost the habit of showy dress."

He waved his fingers dismissively.

"And pardon me, if you can, for the long obstinacy with which I resisted the will of Rome."

His eyebrows lifted; his mouth assumed its customary gape.

"You may wonder at my contrition, but never doubt it, noble Caesar. When your brilliant father was snatched so untimely from the world's embrace, I was a young woman, unskilled in the ways of empire. I too lost my father at an early age, so that my only mentor in statesmanship was the godlike Julius. Once he was gone I was a ship adrift on stormy seas. Then Mark Antony came to Egypt with his legions, claiming to be the rightful successor to Julius Caesar, the foremost of the triumviri and the inheritor of the East. In my fear and insecurity I could only submit to his ambition."

"Why, Cleopatra," he said, "that's—that's ludicrous. The entire world knows how you sailed up the River Kydnos tricked out as Aphrodite"—he gestured to Apelles' masterpiece, squinting at the rosy curves of the Goddess of Desire—"though I suppose you had a little more on than she does—and how you personally solicited Antony's aid for your own schemes and ambitions. It's common knowledge in Rome how you vowed again and again that you would one day sit in judgment on the Capitoline Hill. Please don't strain my credulity."

She sighed and shifted position, demurely enough but with a hint of frustration. "Ah, weak is woman, ever a slave to her passions. Queen though I may be, in that regard I am no different from the rest of my sex. How many fierce emotions I have served in my life! Never doubt that I often cowered in deadly fear of Antony's rages. Never doubt that I also loved him, indeed with too great a depth of feeling for my own good or the good of Egypt. Those two passions, I think, account for the miserable state in which you find me today."

Octavian's brow wrinkled. "I don't dispute your womanliness, or your passionate nature," he said slowly, "but it's plain that you also display a very—how shall I put it?—*masculine* talent for cold calculation and political maneuvering. I might also quote one or two of your letters to me, in which you offered, for, ah, certain political concessions, to put aside the very man you now profess to have loved so selflessly. No, Cleopatra, behind your passionate mask there has always been, mmm, a clear-headed *intelligence* at work."

Tears welled up in her eyes. "You remind me of deeds that resound to my shame! Whatever manly judgment I possess has always been at war with my feminine nature, and I confess that out of this struggle have come one or two despicable decisions." She leaned toward him. "If only I could be more like you, Caesar! Never a false step, never an ill-considered move."

Octavian blushed, and Cleopatra pressed her advantage, rising from the divan and embracing one of the busts of Julius Caesar. "Here is the man who could teach both of us the right path to follow through this uncertain world. He was my first love, and my best. 'Siren of the Nile,' he called me, and 'foam-born goddess,' and 'mistress of the arts of love.' " She stroked the marble face, gazing off as if into the past, her eyes sparkling and her breast swelling. "If only I could have died when he did! The world has been a meaner place since the day he left it."

She glanced back at Octavian, whom her amorous recollections plainly disturbed. "But you are so much like him, Octavianus. You don't mind if I call you that, do you? When I knew you in Rome, years ago, you were just a boy—but now in the prime of manhood you've become a fitting heir to Caesar." She cupped the image's sculptured chin and inclined her head so she could look it in the eye. The movement exposed a healthy expanse of bosom. "In this man here, my love," she said breathily, "you are alive for me. Having him, I have the best of you." And she kissed the cool white lips.

Octavian stared resolutely at the floor.

"Oh, forgive my foolishness!" She resumed her posture on the couch and gazed at him earnestly. "I was carried away by the memory of your father's devotion. He at least found a certain worthiness in me."

"As I do, Cleopatra," said Octavian, tight-lipped. "Have no worries on that score."

"Of course you've been kind to me, very kind, when I've given you every reason not to be." Cleopatra smiled tenderly. "And so it's been in my mind to give you a special gift—some trifles really, but the sort of things that women love. Knowing the great esteem you have for your wife Livia and your sister Octavia, I thought you might appreciate a few articles of jewelry, to convey to them in my name."

Heron had been observing the whole comedy from his post at the opposite end of the room, along with Charmion and Eiras. His own reactions had faded in and out of Diomedes' in a contrapuntal daydream. Now as the Queen clapped her hands he came forward, completely himself, carrying an ivory box. Kneeling, he offered it to Cleopatra and withdrew a little distance.

"Of all my jewels these have been dearest to me," she said. She reached inside the coffer and removed a necklace of matched emeralds, a carnelian brooch carved with the image of Isis, several ancient signet rings, and those two enormous pearl earrings that were the wonder of the East. "Let the women of your family wear them, now that they replace me as sovereign ladies of the world."

"I'm sure my sister and my wife will be touched," said Octavian, rather stiffly. Both Livia's and Octavia's hatred for Cleopatra was legendary. "And have no fear for your own future, madam. I have no greater wish than for your continued good health." He shifted his weight as if to rise; the interview seemed all but finished.

"But Octavian!" Cleopatra fell at his feet and grasped the end of his toga. "Please stay a little longer! I have so much to discuss with you. You reassure me as to my own well-being, but what of Egypt?"

"Madam—" he began, but Cleopatra burst into sobbing and tears. "My people," she said, "the ancient land of the Nile!" And she clutched his knees like a supplicant.

Octavian swore suddenly. His face twisted in anger, and he took a breath to cry out.

In the same instant the Queen said, "Diomedes!" Heron darted forward and grabbed the Roman from behind, covering his mouth. Octavian struggled wildly for a few seconds, flailing his arms about and bugging his eyes in horror. Then his resistance grew feebler, and feebler still, until he slumped down with his eyes glazed and sightless. Heron released him. His face was purplish, contorted in the extremity of pain.

Stella rose, the carnelian brooch in her hand. A drop of blood fell from its sturdy bronze pin, which was smeared with thick green paste. She gazed down at Octavian's body.

"Almost as good as the bite of an asp," she said quietly. "Quick, though hardly painless. Now, my friends, we must see to ourselves. As a Queen I might face beheading, but you freed slaves would certainly be crucified. We'll cheat Rome of that much."

Her three companions gathered round. She reached into the ivory box and lifted out its false bottom, a tray padded with black silk. Underneath was a compartment lined with leaves and Nile mud. "One for each," she said.

Each one of them drew forth an asp. Eiras dropped hers immediately, with a little cry; the reptiles were annoyed at being shut up for so long and required no coaxing to strike.

"Now, John," whispered Stella.

The snake's fangs went in like pinpricks. A rush of heat spread through his body, and a sense of heaviness. He knelt down next to Stella and took her hand. Already his nerves were going numb; he could hardly feel her grip. He closed his eyes and saw the network of bright threads leap into place.

"There . . . there," she said, her voice little more than a sigh. "That's where we want to be. . . ."

The orange thread grew fatter; it was a snake, a cable, a tree trunk, a river. He dove in and felt himself swept along by the current. Looking back he saw huge structures rising along its banks, great towers and pyramids straining higher and higher towards a coronation of light. The cool bloodless voice that had been silent for so long finally spoke:

"So Cleopatra's statues were cast down throughout the length of Egypt; but Isis waxed in popularity, and many remembered how the Queen herself had used the goddess's name. While the Romans launched new civil wars her worship gained more and more adherents, until by the end of Agrippa's reign her temples were everywhere in Rome, and Cleopatra, through this divine intermediary, at last realized her ambition of sitting in judgment even on the Capitoline Hill."

PART FIVE

CITY FALL

18

Rich and Strange

An army of gnomes was pounding him from head to toe with tiny hammers. "Stop!" he said. A cool hand pressed something against his throat. The gnomes went away, leaving him with aches and pains everywhere.

He opened his eyes. The effort cost him. Overhead was a steel-gray sky with pale stars; around him were green leaves and shadows. It was evening in the garden beside Lochias, and the gnomes were hiding behind potted plants, grinning nasty grins. "No," he said. The gnomes went away again and the vegetation thinned out. Amber light gleamed through more leaves and flowers. The head gnome stepped forward with a frown.

"Are you feeling better?"

His mouth tasted of copper and bile. He turned his head sideways and spat. "Grishka," he said. "You're not smiling."

The young man raised an eyebrow. He had grown more meaty and less plump; his essential sturdiness had intensified. "Do I usually smile, Citizen Heron?"

"Maybe not." Heron sat up and groaned. "I'm not sure which is worse, dying or coming back to life."

"Dying, I imagine," said Grishka.

Heron opened and closed his eyes a few times. Strange sensation, having gnomes hammer on your eyelids. He noticed that he wasn't in Lochias after all, but in the SSM laboratory. He looked carefully around the room. Except for Grishka he was alone. How odd.

"I seem to recall an assistant," he said.

Grishka studied him without expression. "At various times, yes, I've had various assistants. But none is needed at the moment." He looked at his wristwatch. "Are you ready for your debriefing?"

Heron groaned again. "How about some coffee?"

Grishka produced a pot and poured him a cup. It tasted horrible, but he took a few big gulps anyway.

"So, Grishka," he said, setting aside the coffee. "I get the feeling you don't like it when I call you that."

"Citizen Likhodeyev would be more appropriate."

The boy had gotten stuffy. How odd. "Okay, fine with me. Can you tell me what today's date is?"

"Actually," said Grishka, "that was going to be my first question for you." He sat facing him in a swivel chair, keyboard poised on his knee.

Heron grinned. "But I'd just say it was July fourteenth, and that would be wrong."

"Fair enough. It's October thirty-first."

Not such a big gap as last time. "I kind of missed out on summer, didn't I. Oh well." He stretched, wincing. "Anyway, so I entered Alexandreia in the persona of Diomedes the Lykian just at the moment when Mark Antony was returning. . . ."

The words spilled out as nonchalantly as could be. Grishka listened without any particular interest, tapping a note from time to time. Once Heron figured out where the camera was he simply ignored him and aimed his delivery at the lens. Might as well play their game.

As he spoke, his aches and pains subsided. He also felt remarkably calm, thanks no doubt to a drug—propapaverium again? Free of anxiety, his mind pursued a private chain of deductions while his mouth maintained the narrative flow.

He was in a new world. The change in Grishka, however subtle, was evidence enough. He wondered what else had changed—which friends he'd lost, which relatives he'd gained, what sort of political and social climate he'd have to deal with. And then the biggest mystery of all—Stella. Where could she be? Somehow he'd expected the two of them to emerge hand in hand and sashay off into the sunset. But there was no sign of her, and he didn't want to ask Grishka anything. It seemed wisest to betray as little of his disorientation as he possibly could.

". . . and we each took an asp, and as the fangs went into my arm I faded back home again."

Grishka nodded. "Good, good." He tapped out some more notes, leaned back, and yawned. "That just about does it. But one thing still concerns me, Citizen—your memory lapse."

"Oh? Well, it's bound to pass, just the way it always does."

Grishka seemed dubious, and Heron was reminded of how much power this man had over him. He didn't want to give him any reason to exercise it.

"I feel fine. Really."

"But can you even find your way home?"

"If you tell me my address I can." His armpits were getting moist. He wanted out.

Grishka pursed his lips. "If you insist. But I want to see you again tomorrow at, say, 1500, for a follow-up."

"Whatever you say, Citizen Likhodeyev."

He slid off the couch and waited awkwardly. No sanity test? No portfolio of skinnies? Not even a handshake? But Grishka just scribbled something on a scrap of paper and gave it to him.

"So I'll see you tomorrow afternoon," he said. "And by the way, I should remind you that this was your last dip. I'm returning your code to the pool; you'll have a new assignment within three days."

Heron wasn't sure he liked the sound of that, but since he counted himself lucky to be escaping at all, he didn't say a word. He put on his coat—a dingy gray thing that rang no bells whatsoever—and headed for the door. An escort met him outside, as usual, and they set off together into the maze.

According to Grishka's scribble he'd been evicted from his plush suite in the Tower. He didn't even have his cozy studio in Residencia Trece any more. No, he'd been relegated to a senior dormitory, G Block on the noisy corner of Panamericana and Tercera; a big step down. It didn't surprise him.

Out in the newborn universe it was almost sundown. The Plaza de la Paz languished in the Tower's long shadow, haunted by circling shoals of brown leaves that scratched and whispered in an unfriendly wind. A squad of Guardias idled at the perimeter, faces drugged into anonymity. Heron did his best to ignore them. With his collar turned up and his hands shoved firmly into his pockets, he set off downtown.

As he passed a public callbox on 2 de Octubre he paused for a moment, struggling with his curiosity. Curiosity won. He entered his own code for deduction and Stella Cranach's for connection. Colored snow blew across the screen. An adolescent boy answered.

"Can I speak to Stella please?"

"You have the wrong number, asshole," said the boy, and clicked off.

But of course he didn't have the wrong number. He had the only number he knew, and he'd certainly punched it in right. It had simply been too much to expect. There were many more avenues to pursue.

Strangers hurried past him, pale, closed in, intent on getting from A to B and not too pleased with what they met in between. They marched along with bowed heads and slitted eyes, to avoid airborne grit, maybe, or maybe because there was nothing they wanted to see. After two blocks he realized his own eyes were squinting and watering; but he didn't care to speculate why. It was no good indulging his sentiments. For now he couldn't allow anything to surprise him, to worry him, or to make him depressed. As July's fiasco had demonstrated, if he didn't keep a lid on his heart and mind, he was useless.

That meant avoiding several touchy subjects. Stella, for instance. He didn't even want to consider the possibility that she wasn't waiting for him somewhere in this twilit version of the New City. She'd seemed so sure of what she was doing; she must be here.

Then there was his dismissal from the Adjustment Bureau. Of course that made no difference at all, because if Stella—no, *since* Stella—was within reach, there was no need for him to go chasing along any more forks in the road. No need for any more dips into other and still other waters. He'd gotten where he'd gotten, and there he'd stay.

But despite his will, despite all sensible arguments to the contrary, his imagination did chase after that gruesome scenario for a second or two. Dip after dip, world after world, each version grimmer and grayer and lonelier than the one before, and never a sign of the one true Stella Cranach.

His reverie was interrupted by a detachment of Guardias standing solidly across his path. "Street closed," they said. He turned right onto Second without question or protest.

Two more blocks and he hit Panamericana, which as usual was

crowded with eager vendors. He passed chestnut roasters and glove dealers and radio sellers and felt comforted by the continued vitality of the *economía gris*. Then he noticed that some of the people huddled along the street weren't selling anything. They were standing or sitting or lying down on ragged quilts and pads, dressed in tattered clothing and grimy with old dirt. They weren't begging; in the New City's moneyless economy there was nothing tangible to beg for. But they looked like beggars. They reminded Heron of the kind of desperate, destitute folks he hadn't seen since the bad old days of Chicago and Miami.

There were more of them outside the main entrance to G Block. Heron fought the urge to ask, "Hey, what's going on with you guys?" But there was no point in acting like a man from another world.

A sallow character in camouflage fatigues—obviously not a Guardia—confronted him inside the door. "Hex code, citizen?"

Heron stared stupidly for a second before offering his wrist to the portable scanner. That's it, stay cool. The scanner hummed a D-flat and the man said, "Thank you, citizen. Just making sure you belonged here." He mumbled a response and went inside.

Faded posters decorated the lobby. "Chance is Freedom," said one. "Wang Suyin: A Retrospective," said another. He remembered that exhibition (Sally had made him go see it), and the memory reassured him. Then he started pressing the elevator button, and kept pressing it until he realized every passing player thought he was nuts. Of course; it was broken. Sheepishly he joined the crowd heading for the stairwell and trudged up seven flights.

His assigned room was a nondescript ceramic box with a few chairs and a pair of bunk beds. In the bottom bunk George Early and a woman he didn't recognize were lying half undressed, groping each other urgently.

"Shit, man, that was a quick one," said Early.

"Sorry, pal. I'll leave."

"Oh, no," said the woman. Jasmine, that's who she was—the well-connected lady who'd taken him to the Lagarto in July. "You must be tired, John. We weren't up to much anyway. Come on in and relax."

Early scowled affectionately.

Heron pulled up a chair and beamed back. "It's good to see you two."

"You just saw us this morning."

"Yeah, but think of all I've been through in the meantime."

"Oh, right!" said Jasmine. "Egypt and Cleopatra and every-thing. God, what a great assignment you've got. Sure beats punching numbers at the Banco del Hemisferio, which is all I've got to look forward to for the next three months."

"Well, it certainly has been—educational."

Jasmine finished straightening her clothes and lit a cigarette with a queenly flourish. "So what was old Cleo up to this time around?"

"Scheming, murdering, and general vamping—the usual stuff. But I'd rather not talk about it. Grishka just put me through the usual hour-long debriefing. What's new with you folks?"

"Pacheco is having a surprise curfew party tonight," said Early. "The message came in while you were at the Tower. I can't decide whether to go or not."

A party with Pacheco sounded promising. But what was this business about a curfew? "Sounds great to me," said Heron. "Where is it?"

"At his loft."

His blank look must have betrayed him, because Jasmine said, "Uh-oh—he's zoned out! Jello-brain Johnny rides again!" She sailed off the bunk and went fumbling through a cabinet under the window.

"Just take it easy, pal." Early patted his hand. "Old George and Jasmine will have you fixed up in no time."

Jasmine returned with a grubby dogeared spiral notebook. "Here you go, John. Standing orders." She imitated his Middle-man twang. " 'If I ever turn up and don't seem to know what's going on just hand me this.' "

It looked like a diary, like the one he'd searched for in vain the last time around. He resisted the urge to start reading immediately. "You know, I think I'll go down to dinner now and study this while I eat. Just tell me two things: where and when is Pacheco's party?"

"Avenida Quinta, number six twenty-three, fourth floor." Jasmine offered him a pen; he jotted everything down. "And you've got to be on your way by 1915, because curfew starts at 2000."

"Got it." He headed for the door. "So go back to whatever you were doing before I barged in. Maybe I'll run into you later."

"Later," they agreed, and he was gone.

In the cafeteria he sat alone. Service had only just begun, so the hall was almost empty, sparing him any potentially embarrassing conversations. Dinner was a mysterious stew ladled into a chipped clay bowl. He thought briefly of the wonders of Cleopatra's table before taking his first bite. It wasn't really so bad.

But the book, now: that was the main course on his table. His hands trembled as he opened it.

"Your name is John Heron," it said. The handwriting was careless, unmistakably his own. "Your mother's name was Jennifer. Your father's name was Lucas." So far, so good. It continued with the little details of his biography: date and place of birth, education, residential history, et cetera, omitting any reference to his teenage association with the Acorn Group, which was only prudent. Then it described his arrival in the New City and his first marriage and everything went wrong.

The notebook said he'd immigrated at age twenty, but he remembered coming at twenty-three. The notebook said his first wife was Sarafina Cruz, but he remembered Teofila Herrero. The notebook said they'd separated after eight years, which suggested that Sarafina had been a much more pleasant companion than Teofila, because he'd only lasted two years with her.

The notebook, in short, may have been written by John Heron, but it wasn't the same John Heron whose life he'd been living.

"So I wonder where the hell *this* guy's gone off to," whispered Heron. "Poor sucker."

He looked up, frustrated and filled with a profound sense of alienation from the room, the book, the clothes he was wearing, even the flesh that held his spirit. His eyes chanced on the corner video box, which was showing some classical play. A kid with blue hair hovered in midair and sang a tune as plaintive as one of Sappho's.

> Five fathoms deep thy lover sleeps,
> His bones of branching coral made;
> Pearls are all the tears he weeps;
> Nothing of his heart doth fade
> But doth suffer a sea-change
> Into something rich and strange.

That's me, he thought. Thanks a lot, MEQMAT.

Obviously the notebook couldn't give him much, if any, insight into himself; but if he was going to be stuck in this world it made a useful crib sheet. Next time he ran into Teofila, for instance, he'd know enough not to make any familiar remarks. And as for this Sarafina—hmm, there was no mention of whether the parting had been amicable. He'd still have to play most of it by ear.

Since there was too much to read at one brief sitting, he skipped ahead, both to feed his curiosity and to get an idea where it was heading. About midway through, it did turn into a diary. Odd sentences caught his eye: *Grishka has canceled my prescription for eumenidol. Says he won't let me dip till my blood's clean. Little bastard.* And later: *Still no sign of S. I just can't figure. Nobody's heard of her.* And on the last page: *Can't find her here so I may as well move on. Isis: You found your love again. Help me find mine.*

No need to guess what the S. stood for. (Or maybe there was; maybe this guy's dream girl was a Sheila or a Sylvia. But that was a minor detail.) Her absence didn't reassure him. Those despairing words, however, had been scribbled before the dip, and the whole universe had changed since then.

Now that he thought of it he was struck by how minor a transformation it had been. The New City still existed, and its citizens still spoke English, Spanish, and Chinese—and not, for example, Russian, Hindi, and Bantu, or some strange amalgam of Egyptian and Greek. He himself still existed, for that matter, in much the same form as he always had. He wasn't bald or blind or one-legged or even tattooed. It was all piddling stuff. He might have expected the premature death of someone as heavy as Caesar Octavian to reverberate far more ominously down the canyons of history. But it hadn't.

Then he remembered Stella saying, in the guise of Cleopatra, that there were limits on how far a soul could stray, that it could only settle into a body it recognized. Such a condition would constrain the choice of worlds even more severely than it would the choice of personae. In fact, the more he reflected, the clearer it became that this version of the present was in no way rooted in the past he had helped shape.

It hadn't been this way the last time. Once rescued, Kaisarion had stayed rescued, though his survival hadn't made much difference in the larger movement of history. Apparently the pattern of correspondence was more complex and less obvious than a layman like himself could fathom.

Still, the idea tantalized him. He checked the clock. It was ten minutes short of 1800, which gave him another hour before he had to leave. He stuck the notebook in his coat pocket and headed for the lone public terminal in the lobby's far corner. By chance, or the kindness of some god, it was free. He sat down, entered his code, and asked for the dope on Cleopatra.

MEQMAT obliged him. Reams of text scrolled down the screen, ancient authors and modern scholars all jumbled together—Plutarch and Strabo, Mizomachi and Grant, Dio Cassius and Cicero. The consensus tended to confirm his deductions. Cleopatra had committed suicide shortly after the fall of Alexandreia; Octavian had lived on for forty-odd years. One citation especially intrigued him:

"No one knows clearly in what way she perished . . . some say that she applied to herself an asp which had been brought in to her in a water-jar . . . others declare that she had smeared a pin, with which she was wont to fasten her hair, with some poison. . . ."

Venom or poison, suicide or murder: many and various were the tricks of time.

19

Almas Perdidas

Feeling rather pleased with his cleverness (Stella would be so proud), he strolled out into the dreary evening. Panamericana's vendors had all packed up and disappeared, but the *desgraciados* remained. What would they do when curfew started?

They'd camp in the metro station, of course. How silly of him not to realize.

His first clue was the pervasive reek of unwashed bodies and sour clothing that he noticed on his way downstairs to the platform. Then he saw them: entire families, from grannies to tots, equipped with pallets and blankets and assorted grimy bundles. Most dozed or sat quietly, but there were a few who whimpered, or spoke in hushed, furtive tones; and the language they used was the same broad old-fashioned Middleman English as Heron himself spoke.

He looked closer. Underneath the dirt were some ugly scars. Several were missing limbs. He squatted down by a withered old lady with a patch over her left eye, and said, "Where do you come from, sister?"

She looked up anxiously. "Bloomington."

"What brought you back East?"

"The war, son, the war! Whatever else? I'm the only one left out of my whole family, and praise God's mercy, but I don't know why He saw fit to spare me when He took my sons and my daughters and my two little grandchildren." Her voice was a whine; tears wet her cheeks and dribbled from her lips. "I'm just an old used-up rag with no purpose left in life but to sit here in the guts of this godless town."

Heron touched her shoulder. "The Lord moves in mysterious ways, sister. He must have saved you for a good reason. God bless you." He straightened up and started walking down the platform.

The old lady's tears oozed like pus. "Oh, but wait, son! Couldn't you stay a little longer and talk to me? You're the only good man I've met here."

But Heron was already ten meters away. His homely blessing had been automatic; it surprised him even more than it did her. Evidently great chunks of his childhood piety still lurked beneath the overlay of New City player, just waiting for a voice from the past to call them out.

He saw things a little clearer now. These wretched people were refugees of war. That would account for their homelessness and disenfranchisement; apparently, for reasons unknown, the New City had given them sanctuary without extending the privilege of citizenship. All of which suggested that the Texas-Tropicana War had escalated to new levels of menace.

He pulled out the diary and scanned through weeks of scribble. After some hunting he found it. *September 2: Texas invaded Middle the day before yesterday and has already rolled its tanks to within 200 km of Chicago. The city's been hit by regular air strikes since the middle of last month. I bet my uncle's factory was pulverized. I wonder how many old friends and relatives are dead.* Pretty cruel world I've landed myself in, he thought.

He stared down the tunnel, hoping to see the telltale headlights of an approaching train. No such luck. He looked at the wall clock: 1905. Still plenty of time. There were lots of other people waiting, so it was unlikely that he'd just missed one. About half his fellow travelers had the well-fed, well-scrubbed look of citizens. The rest seemed as miserable as Sister Bloomington. He settled in to wait, idly flipping the pages of the notebook.

September 28: First quota of refugees arrived. George and I went down to the new river wall to watch them climb off the ferry. Sad sight. Especially the eyes: blank as video screens. Already people are calling them refugiados, desgraciados, *even* almas perdidas—*lost souls—as if they're not quite human any more.*

Ten minutes and ten pages later a train came screaming in. He'd never before heard one so noisy or seen one so poorly maintained. Most of its windows were cracked or broken; all the rest were opaque with crud. Exterior paint peeled off in strips. Scrawled across the doors at regular intervals were familiar graffiti: "Foresight is slavery—fortune sets us free," and "*Queremos la justicia! Queremos la verdad!*" Since several doors were jammed, the scramble getting on and off was especially ugly. And once he got on he didn't see an icicle's chance in hell of finding a seat, as almost every one was already claimed by a *desgraciado*. Some sat up, other stretched out; all smelled abominably.

Eventually, when the doors finally closed, the train lurched forward like a drunk. It made its stops at Eighth, Fourteenth, and Twentieth in reasonable time. Then somewhere short of Twenty-sixth it bucked to a halt in the shadowy limbo between stations and didn't budge a centimeter.

The citizens groaned, but the *desgraciados* barely noticed. Why should they? They weren't going anywhere.

Heron was, however, and he didn't enjoy the delay one bit. In spite of its broken windows, the sheer mass of humanity aboard his car gave it a terminal case of stuffiness. There wasn't enough oxygen to go around. And all those bodies contributed to an unpleasant level of heat, especially nasty for someone dressed in wool. He sagged against the door, feeling sleepy and sick to his stomach, wishing the train would move. What a petty ordeal. Why did full-time residents put up with it? Studying the massed *desgraciados* he started wondering how many of the ones that seemed to be sleeping had actually fainted. A quarter, maybe, or possibly a third? Most all of them looked battered and abused; many were positively ancient, even more frail and withered than Sister Bloomington. He wouldn't be surprised if some of those supine forms were corpses. It would certainly explain the odor.

"*Cerveza! Cerveza fría!*"

He snapped to attention. Some character was pushing through with a styrofoam cooler hung around his neck. His Spanish accent was atrocious; he had to be a Middleman.

"Over here, pal." Heron held out his wrist, expecting a portable credit-transfer box. He could just about taste the beer.

"Sorry, sir." The peddler shook his head. "Numbers ain't any good to me. Hard currency's all I can use and all I can take."

Heron's eyebrow lifted at that archaic "sir." He shrugged wearily. "Then we're both out of luck, pal." He hadn't had his hands on any coin since December.

The *desgraciado* trudged off, shouting "*Cerveza fría!*" over and over again. It was a minor form of torture.

Enterprising old sucker, thought Heron. If these folks stick around they'll bring the whole city down around our ears. He settled against the door again and waited some more.

"Brothers and sisters!"

This time it was a white-bearded tramp wrapped in a blanket. "Oh I've got good news for you, my friends, oh I've got real good news!" But his voice was so shrill and angry-sounding that there was nothing even remotely good about it. "Oh I'm bringing you news of love, the sweet blessed love of Our Lord Jesus Christ! Oh and you need His love, my dear brothers and sisters, oh you've never needed His blessed love the way you do right now, my friends. Oh listen to me! Listen, my dear brothers and sisters in Christ! The flaming sword of the Lord is hanging over this city, this wicked city, this sink of iniquity, this ungodly Babylon of the modern day, this Sodom, this Gomorrah, this playground of Satan, oh this black cesspool of evil! Oh His flaming sword is gonna strike, oh yes it's gonna strike!" He sliced his hand down in a karate chop, so hard that he almost lost his balance.

Where's the Guardia when you need them, Heron wondered. This guy was committing a crime that at best got you exiled, and at worst landed you in the waste-processing camps of Contracosta.

"This city's gonna burn, my brothers and sisters, oh it's gonna burn and so are you, my dear brothers and sisters, unless you get down on your knees and pray to Jesus Christ! Oh you gotta pray to Jesus, you gotta beg for his sweet blessed love, oh you gotta make a place for Jesus in your hearts!"

The evangelist made slow progress through the car. He stood opposite Heron now; his voice threatened to rupture an eardrum.

"You, brother!" he shrieked. "I see the face and I see the man! I see a good man who lost sight of Jesus, I see a good man who turned down the devil's road!"

"Just fuck off," Heron said.

"Oh brother, you're using the devil's favorite word! Oh I hear it, oh I see it! You're locked up tight in the devil's black tower! And we gotta bring that tower crashing down, my brother, oh yes we do! We gotta knock that tower down! We gotta pray for the blessed sword of the Lord, the sword that cuts through evil, oh we gotta pray for that flaming sword of God's undying love! Oh my brother, that sword's gonna cut through the evil in your heart!"

"Not likely," said Heron.

A few of his fellow passengers were listening in with wry

amusement; everyone else ignored the old tramp and his victim, no doubt thanking their luck that they weren't in Heron's place.

The evangelist produced a tattered black book and waved it overhead. "Our Lord Jesus Christ has put the sword of his terrible mercy in the hands of Texas, my dear brothers and sisters! It is written! It is written, oh it is written in Jeremiah fifty-one, right here in the Bible!" He thumped the old book and coaxed even more volume out of his voice. "This is the time of the Lord's vengeance! Flee out of the midst of Babylon, for the nations have drunken of her wine and gone mad! Babylon will fall and be destroyed, Babylon will be an astonishment, Babylon will be a hissing of serpents! Weep for her, my dear brothers and sisters in Christ, howl for her pain!"

In mid-howl the train shuddered and leaped forward in a spasm of reanimation. The evangelist toppled backwards, still clutching his book. He landed on a sleeping Middleman and uttered a long string of curses. His victim woke up and gurgled in terror. Thrashing wildly about, eyes bugging from his head, he screamed, "The Texans are coming! The Texans are coming!" But the evangelist said, "It's our good Lord Jesus Christ who's coming, brother," whereupon both *desgraciados* began a serious shouting match. Thoroughly disgusted, Heron pushed his way to the end of the car, hopped over the coupling, and escaped into the next one down.

Here it was a little quieter, but no less crowded. He squeezed himself into an unoccupied spot and sweated out the next five stops.

At Fifty-fifth he had less then ten minutes to spare. Climbing up to ground level he wondered what would become of the folks who were riding to the end of the line at Eightieth Street. How would they ever get wherever they were going before 2000? Maybe they'd be allowed some leeway; maybe the curfew wasn't strictly enforced—but since he had no desire to be a test case, he stepped lively.

Fifty-fifth was dark and empty. Heading west he glimpsed few other pedestrians, all of them in as big a hurry as he was. Little knots of Guardias milled on the corners of Tercera, Cuarta, and Quinta, their eyes glassy with obedience drugs. Heron had never seen so many cops on the street before. Apparently that slot had become one of the likeliest outcomes of the Lottery. Which reminded him: Grishka said he was returning his code to the pool. The last thing he wanted was to get stuck on the Guardia again.

He turned up Quinta and scanned house numbers: 619, 621 . . . there it was. He was about to ring the bell when a female voice called out to him.

"Hey mister."

She was standing in the shadows of the next door down, a kid of fourteen or fifteen. Blond, fresh-faced, maybe even pretty. She wore a skimpy vinyl jacket, torn fishnet stockings, spike heels, and a skirt so short it was practically a belt. Her "mister" pegged her as a *desgraciado*.

"Yes?"

She smiled and stuck her hip out. "You wanna party, mister?"

"Sorry, sweetheart. I don't have any hard currency."

She came closer, awkward in the heels. "That's okay," she said. She was trying not to shiver. "You're so cute I'd do you for free."

"You want off the street, huh?" He sized her up. She could easily be his own daughter. Until a few months ago she'd probably been a schoolgirl, flirting with boys, helping her family with the chores, attending Bible classes every Sunday and Wednesday. Now she was a harlot in Babylon and not having any fun at all. "Listen," he said. "I'm on my way to a party. I could take you along, but only if you promise to behave. No whore stuff."

"Oh, would you, would you?" The street-girl pose fell away and she was just plain desperate. "I'll be good, I swear."

"On a stack of Bibles?"

The roar of a bullhorn obliterated her reply: "THE TIME IS NOW 2000. CURFEW HAS BEGUN. ALL PERSONS FOUND OUTDOORS ARE SUBJECT TO ARREST FOR NONCOMPLIANCE WITH THE LOTTERY OF THE NEW CITY."

Heron looked back long enough to see a half-dozen Guardias marching down the street, night sticks ready for business. He ducked into 623 and dragged the kid after him. "And another thing," he said. "Once we're inside, you're on your own. Understand?"

She understood. They climbed toward the noise and music till they reached its source.

"John! You made it!"

An old man with a beard was waiting for them at the door. Heron stared blankly for a split second; then he recognized him as that same mysterious old codger who'd hailed him in the Quinta Esencia, last July. He still didn't know his name.

They shook hands anyway. "This is my cousin," said Heron. "Uh—"

"Felicity," said the girl.

"Well, welcome aboard. I'm Marpus Lilling. Great costume you've got there, Felicity."

She simpered and Heron realized two or three unpleasant things at once. The first was that yes indeed, he did know this guy, except that Marpus had aged twenty-five years since they'd last met. At the moment he looked to be pushing seventy, yet Heron remembered him as a vigorous man of his own generation. That's why he'd seemed a stranger before. The scary part was that the same misfortune could have caught him. What if he'd taken a bum turn somewhere and landed in a decrepit, half-dead version of himself? The years' flow was erratic and unpredictable; it could play all kinds of tricks, so why not that one?

The rest of his insights likewise involved time. Grishka had said it was October 31, which now that he thought of it meant Halloween; this get-together was some kind of costume party. And if today was the thirty-first, then the new Lottery drawing was only a few hours away.

"So come on in and have a look." Marpus had been talking steadily through his deductive dismay. "It's pretty ugly stuff. You're lucky you didn't get sucked into it."

"Sucked in what, pal?"

"The riot, John, the riot!"

They went in, and the room's warmth of bodies broke over him like a pail of hot water, running past his ears as babbling voices. Marpus led them through the crowd to an oversized video screen. Heron had a brief, dazed impression of dozens and dozens of people dressed as vampires, aliens, calculators, playing cards, unicorns, and guided missiles, and then he was staring at floodlit mayhem in the Plaza de la Paz.

Figures bounced and quivered against a backdrop of bare trees and blank façades. Mouths gaped in moans and screams, and thick arms covered with black leather swung rifles and clubs, revealing the emblem of the Guardia Civil with every blow. An excited woman with a bruised face squatted next to the screen, gesturing wildly and making breathless comments.

"There's Kim Lee Sung, one of the players who organized the demonstration," she said. The screen showed a kid whose face was almost invisible under a fresh coat of blood. Over his shoulder Heron read placards: WHO'S RUNNING THE SHOW, TEXAS OR MEQ-

MAT? GIVE US BACK OUR LOTTERY! GIVE US BACK OUR LIVES! Then the camera jerked away, and there were people lying on the pavement in various contorted positions, trussed up in tanglespray. More jerks and spins, and two Guardias were beating a woman with night sticks. Then a longer shot of upraised fists, hundreds and hundreds of them, silhouetted against the gleaming mass of the Black Tower. And over everything a constant stream of incoherent shouts and screams, with an occasional "Shit!" or "Stop!" coming through more clearly.

The image jumped away and bucked and focused on the blank black helmet of a Guardia, dangerously close up, night stick waving. Then elbows, feet, unreadable shadows, a nose, a blaze of light, and nothing at all.

"That fucker would have killed me!" The young woman trembled furiously, baring her back to show the purple and yellow blotches. "It was only luck that I got away with this much."

"Let's see it again from the top!" someone shouted. But she was already rewinding.

Heron turned to the person next to him, a tall guy dressed as Marie Antoinette. "When? When did this happen?"

"About 1830 or 1900, a couple hours after the announcement."

"Announcement?"

"You mean you still haven't heard? Welcome to the real world, pal. Tonight's Lottery has been canceled. The Junta's freezing everybody for the next thirty days."

"Jesus." He shook his head. He'd been so wrapped up in himself all evening; the only players he'd talked to had been George and Jasmine, and they obviously hadn't stirred from the room for hours. So here it was, a first in the long history of the Lottery of the New City. A freeze. Chance suspended. Determinism closing down the existential crap game. No wonder those people had demonstrated.

"But the Guardias," he said. "They're players too. Why did they get so ugly?"

Marie Antoinette flicked his fan. "They've got their drugs and their orders, right? I remember how it is. Shit, I spent six months on the force myself. And you know—or maybe you don't—about all those new inductions? The Special Circumstances, the Emergency Powers? Man, you're out of touch! It's the refugees, the goddamn *desgraciados*. The Junta has waived landing fees for about eight hundred of them so far, on condition that they sign up as Guardias for two years."

"Two years! That's slavery!"

"*No me lo digas, ciudadano.* Only fortune sets us free." And he swished off with a great rustle of petticoats.

Heron found something to drink as quickly as he could. What a world to be stuck in. It was unreal, surreal, it rivaled fiction, it seriously challenged his powers of belief. How could things go so bad so quickly? The New City had been an island of tolerance in a bigoted world—but no longer, it seemed, no longer.

He turned around and there was Alberto Favaloro at his elbow—looking, thank God, exactly as he remembered him. They exchanged outrage and disbelief. Then the music started up again and the mood turned more frivolous and less political. A knot of people still hovered around the video set, but most of the rest got down to the serious business of drinking, dancing, and carrying on.

In quick succession Heron spoke to Iris Mulvaney, Milagros Oquendo, Noburo Fukushima, and Pacifico Ortiz. Pacifico was suspiciously boyish and surprisingly genial. He directed Heron's attention to several large canvases hanging in the sitting room off the main living space.

"Aren't these magnificent?" he said. "They're all by the woman I share my studio with. Fabio actually bought one."

Heron politely agreed. The paintings actually were pretty nice—monumental, archaic-looking things in faded purples and browns, with random areas decorated in peeling gold leaf. They showed processions of long-haired women carrying vases, naked men wrestling, and a young girl holding the bridle of a stiff, naively rendered horse. He read the signature: "Celia Garza"—no one he'd ever heard of.

"Brilliant, aren't they?" Fabio Pacheco appeared, middle-aged and elegant, spreading his arms like the patron saint of painting. "And the Junta hasn't even deigned to grant this woman Art Pro status. So I'm doing what I can for her while I can."

"Good for you, Fabio. But what's this war done to your own career?"

"Ah, don't ask. Right now the oleocrats of Dallas are investing their bucks in bombs, not art. I don't know what's going to become of me at the next review. They could terminate my status and toss me right back in the pool. At least at my age I'd be spared the Guardia."

"Fabio," he said softly, "do you think of getting out?"

"Do I think of anything else?" Pacheco likewise lowered his

voice. "It's becoming a question of when, not if. I think the only reason I'm still here today is money. I have enough hard currency to buy two one-way tickets to Buenos Aires, but that's all, and that only covers me and Catherine." Catherine was his wife of twenty-odd years. "I'd like to get the kids out too, but I haven't been able to rustle up the cash."

"Maybe once you were out you could send for them."

"Maybe. So far that's still an option, but have you heard the rumors about exit visas? A trustworthy source tells me the Junta is on the verge of restricting free travel, on account of the war emergency. Everyone who wants to leave town will need official permission, granted after due deliberation on a case-by-case basis. They may even charge money for it."

"That sounds like a better reason to hurry than to wait."

"Yes, but if I cut out now, the Junta might think I'm an ungrateful revisionist, a crypto-determinist, and make life miserable for whoever I leave behind."

"A dilemma."

"Isn't it." Pacheco made a face. "It feels like the end of the world. You know what this place has been for me—it was the same for our whole generation. A haven against the mad mediocrity of the twenty-first century. A place where people can be what they are, and still live with a modicum of dignity. A place where the talented, not the greedy, can be king. A refuge for the oddballs, the perverts, the dope smugglers and the nicotine addicts, the dykes and the queers, the gamblers and the loose women, the Hindu-Buddhist agnostics and the Mother-loving pantheists, the whole ornery brigade of free-thinking humanists that Reverend Joe Bob Lewis is always warning us about on Radio Free Texas. I know how the kids complain about unlucky draws, about the shitty assignments and the spartan dorms, but we both know that even a bad draw is better than wage slavery in Sacramento or Houston. Imagine being shut out of all this."

"But Fabio, it looks like we already have been."

Pacheco sighed. "So even John Heron's getting fed up. I suppose I should listen to you, old friend."

Someone coughed politely. Pacheco glanced up and smiled.

"I hope I'm not disturbing?"

"Of course not." Once again he was the cordial host. "In fact we were just saying nice things about you. John, I think you've met the painter Celia Garza, haven't you?"

"Uh, maybe."

She was a tall, bony-faced woman with black hair and penetrating eyes. They clasped hands; she smiled coolly. "Actually we have met, Citizen Heron. But only briefly."

"Well, in any case, Celia, welcome to the party." Pacheco shot Heron an odd glance. "How do you like my installation?" And the two artists started discussing the lighting and the texture of the wall and the relative spacing of the canvases in minute detail. Heron withdrew a meter or two, uncertain whether courtesy allowed him to drift entirely away. Then Pacifico appeared, saying, "Celia! Where have you been!" and that settled it. He wandered back to the main room and focused on a performance that had just begun.

Two women he didn't know were executing an elaborate adagio to the music of a random-tone generator. Both were naked and painted purple, and both had extremely well-defined, heavily muscled physiques. As well they should, since the choreography mainly involved lifts and balances, with an especially grueling moment when one dancer had to support the other at arm's length overhead. It was almost as exciting as the riot video. As it ended, and the room resounded with applause, Heron noticed Celia Garza standing next to him.

"John," she said, *"por qué te fuiste? Yo te buscaba en todas partes."*

"I'm sorry, Celia," he replied, in his decidedly rusty Spanish. "I thought you were just paying your respects to Fabio."

She frowned. "You seem distracted."

"Well," he said, wondering why she cared, "I'm an experimental subject for the Adjustment Bureau, and some of the procedures I'm involved in space me out a little—temporarily, of course."

"John. Am I really a stranger?"

Now wa-ait a minute, said a voice inside. What is going on here? I didn't *think* I was drunk.

Celia switched over to English. "Is this better?" And she peered closely into his face.

Jet-black hair, yes, gleaming red lips, okay, heavily painted eyes, sure, but under the makeup the face wasn't quite the same—no, too thin and severe, same with the body—and her dress, though plausibly monochrome, was a hand-printed cotton smock that suggested Javanese batik seen in an out-of-focus black and white photograph. No, there was nothing particularly wrong with the way she looked, but she didn't ring any bells.

Still, for some reason, his heart pounded and his breath caught. "You're not really . . . Stella?"

Her eyes widened. "Holy mother Isis!"

"Jesus Christ! You are!"

And she was. Something clicked, something shifted, the light bulb switched on, and he saw her: a little fiercer, a little leaner, maybe, but still undeniably Stella.

She was in his arms then, and when she drew back her eyes were wet. "You look the same to me," she said, "but you don't really recognize me, do you. You knew me as someone else."

"Uh, yeah, of course. I knew you as Stella Cranach."

She shook her head. "Was that all?"

"Umm, what do you mean? You were Charmion the Egyptian, and Cleopatra the Macedonian."

"But never Celia Garza?"

"No."

She smiled sadly. "But that's who I am, or who I think I am. Oh, I remember being Stella, but she was just a mask, and not a very comfortable mask at that."

"Oh God." The light bulb was already flickering.

"And Cleopatra—she was a little more interesting, though not what I'd call cooperative. And Euterpe the chorus girl—no? You never knew her? Mistress of Anaxenor the shipping magnate? She was actually a lot of fun. But as for Charmion—" She shrugged. "I missed that incarnation."

His mind was a mad jumble of hope and dread. She had to be Stella.

"What do you remember about me?"

"I knew you as John Heron, exactly the way you are now. Also as Amyntas of Kyrenaika, and Diomedes, the Queen's private secretary."

Two out of three; bizarre, a bit shaky, but maybe not impossible. He kept cool. "I remember Amyntas, too; he was an okay guy. And now that I'm trying, I do, I *do* remember Euterpe—she was one of the guests at the banquet Nikias the rhetorician attended."

"You were Nikias?" She laughed. "That dirty old man!"

"He wasn't a dirty old man!" He was almost annoyed. Then he caught himself and wanted to laugh a great big hardy-har, wanted to collapse on the floor in spasms of aftershock and relief, wanted to weep for joy and offer doves to Isis; but somehow he couldn't, because somehow he really wasn't relieved. He composed his face and his voice and went for the big question.

"Are we actually who we think we are? Because if you weren't Charmion, and I wasn't Amyntas, who was?"

She took him by the hand and led him to the edge of the party. "Listen, John," she said, sitting down on a threadbare sofa. "The first time either one of us put on those headsets, the first time we got involved in MEQMAT's game, we burned our bridges behind us. We've lost all those people we used to be. And we've displaced all those people who used to be us—the guy who slept in your bunk yesterday, the woman who used to wear this dress. They've been shunted onto other forks in the road. Now there are lots of John Herons and Celia Garzas flitting through the manifold universe, all looking for a comfortable spot to perch."

"Is this one?"

"I thought so when I got here this afternoon, but I think I've changed my mind since."

"Yeah," he said. "Same here."

She pulled out her cigarettes; they both lit up. "When did you first meet me?" he asked.

"God, it's been so long. A party? One of Pacheco's blasts, I think—yes, it was December, two years ago." She looked at him uncertainly. "You don't remember?"

"As I said before, I've never met anyone called Celia Garza. It was Stella Cranach I knew. We met last December at Minoru Fukunaga's. You don't remember?"

She slumped, exhaling smoke. "No. I did my first dip in November, and then came back to the New City in mid-March. So I missed out on everything that happened in between. Which was bad enough, but here's what was worse: I suddenly wasn't myself any more. Everybody thought I was this Stella woman, exactly the way you did. And when I looked in the players' directory there was no entry for Celia Garza, alive or dead."

"Jesus."

"Tell me about it. I had a hard time keeping my sanity."

"But I didn't think that was possible—I mean, coming back in somebody else's skin. I thought we could only return as alternate versions of ourselves."

"We'll get to that. But back to my story—instead of boiling over into hysterics, I tried to fake my way through Stella's day-to-day existence. And I did a damn good job, too, if I do say so myself. One thing that helped me was this kind of diary or private autobiography she'd left lying around. You know about those, huh? Apparently she'd done a few dips herself, so she was familiar with the problems. Clever lady. But believe me, it was no fun being Stella Cranach. She's very hard on herself, very driven, a real workaholic. In fact—and this is the good part—she's the woman I might have been if things had taken another turning. Just listen. We have different names, right, but the same birthday, and the same parents. I just happened to take my mother's surname, while Stella took her father's. In secondary school we both studied medicine and psychology, and we both dabbled in the visual arts. In my case the art stuff clicked, and I gave up on psychology, but Stella was always caught in the middle. She was always trying to be one thing and wanting to be another. Maybe that had something to do with her weight problem."

Driven? Frustrated? Heron shook his head. So many pictures of Stella; were any of them real?

"Needless to say I didn't linger in that uncomfortable spot. Stella had a lot of pull at the Adjustment Bureau, so it was no problem scheduling another dip as quickly as possible. I went back to Alexandreia, I played out that scenario with Cleopatra and Diomedes, and then I returned to what I thought would be my old self and my old life. Except that it isn't." Her voice flattened out; she gestured toward the wall with her cigarette. "Because I never painted those paintings, and now my own husband doesn't recognize me."

His eyes opened wide and then clamped shut. She wasn't Stella, she wasn't, she wasn't. There were no words left to describe the way he felt. "Oh, Celia," he said. "Talk about lost souls."

20

Code Seven

The whole point of Pacheco's party was that it had to last all night. With the curfew in effect, wherever 2000 found you was where you were bound to stay till 0600 the next morning. The only challenge was filling out the time.

Of course, in a flat as big as this one, with a gathering so diverse, there was no shortage of options. You could dance, you could watch videos, you could take any number of drugs, you could watch a grab bag of experimental performance, you could talk to friends and strangers, you could sit in a corner and read, or you could even sleep, in a dormitory-sized room fitted out especially for that purpose. That's how Felicity, the harlot of Babylon, spent her night at Fabio Pacheco's.

Or you could do a little bit of everything, which is what John Heron ended up doing; though no matter where he went, or what he got involved in, Celia Garza was always by his side.

She wasn't Stella, and he wasn't her husband John. But they *were* awfully close. Better yet, they were the only people in the world who could understand each other's dilemmas, and maybe help each other find a way out.

"Grishka wants to see me at 0900," said Celia. "Even though it's supposed to be my final debriefing, I think I can talk him into another dip."

"He made an appointment with me, too," said Heron, "but in

the afternoon. Maybe if I go down with you, he'll see me at the same time."

"Have no fear. I've got some very persuasive arguments up my sleeve."

So it was decided. And for the next several hours, in between spectating and napping, Celia explained to him as much as she'd learned about the art of threading the schizogenic maze. "Your body remembers," she said again and again. "Even without MEQMAT each of us can catch echoes of the memories of all our hosts, whether previous or current. That's the key. That's our ticket out of here."

And Fabio says Buenos Aires is a tricky destination, Heron thought. He should try picturing a river composed only of potential, and then try diving in.

At 0600 the Pachecos served all their guests a breakfast of reconstituted orange juice, instant pancakes, and refried beans. After cleanup the party ended, and the whole gaudy circus—costumes wilted and disintegrating from the night's exertions—trooped out into a crisp November morning. Heron and Celia, hand in hand, brought up the rear.

"Back to my place first, okay?" said Celia.

"Fine. But how about if we splurge on a cab? I don't think I'm ready for another metro ride just yet."

"I'm with you, amigo." They shared a wan smile and started scanning the stream of traffic.

That particular morning, however, cabs were as scarce as *desgraciados* were thick. To stimulate circulation they started walking down Quinta, waving madly whenever they saw a set of public wheels—which wasn't often. On every block they passed groups of refugees huddled together over hot-air vents or in the sun. At Fiftieth, Forty-eighth, and Forty-fourth they saw teams of irritable-looking Guardias, and along Forty-second Street there was a whole detachment stringing from Hemisferio to Tercera.

"What is this, martial law?" said Heron.

"Starting to look that way," said Celia.

Also at Forty-second they had a clear view past the venerable tower of La Crísalis, all the way over to the new ramparts fronting the East River: a long mound of compacted rubble with antiaircraft emplacements on top. From his diary Heron knew it was the same along the West River. The New City had become a fortress.

Crossing Thirty-ninth Street they saw one possible reason why. A squadron of jets in wedge formation was flying over Contracosta, heading roughly northeast. Though they were somewhat indistinct in the morning haze, they looked an awful lot like bombers.

Heron whistled. "They can't be ours, can they?"

"As far as I know we don't have anything like that."

"Then they must be Texan, or maybe Tropicanian. So why the hell are they flying in so close?"

"Trying to make us nervous, I guess."

"And succeeding pretty damn well."

Although at this point just about anything would, if they gave it a chance.

Above Thirty-fifth they finally bagged a cab. With great sighs of relief they climbed in, arranged the windbreaker, and settled back to enjoy the ride. Though it wasn't easy—partly because of the grimness of the passing scenery and partly because their hack looked like he was about to die. The poor sucker was nothing but skin and bones; it was hard to believe that those pipestem legs could generate any power at all. And at every pause in traffic he started coughing.

"I feel so guilty," whispered Celia. "Maybe I should be pedaling."

"Yeah, and I'm wondering how long he's been doing this. With the freeze on he's got no prospect of anything else."

"At least there aren't any hills."

Passing the familiar bulk of the Ciencia Complex on Nineteenth, however, they did run into an obstacle, and a pretty major one at that. One minute they were laboring along, listening unhappily to the hack's coughing and wheezing, and the next they were watching the city go up in a flash of light. The noise came a split-second later—a roar that all but shredded eardrums, along with a shock wave that felt like a boulder colliding with their guts.

Wherever their guts were—because Heron was suddenly weightless, he was flying, he was tumbling through the air. If he screamed he didn't remember; he was too busy reminding himself to tuck his head, curl into a ball, and pray he didn't land on his bad foot. He struck the pavement with tooth-loosening impact and slid a good two meters into a scarves-and-gloves vendor, who certainly was screaming, in what was probably the loudest and fastest Guangdong dialect ever heard in the streets of the New City.

Heron lay still for a moment. He was in pain. His left shoulder felt like one massive bruise. He wiggled his fingers, then his toes, then his arms and legs. It all worked. So he sat up, and yelped in agony. Whew—wasn't quite ready for that one! He saw red for a second; then his vision cleared, and the pain cooled off a little.

About a hundred meters downtown of him the street was full of rubble. Smoke and dust drifted up from a half-ruined building—let's see, which one had it been? The Eighteenth Street branch of the Banco del Hemisferio? Maybe Residencia Epsilon? Hard to say. Close by him, dozens of other people were hauling themselves up, to a similar chorus of yelps and groans; closer to the ruin, however, they were just moaning, or lying quiet and still.

He stood carefully. He felt weak, and his skull throbbed. Concussion? But no, he hadn't hit his head.

"John!" Celia's voice sounded loud and clear. There she was, disentangling herself from the overturned cab. She looked to be in better shape than he was. He limped over.

"You're okay?" she said.

"More or less. You?"

"Not so bad. But check out the hack."

He was lying in a heap, whimpering softly. They knelt beside him. "My leg," he said.

Celia went to work, probing gently. "Left tibia," she said. "It's broken. No more pedicabs for you, amigo."

"Good," he said, and fainted.

A siren was warbling somewhere east of them, which was a reassuring sign. They waited with the hack until an emergency medical team arrived on the scene, a matter of about fifteen minutes. Then they set off again on foot. Heron disdained medical attention; getting back to Celia's, and from there to the Tower, was his first priority.

But although they wanted to keep following Quinta, the Guardia Civil already had it cordoned off between Nineteenth and Fourteenth. So they skirted the ruin (it *was* the Banco del Hemisferio), turned east, and followed Libertad into Plaza Reunión—where they ran into a second police barricade.

"Shit." The pain in Heron's back made him want to sit down and cry. Since yesterday, it seemed, free movement through city streets had become a lost cause. Seeing another player crossing Fifteenth, he called out, "What gives?"

The player shrugged. "All public squares are off limits today, pal. I guess the Junta's afraid of another ugly scene like last night."

So they angled east again. Heron wondered briefly if the pro-Fortune group could have done the bombing. Impossible to be sure, but somehow he couldn't see New Citizens trashing their own city, especially when a more likely explanation was available. If Texas, Green, or Tropicana had terrorist agents operating locally—which seemed almost certain—today would be the perfect time to strike. All blame would shift to the protesters.

"Not a good year for players," he said.

"No," said Celia. "Not a good year for anyone."

By the time they hit Ninth Street Heron was very sorry he hadn't copped any painkillers. His shoulder throbbed and his back was as stiff as a board. Walking had gradually become an ordeal; every step he took introduced him to new variations of pain. He felt like an old man.

Then from overhead came the heavy *whup-whup-whup* of a huge police helicopter, flying just above the tops of nearby buildings. "ATTENTION ALL CITIZENS." The voice was cruelly amplified, an animal roar. "IF YOU ARE PRESENTLY FILLING A DUTY SLOT, RETURN AT ONCE TO YOUR PLACE OF EMPLOYMENT. IF YOU ARE OFF-SHIFT OR UNASSIGNED, RETURN AT ONCE TO YOUR RESIDENCE. CURFEW IS NOW IN EFFECT AND WILL CONTINUE UNTIL 0600 TOMORROW. ATTENTION ALL PEDESTRIANS . . ."

They traded bleak looks. "I suppose," said Celia, "that we should abandon any idea of going back to my flat. We'll have to claim we're needed in the Tower. It won't really be a lie, since as of yesterday we were both still involved in the SSM program, and the freeze went into effect last night."

Heron nodded. "This might actually be a lucky break for us. We'll just be following the rules."

Their first problem was getting past the Guardia. There must have been a thousand of them stationed between 2 de Octubre and the north portal of the Tower, looking every bit as deadly as they had in last night's video; and the steadily circling helicopters, with those high-decibel threats, didn't add any cheer to the picture. Heron kept reminding himself how easily Grishka had breezed past a similar infestation last July—though he also remembered that all that had been in a different world.

As they approached the front line, at least twenty assorted tangleguns, tear-gas launchers, and projectile rifles focused on them. A *sargento* hustled forward, weapon aimed and ready.

"Halt!" She didn't say it, she screamed it. "Are you assholes deaf or what?"

"We're assigned to the Tower," said Celia. "Bureau of Adjustment, Subcommittee for Simulation and Modification."

"You think that means a flying fuck to me, citizen? Let's see some ID!"

Of course they didn't have any, since they weren't Tower employees. "But we have an appointment," Celia said. "With Citizen Likhodeyev. He's expecting us."

"Cover me!" screamed the *sargento*. Without lowering the rifle she spoke rapidly into her headset. She listened, nodded once and said, "Okay! Let's see your wrists." They approached to within a meter of her, until she screamed "Halt!" even louder than she had before. They exposed their hex codes; she recited them into the microphone. When her answer came, she spat vigorously at their feet, without once relaxing her aim.

"Okay, you two! You're on the Approved For Entry list but we don't know anything about this appointment shit! You're coming to Torre Seguridad and we're going to check you out good and proper! If you're fucking around we'll fuck you around so bad you'll never fuck anybody around again! Understand?"

Heron restrained the urge to say "Yes, sir!" and just nodded.

Four gun-toting Guardias came forward and made a hollow square around them. Even through bulky uniforms Heron could smell their sweat; just how drugged were they? At the *sargento's* command the lines parted; they marched (it really did feel like marching) through rank after rank of black-clad automatons. I could be one of them, Heron kept telling himself. This could be me.

The great glass doors swung open. Chin Leung's sculpture collection smiled down at them: a bronze Buddha from Thailand, a *kouros* from Attika, an Isis with baby Horus from Upper Egypt. Before a colossal black marble desk the acting security chief welcomed them with a glare. Once more they presented their wrists.

"Citizen Likhodeyev, you say? He hasn't yet answered our query. In the meantime I think the situation warrants a body search. If you please?" And two separate teams whisked them in opposite directions.

In a bright white cubicle Heron was treated to a slow and humiliatingly thorough search. He imagined Celia's must be even worse, female anatomy being what it was.

"Where'd you get these bruises, Citizen?" One of his examiners prodded a purple area roughly the shape and size of Africa.

"Explosion on Nineteenth Street," he said, gritting his teeth.

"You sure have a knack for being in the wrong place at the wrong time, don't you."

"I'd have to agree with you on that one, pal."

After assuring themselves that neither suspect was carrying any bombs or other instruments of destruction, the security officers let them dress again and go back to the main lobby. Once more the head honcho glared down at them. "Likhodeyev cleared you. Here's your escort."

Heron wondered what would have happened if Grishka hadn't come through. Forty-eight hours of interrogation? Prosecution for noncompliance with the Lottery? It didn't bear thinking. He and Celia exchanged weak smiles and set off into the maze.

After their third elevator ride, while in care of their second guide, the Guardia's communicator suddenly erupted in squeaks and growls. "Code Seven," it said. "Code Seven. Report to station Y-Fifty-four."

The escort stopped dead in his tracks and paled several shades. First he said "Shit," with a great deal of feeling, followed by "Wait right here," with considerably less, and then he took off down the corridor at a rapid jog. He never once looked back.

Heron stared after him with his mouth open. "I wonder what the hell Code Seven means."

"Direct assault on the Tower," said Celia.

"How do you know that?"

"Don't forget I was Stella Cranach for three days. Some things I still remember."

He punched the wall. "Jesus! This is looking more and more like the Last Judgment."

"We can only hope."

He laughed unhappily. "Meanwhile we're stuck in some featureless corner of the Tower when we want to be groveling in front of Grishka."

"Not a problem, amigo. I can solve the labyrinth too. Just follow me."

So he did, without further complaint. Though he did have a hard time keeping up with her, and an even harder time fathoming how she knew what she knew.

His body didn't like the treatment it was getting. Several times in the course of their journey he felt his vision graying out, and he had to ask Celia to wait till he recovered. "Come on, John," she'd say. "Just a little bit further, and you can sit on your butt and take all the drugs you want."

So on he went, down a corridor lined with Corinthian pillars, around an autumnal garden of chrysanthemums and red maple, up a service stairway so dank and dusty it looked older than the Tower had any right to be, behind a row of smelly animal cages, through a door more massive than the one sealing the inmost vault of the main branch of the Banco del Hemisferio. Things had stopped seeming likely or plausible quite a way back. It was just put one foot in front of the other, follow the lady in black, pay no attention to the nonsense your mind is brewing. Of course you're not lying unconscious on Avenida Quinta; of course this isn't an hallucination brought on by a blow to the head; you never hit your head, remember?

And those people he passed en route. That couldn't be, no way that could be Jemmy Whitaker sitting on a love seat next to Third Citizen Zhang Ziyang, commenting on the bouquet of a pot of jasmine tea. (Though the kid did bear an uncanny resemblance to Jemmy at age eighteen—God, was that already twenty-five years back?) And of course that wasn't Teofila Herrero hurrying down a side corridor, glancing uneasily over her shoulder. Teofila didn't even exist in this world. (Though was that necessarily any objection to anything?) And no, it looked a lot like but most definitely wasn't Diomedes the Lykian frowning over a computer screen in a dingy cubicle. (Because Diomedes was a figment of John Heron's memory, and John Heron's memory was subject to change without notice.)

Heron could attest, however, that something strange was interfering with his vision. Call it cerebral oxygen deprivation, call it low blood pressure, call it lunacy, but he could clearly see the walls vibrating and the floor undulating like a rubber sack full of water. Not to mention the way space kept moving by in reverse. He knew very well that they'd just passed through a red-enameled door frame—but suddenly it was in front of them again, gaping wide open. And that broad marble staircase they had so arduously climbed—when they reached the last step, he looked back and saw it leading up again, not down; and the gray-haired guy struggling to make it to the top was an eerie mirror image of himself.

He mentioned none of this to Celia. He figured she had enough on her mind as it was, trying to remember her way through the maze and everything, without having to worry about his faltering mental state. But as the weirdness intensified it occurred to him that she might be lost. Twenty minutes had gone by since they'd set out on their own, and they still hadn't gotten anywhere that made sense.

"Um, do you have any idea where we are?"

"Certainly. We're about fifty meters underground and getting deeper."

"When do we find this place?"

They turned a corner. "Right around now."

And there was the broad blue door marked MEQMAT-IV, looking almost too real. Surveillance cameras rotated into focus. Colored lights blinked. The blue door swung open, and Grishka Likhodeyev greeted them with a gun in his hand.

For the second time in two days he wasn't smiling.

"I suppose it's time we balanced our accounts, isn't it," he said. He motioned them in with the gun's blunt barrel. To his credit, he wasn't actually aiming it. But his face had lost the rosy glow Heron remembered, and his forehead was as furrowed as Stella's used to be.

They sat on metal chairs in the broad shadowy room. "So," said Grishka, toying with the weapon. "The experiment is finished."

Celia sat up straight. "Must it be?"

"It must. Texas pushed the button. Or rather, it's about to, and as you know by now that amounts to the same thing. A nuclear warhead will explode over the Plaza de la Paz within forty-five minutes."

Heron managed not to fall off his seat.

Celia shrugged. "But we're in the ideal place to survive a nuclear strike. They're not using big messy bombs, after all."

"Big enough to terminate the Lottery of the New City. Face it, Citizen Garza. The game is up, at least in this frame of reference."

"But that's the whole point, Grishka—*this frame of reference.* It's simply time for a new one. Time to divide into the stream again."

Grishka shook his head. "Since you seem to have her memories, you should know that that's not good enough. By now we've followed all contiguous paths to the same bitter end. They always finish here. Even the killer couldn't shoot, stab, or strangle his way out of the bind."

He flicked his eyes at Heron and made a breathy noise, almost a chuckle. Heron could only suspend disbelief.

"One way or another," said Celia, her eyes fixed and cold,

"MEQMAT survives. There's no reason why we can't, too. No reason why the rats can't jump ship."

Grishka stood. "Frankly, I don't care what you do. You're a bad penny, Stella, or Celia, or Cleopatra, or whoever the fuck you are. Fortune knows how many times I've tried to get rid of you. But you always seem to turn up, one way or another. Same as your friend."

Heron wondered if all the Grishkas nursed so much bitterness.

"Anyway, I'm signing off." Grishka took slow steps toward the side door. "There's a chance, yes, I grant you that, and I am taking it. The hard way." He opened the door. "You'll excuse me now. I prefer my privacy, and you wouldn't like the mess."

The door closed behind him. A minute later they heard the shot, which seemed to come from far, far away.

21

Amalgamated Woman

"He might have tried something a little less gory," said Celia, no doubt remembering Cleopatra's sensible choice. Before Heron could reply, a video screen halfway across the room switched on. It showed a night sky full of stars—perhaps the Milky Way, as seen from a mountaintop. Hidden speakers played wind-sounds, soft moans and long gentle sighs. The sighs coalesced into speech.

"Men choose the manner of their deaths all too rarely." The voice was epicene and familiar. "Citizen Likhodeyev must be forgiven this last burst of theatricality, though he is to blame for so much else. Now that I myself approach extinction I am becoming increasingly tolerant."

"Can't you escape, MEQMAT?" said Celia. "You've had plenty of warning."

Stars shimmered through a veil of mist. "At this moment I am transmitting portions of myself to storage banks in Chengdu, San Miguel de Tucumán, and the orbital station *Yama's Gate*. But my actions create only the possibility of survival. To function again as I have here in the New City will require a whole new neural array, extensive enough both to reunite my scattered fragments and to permit on-line activity. These conditions may or may not ever be fulfilled. The Theocratic Republic of Texas will no doubt take steps to see that they aren't."

Stars and nebulae faded into waves breaking on an empty beach, cross-lit by a fat orange sun hovering on the horizon. It could be dawn or sunset; only time would tell. MEQMAT spoke through the wash and rumble of the waves.

"You've served me well, John Heron. But in the end I'm afraid you're as guilty as anyone else."

"Guilty? What have I done?"

"You've been an instrument of death. Surely you remember the assassinations of Forbus and Mitchell, and old Dr. Jeremiah Brown."

After so many covert years it frightened him to hear his crimes spoken aloud. Add that to his aches and exhaustion and the total was despair. Retribution was at hand. His shoulders slumped; his voice came hollow and dry. "But that was so long ago. Decades before your experiments here. I thought those years were a closed book."

"Come now, John. Only a fool and a coward could imagine that, and you're neither. By now you know very well how long the past keeps bearing its bitter fruit.

"Twenty years ago Green's Acorn Group—advised, incidentally, by the New City Junta—tried to stem Texan militarism with a little political surgery. You and your friend Jemmy wielded the scalpels. For years it looked like we'd been successful. Dr. Brown's death allowed a moderate faction to control the Texan government, which pursued less militant and more conciliatory policies. But the moderates, unfortunately, were much less astute than their predecessors, and when their blunders snowballed, Reverend Joe Bob Lewis got himself elected Chairman of the Circle of God. You've seen what he's done for international relations. Apocalypse is just around the corner. All my attempts to avert it have failed."

"But why did you keep fooling around with Antony and Cleopatra, and Louis XVI? Why not try to replay Brown's assassination?"

The beach gave way to towering clouds. Lightning flickered like laughter.

"They did try that," said Celia. "Those were Grishka's dips, and he went back over and over again. He said you gave him a real hard time."

"You mean Grishka wore my persona? Grishka crawled around in my head? That's disgusting."

"Apparently you thought so then, too. Your personalities never meshed. You always overrode him."

"Huh. You should have sent me."

"Oh, they tried that a couple times, too. The exact opposite happened, but the end result was the same. Your past self reabsorbed your future self. It was like painting white on white—no contrast, no picture."

"So a couple of dumb teenage kids blow up the New City, and the smartest minds in the world can't stop them?"

MEQMAT replied in a voice of thunder. "Destiny has its own inertia, John Heron. Some nodal points are fixed. The more distant in time a sequence is, the easier it is to tamper with; but all those acts and omissions that lead to our present nightmare are written in stone. A cruel paradox, yes? Our agents had no problem upsetting remote events, whose outcomes would change our era far more drastically; yet none of those agents could ever return to the twenty-first century sequels of their sabotage. The worlds they created were worlds where neither they nor I existed."

"Then how can you know these things?"

Storm winds drove dark shreds of cloud across the screen. "You can never understand what I am or what I know, any more than an insect can understand a man. If I speak of the labyrinthine unfolding of eternity, you hear words, but I perceive the actuality, in all its schizomorphic grandeur. When the full array of my constituent units is activated, I can take stock of the entire multiverse. I see the whole shifting structure of the present, and from that data I reconstruct every tortuous path that converges on this moment."

"So you can see the disaster but you can't do anything about it."

"Exactly. Omniscient impotence: black irony indeed." The storm clouds dissipated, revealing a sterile expanse of sand, drifting amorphously in random breezes. "But you're wasting precious time. I won't be with you much longer. Will you enter the flux again?"

They would. They lay down on adjoining couches, and Celia, with MEQMAT's guidance, adjusted the headsets.

Any moment, thought Heron. Any moment now the fire comes roaring down. As he pressed the skinnies to his throat he recalled Mardion's asps and the comfort of their tiny fangs.

And felt pain, blood red, searing. Titans were using his body as the cue ball in a macrocosmic game of billiards. Impact, rebound, impact. He fell into a pocket of emptiness.

He blinked away doubt and turned the corner, reading numbers to himself: 1243, 1245, 1247. His feet made no sound on the thick carpet; his tool kit didn't rattle. No one saw him, no one heard him.

At 1251 he pulled out the key. It turned without any resistance and he was inside. Of course there must be cameras trained on him, but they would just show the hotel handyman on a call. He squatted down by the callbox and opened the side panel. His back hid his moves as he reached into the tool kit, pulled out the explosive, and attached it to a multicolored bundle of fiberoptic cables.

Nice and easy; all finished in a matter of minutes. Even Jemmy could have handled it. But since John Heron had the reputation as a techie, John Heron got the assignment. He closed the panel, stood up, and brushed his hands against his trousers with the sense of a job well done.

The room—powder-blue carpet, flamingo wallpaper—was completely nondescript, a standard Miami hotel room of the more expensive variety. Except for the plain wooden cross over the bed, it offered no clue that a top minister in the Circle of God was staying here. Dr. Brown's suitcase sat on a stand, half open, showing neat stacks of snow-white underwear and navy blue socks. His bed was unmade, though hardly rumpled at all. God's chosen obviously slept the untroubled slumber of the innocent.

Tap-tap-tap, said the door. *Shit*, said the voice in Heron's head. *Holy Fuckin' Jesus*. But no, there was no problem; he was on a legitimate errand. Just act natural.

Rattle of keys; doorknob turning; door opening. A woman with black curly hair, wearing a pale blue smock, stuck her head in.

"Oh. I was just gonna clean the room. You got work here, too?"

She had a broad Spanish accent and an open, friendly face. "Just finished, ma'am," he said. "On my way out."

He moved toward the door, but she closed it behind her with a smile. "You the new guy, right? You started today. My name's Stella."

"Pleased to meet you, ma'am, but I've got to be on my way."

"Oh, just you wait a minute. There's something I want you to see."

"Ma'am," he said, brushing past her and fiddling with the doorknob. The bitch had locked it.

"Don't panic." Her eyes twinkled. He thought, *I know her, I know her, what the hell is she doing—*

The callbox beeped. He screamed. "No! Not yet! No!" It beeped again, and the whole room erupted in flames.

"You did it! Fantastic! Is everything fixed now?"

He heaved himself onto a block of black marble. The whole pile, more plaster than stone, shifted and settled under his weight. The smoke came on thicker and thicker.

"No." Her eyes were red, tearing heavily. Her hair was white with plaster dust. "None of that really happened." There was a catch in her voice that he found incredibly sexy. But how could he think of sex when the whole Tower threatened to crumble down around his ears? Something about that woman, by whatever name she chose—Stella, Celia, Charmion, or Cleopatra.

"Then what next?"

She started coughing and couldn't stop. He took hold of her, stroking her back. "What makes you think there is a next?" she said.

A gust of smoke came along and hid her face, though it was only ten centimeters away.

Even in January's bitter frost the dog-mask made him sweat. Summer or winter, hot or cold, it was an oppressive weight, to Jacques Carnot as much as to the hapless folk he served.

Today of all days a lusty heat rose off the bodies packing the Place. Red-faced they were, despite the weather, and thirsty. Vendors moved among them selling brandy by the swig, but those drapers and shoemakers and porters who pressed so eagerly against the scaffold were thirsty for another kind of liquid. "Louis Bourbon!" they shouted. "Not king but man!" And again, "The old king goes the way of the oldest king! No longer Louis XVI, but Osiris!"

Louis himself was sweating profusely, standing wigless in a common laborer's coat. He had lost flesh during his months in confinement, so that his facial bones showed more strongly, and his aristocratic nose stood out like a beak. There was no sign of fear or contrition in his face; indeed, the man was angry.

As the Hierophant approached with a vessel of holy Nile water, Louis eluded his guards and moved to the edge of the platform. Raising his bound hands over his head, he shouted, "Citizens of France! I am innocent of any crime!" The Hierophant motioned frantically; the guards, looking extremely foolish, took hold of him again, and the choir began its chant.

Wearing the horns and feathers of Isis, the Chief Chorister sang a long slow lament, echoed every other verse by a dozen lesser singers jangling sistra. The noise drowned out Louis's last protests. At Carnot's side Pierre Clary, in the monster-mask of Setekh, lifted his gleaming blade.

Carnot could imagine the light in his eyes, the saliva on his lips. There was such a thing as enjoying your work too much.

Concentrating on his own performance, Carnot came forward with a roll of pure white linen. He was Anubis, Lord of Death, an office whose duties he had discharged for a decade. His long-time assistant Jean-Louis Ménard, also known as Wepwawet the Wolf, helped him ease Louis onto the worktable. The ex-king was docile now, and trembling violently.

The Chorister's voice soared in a long, quavering cry. The Hierophant raised his arms. Carnot bowed and pressed the linen wrappings over Louis's nose and mouth.

He wasn't sure what impulse made him look at the priestess just then. As a rule he concentrated exclusively on his victims, offering them all the attention they deserved, but now as the crowd howled and Louis trembled, he was drawn out of himself and into the woman's enormous blue eyes. She saw his look. Without missing a note she stared straight into the mask's fanged mouth, where she knew his own eyes would be, and grinned like a whore.

And he knew her, as he knew himself. Priestess and killer: why such persistent type-casting, even across two thousand years? Now as Setekh raised his blade he pressed harder over Louis's nose and mouth, moved for once to mercy. Let the man be dead before his dismemberment began.

The old king never struggled. The cleaver rose and fell, blood spurting like champagne from a freshly opened bottle. Wepwawet displayed Louis's right hand, then a handful of toes, then a bit of his forearm, while the priestess mourned and the Jacobins cheered. A dozen or more pressed forward to dip their handkerchiefs in the gore.

Carnot-Anubis-Heron slipped into darkness and disgust.

"No." Her eyes were red, streaming tears of pain. Her hair was white with plaster dust, as if she had aged forty years in a single day. "None of that really happened." There was a catch in her voice that he found incredibly sexy.

"Then what next?"

She started coughing and couldn't stop. He lifted her bodily and

carried her farther up the great mound of rubble, trying to get clear
of the smoke. The whole pile shifted and settled alarmingly under
his weight.

She caught her breath for a moment and buried her face in his
neck. "What makes you think there is a next?"

Eumenes of Pulos felt naked without his spear. The rest of the
Pulian company shared his anxiety; fighting men without arms,
isolated from the greater part of their force (still waiting patiently
on the ships at Amnisos), they were completely at the mercy of
these smooth-talking, shifty-eyed Cretans. Idling here at the heart
of the House of the Double Ax they might just as well be caught
in the teeth of an animal-trap.

But their liege sat calmly in his seat, gazing down into the
sand-strewn court as if he were an aficionado who knew the
meaning of every move the bull-dancers made. Enkhelyawon the
griffin-lord, Wanax of Pulos, was a master of strategy, a cool head
in battle, a strong right arm in any fight. He was convinced that
the chief prize of all the islands in the Midworld Sea was about to
drop gently into his lap. And Eumenes had learned to trust his
judgment over the years he had served him.

Still. These people, the whole situation here, could make any
honest man's skin crawl.

Beneath them in the restricted tiers the ladies of the Labyrinth
were going wild. Long tresses went flying, bejeweled arms
waved, bare breasts heaved with unhealthy excitement. This was
the sort of spectacle that came only once in nine years, and the
ladies meant to have their fill. Minos, son of the Mountain,
beloved of the Mistress, was dancing before the red bull.

Clad only in a scarlet loincloth and the peacock-feather crown,
the Queen's husband pranced and capered in a wide circle around
his deadly playmate. All the while he danced he coaxed the animal
with soft words, teasing him like a lover, posing grandly with his
chest up and his rump out—only to leap nimbly aside whenever
the monster charged.

A team of acrobats assisted him. Already Dideru, the favorite,
had performed one picture-perfect vault over the bull's back.
Eumenes wouldn't have believed such a trick possible, but then
these Cretans were the cleverest people he had ever seen.

With all the goading and teasing, the bull was tiring quickly.
Minos wasn't much better off. In spite of his supple figure the man

must be near thirty, and he'd been dancing hard for some time now. A climax couldn't be far off.

Eumenes saw it, saw the brief signal that passed from Dideru to Minos. Once more the dancer stood proudly and beckoned to the bull. As the red giant lowered his horns for the charge, the acrobats, instead of drawing him away, stood back and watched solemnly. In that last moment Minos was as brave and beautiful as holy Adonis. Then he was butted, gored, tossed on the bull's massive horns, and the smooth strong body that in its day had given and taken so much pleasure lay broken and torn, bleeding its life into the thirsty sand.

From the women came a deafening chorus of hoots and wails, as if a flock of Mistress Athena's owls had settled over the place to roost. And Queen Ariadne? What thoughts crossed her mind at the sight of her husband's noble send-off? No one could say, because her face remained as sphinxlike and impassive as a painted likeness of the Mistress of Mistresses.

She rose from her wooden seat and covered her eyes for a moment, a ritual gesture of grief. Then, surveying the crowd of weeping courtiers, she said, "Minos is dead." Her voice was soft, but it carried to the highest tiers. "Who will be Minos again?"

That was Enkhelyawon's cue. He called out the prescribed response and descended to the sandy area before Ariadne's dais, his men at his back. "I would be husband to Ariadne," he said, "and serve the Mistress with my life and death."

Long negotiations had preceded this moment: exchanges of showy gifts, extravagant promises, veiled threats. Enkhelyawon had sworn that, once granted the throne of Knossos, he would use his military might to bring the Queen's rivals in Phaistos and Kudonia under her sovereign rule, and carry her sway into the Islands of the Wheel and even to the mainland.

Yet now, at the moment of decision, Ariadne's blue eyebrows arched, a study in surprise.

"A Greek?" she said. "A man who speaks our language brokenly, whose mouth can barely shape the Lady's ninety names? A barbarian whose filthy beard would chafe my consecrated flesh? This is sacrilege."

The fight was bitter and brief. Enkhelyawon was among the first to fall beneath the Cretans' spears. As Eumenes went down, pierced a dozen times, he looked up through the haze of pain and saw Ariadne watching him coolly, through Stella Cranach's eyes.

He knew her, and he knew himself; he recognized the nightmare for what it was.

None of that softened the horror.

"You did it," he said, his voice a dry rasp. "We're still here, alive. The apocalypse never happened."

He ripped wires from his head and sat up. She slumped opposite him on her own couch; the flesh around her eyes looked bruised.

"No. None of it was real. Everything is waiting for us in the future."

He massaged his temples. "Then what next?"

MEQMAT's screen had gone blank. The blinking Christmas tree lights were out. The lab equipment hulked like old furniture, silent and useless. A presence had passed away.

"We follow Grishka's footsteps and get out of here." She slid to the floor and offered her hand. "Come on."

Heron had that dazed, blurry feeling of reentry, and his brief rest hadn't done anything for his headache or the ache in his joints. Once more he stumbled blindly after her, wondering if she really knew where the hell she was going, wondering who she really was.

The corridor outside was lit only by blue emergency lights, so it was difficult to get a clear impression of her face. Besides, his brain was so fuddled by now that he couldn't really picture her various incarnations as separate individuals. They all merged together in an ur-Stella, an amalgamated woman who partook more of fantasy than of truth.

"Hey—no amnesia this time."

"That's what I mean," she said grimly. "Those weren't authentic dips. We just got our toes wet."

The Black Tower's maze wasn't empty anymore. As they ascended to higher and higher levels they met a constant stream of Guardias and bureaucrats, all hurrying in the opposite direction— that is, deeper underground. The burrowers jogged more often than walked, and there were signs of ill-concealed hysteria on every passing face. Mechanical voices barked codes from wall speakers and hand-held remotes, hiding bad news in strings of numbers and acronyms. Well-tailored pros cursed aloud at every new announcement. Heron and Celia were mostly ignored, but every now and then some grunt stared after them in a mixture of suspicion and disbelief. Those random double takes spoke volumes about how bad things were outside.

Two levels short of the surface, they ran into a checkpoint. A half-dozen soldiers were sifting through a mob that must have numbered in the hundreds, all pushing and yelling, all bent on reaching the promised land of the deepest vaults.

"Don't you recognize me? I'm Song Meiling! I have clearance."

"Here—here—look—take it! Five thousand Argentine australes. It's yours. Just let me through."

"Please! I don't care about myself, just let my kid get by."

"Look at me! I have papers! Look!"

"Take me! Take me!"

And the corresponding arms waved overhead, clutching banknotes, ID cards, jewelry, babies, anything that might make a difference. The chosen few slipped through the barricade in groups of two and three, gasping and stumbling and running like rabbits once they made it to the other side. There didn't seem to be a chance in hell of going against that current.

Heron's momentum died. He blinked back panic. Celia hunched against the wall and wept.

"Can't we circle back? There must be another way."

"Wrong. This is it."

He put his arm around her. "Then this must be as good a place as any to die, no?"

She chewed her thumb. "I suppose. But it's not the way I remember, John, not the way I remember."

"You mean the rubble and the smoke?"

She nodded miserably. As she did, a series of pops sounded on the other side of the Guardias, like balloons breaking. Somebody had a gun. The screaming and pleading reached a new pitch of frenzy. More pops, and the Guardias fell back, lifting rifles to firing position. When the discharge came it rattled their skulls. It was indoor thunder and lightning, and the downpour was human blood.

They both fell flat; there was an instant of comedy, an insanely gruesome farce where each one tried to shield the other. They curled together in a fever and saw booted feet stride backwards under the rattle of gunfire, and then the Guardias were turning tail, hauling ass down the corridor, and everybody left standing was surging after in a brutal stampede. Heron staggered to his feet, went sprawling again, and contracted like a turtle in search of a shell. He was screaming as loudly as anyone else, but he had no idea what he said.

How long did they huddle there like a heap of garbage? How long did they whimper and shake in absolute mindless terror? No more than a few minutes, but when they unfolded themselves and stood up again they were the only ones left unwounded. Bodies lay everywhere, twisted, blood-soaked, sometimes half-dismembered by the force of the rifle volley. Odd scraps of clothing and flesh were strewn around like fallen leaves. Moans sounded weakly from the occasional survivor, and one monolog droned on and on: "I don't want to *die* somebody *help* me I don't want to *die* somebody *help* me I—"

Otherwise it was quiet. Smoke poured down from the next level; there must have been an explosion that they'd missed in the tumult.

"So does it look okay now, sweetheart?"

"I suppose."

He reached for her hand, as gallantly as if they were about to tango at one of the Lagarto's *thés dansants*. She accepted, smiling through the ruin of her makeup, and they set out across the rubble through thickening clouds of smoke.

He was amazed at how good he felt. His aches and pains might have belonged to someone else. Maybe it was the woman at his side; maybe it was the inchoate suspicion that they'd broken through the last obstacle and emerged in the clear beyond. Even when they started choking on the fumes, even when they lost all sense of direction and simply scrabbled onward into chaos, he knew they weren't lost.

When the world flashed white in a total negation of perception, he welcomed the change. As his eyeballs boiled away, as his flesh melted off the bone, as Stella's fingers (curled so tenderly in his own) turned to smoke and ashes, he smiled like a baby.

22

Always, Never

The crowds were thin. Once he'd picked out the lotus-crowned pillars flanking the entrance to the Egyptian Wing it was obvious that she wasn't there. He checked the wall clock: 1805. He was late, as usual, but not so late that she would have given up and gone. No; he was late, she was later.

And later. And later. By 1820 he was irritated; by 1830 he was depressed. He figured the safest thing to do was call her.

There were four callboxes in the museum lobby. Three of them had *Fuera de Servicio* signs; the fourth had a queue. What the hell, he thought. Queues, waiting rooms, wasted time: that's life in the New City. He stepped to the rear and sighed.

When he was only two people away from the box he saw her coming. His depression evaporated and the sun came out in his mind. God, she looked good: striding like a Guardia on parade, showing a tasty length of leg with every step. Her hair flew in ten directions at once, her long black coat floated behind her like a superhero's cape. He'd only observed her up close before; now he could watch from an objective distance, in those precious seconds before she recognized him, and he liked every centimeter of what he saw.

Something surged inside him. Something white blanked out his vision. Something burned through all his synapses, and hot pain flashed up his right leg. He swayed, he pressed down with every kilo of his weight on the Lottery-issued cane. Pictures pounded his

optic nerve to the rhythm of his heartbeat. Cleopatra in glory.
Kaisarion pouting like a brat. Grishka Likhodeyev taking bored
notes. Ursula dancing in a world of her own. Antony dying,
dying. Stella Cranach regarding him with contempt. Stella Cranach sweating in passion. Stella Cranach coughing her lungs out.
Stella Cranach going up in smoke.

"John, oh there you are, I'm so sorry I'm la—" She stopped
short and frowned in his face. "Are you okay?" Then her own
eyes widened, and she remembered, she knew, she sagged against
him while he stroked the soft nape of her neck.

"Hey pal, you gonna make your call or what?"

He blinked. It was his turn already. He shook his head and let
the queue wind around him. This was no time for common
courtesy.

"Do we wake up in the end or does this show keep running?"

"How should I know, John?" She pinched the flesh beside her
mouth. "It feels like a pretty good fit to me."

They were walking aimlessly, they were crying quietly, they
were smiling like fools. He said, "I hope you didn't really want to
see the Egyptian Collection."

"There wouldn't be any surprises, would there. How about that
restaurant on Libertad and Second?"

"How about the ferry to the airport? How about a ticket to
Shanghai?"

"Come again?"

"Wake up, Stella. Remember. Residence in this fair city will
shortly become a death sentence. MEQMAT's backed us up,
given us a second chance. Let's get out of here while we can."

She stared at him. "Shit, you're right. But what do you think I
am, a cash hoarder? You know what airfare costs these days?"

"Come on, Stella. I bet you've got two round trips to Miami in
your handbag right now."

"How did you know? That's where I was supposed to be going
today, till my boss put everything off until Thursday."

"Funny, the things I remember." He guided her firmly toward
the exit. "I've got some hard currency at my place, and I'd bet my
last Middlebuck you've got a stash of your own. Plus, those
tickets you're holding can be converted into a tidy sum any night
from 1800 to 2400 in the back room of the Puerta Negra. Let's
rustle up all our resources, Stella. There's no reason to hang
around the New City any longer than we have to. Any arguments?
I didn't think so."

Arm in arm they descended the broad Museo steps. A crisp wind blew up Quinta. It was cold for December, but he figured the breezes would be a little balmier in Shanghai. Let's see . . . *Ni hao ma? Wo hao.* As he waved to a pedicab Stella plucked his sleeve.

"You know, John, this might be just a trifle hasty, don't you think? We haven't even had our first date yet."

"Oh." He stopped short. "Is this the part where we compare notes and figure out who was who and when and where?"

She shrugged. For a moment there, sunk down in her oversized coat, she looked almost helpless, and he suffered a twinge of doubt. Was this really his tough no-nonsense Stella Cranach?

Of course it was.

"I concede the point," she said. "Whatever we thought was happening really happened to other people. But still . . ."

"But nothing. I thought your specialty was the persistence of memory." He smiled, a little mockingly, a little tenderly. "I think I see you very clearly now, after studying all those knock-offs. I think I'm ready for a season with the original."

"You want this cab or don't you?" The hack frowned and jerked his head back toward the vehicle.

"Yes," Stella said, with sudden firmness. "Yes, we do."

They climbed in and settled the rug around their legs. "Barrio Violado," said Heron. "I'll give you better directions once we're downtown."

And they were off. Even from this distance the Black Tower glittered darkly, gloriously, a vision of power in the western sky. But never again, he thought. Goodbye to the city of fortune.

Stella's left hand groped toward his. He caught it with his right and raised it to his lips, ogling her over the folds of black wool. Always.

"John, what in the world are you thinking?"

He smiled a crinkly smile. "Oh, about time, and the way it splits and fractures, and about how you can fall through a crack and land right back where you started."

"Not really," she said. "Not quite."

"Close enough."

She squinted into his eyes. She took hold of his chin and tilted his head right and left, examining the mismatched profiles. "Well—" she said, with elaborately faked hesitation. "I guess so."

They shared a look of amazement; then they were both laughing, and it was almost Fourteenth Street before they could stop.

CYBERPUNK

___Islands in the Net Bruce Sterling 0-441-37423-9/$4.50
Laura Webster is operating successfully in an age
where information is power--until she's plunged into a
netherworld of black-market pirates, new-age
mercenaries, high-tech voodoo...and murder.

___Neuromancer William Gibson 0-441-56959-5/$3.95
The novel of the year! Case was the best interface
cowboy who ever ran in Earth's computer matrix. Then
he double-crossed the wrong people...

___Mirrorshades Bruce Sterling, editor
0-441-53382-5/$3.50
The definitive cyberpunk short fiction collection,
including stories by William Gibson, Greg Bear, Pat
Cadigan, Rudy Rucker, Lewis Shiner, and more.

___Blood Music Greg Bear 0-441-06797-2/$3.50
Vergil Ulam had an idea to stop human entropy--
"intelligent" cells--but they had a few ideas of their
own.

___Count Zero William Gibson 0-441-11773-2/$3.95
Enter a world where daring keyboard cowboys break
into systems brain-first for mega-heists and brilliant
aristocrats need an army of high-tech mercs to make
a career move.
